CHARLEEN SWANSEA is editor and founder of Red Clay Books, a small press located in Charlotte, North Carolina. With associate editor, **BARBARA CAMPBELL,** she has been publishing collections of original poetry and *Red Clay Reader,* a literary magazine designed to give southern artists and writers a forum for their work, since 1963. LOVE STORIES BY NEW WOMEN is their first volume of short fiction. These eighteen stories were selected from 300 sent in by women from all over the United States, and compiled over a two year period. The authors range from unpublished novices to well-known writers, and in addition to writing, they teach, build houses, make films, sculpt, and practice law.

LOVE STORIES BY NEW WOMEN

Edited by
CHARLEEN SWANSEA
and
BARBARA CAMPBELL

 A BARD BOOK/PUBLISHED BY AVON BOOKS

AVON BOOKS
A division of
The Hearst Corporation
959 Eighth Avenue
New York, New York 10019

Copyright © 1978 by Red Clay Books
Published by arrangment with Red Clay Books
Library of Congress Catalog Card Number: 79-90727
ISBN: 0-380-48058-1

Cover painting by Gina Gilmour
Cover design by Ena Whisnant
Cover photography by Bill Scott

First Bard Printing, December, 1979

BARD IS A TRADEMARK OF THE HEARST CORPORATION
AND IS REGISTERED IN MANY COUNTRIES AROUND THE
WORLD, MARCA REGISTRADA, HECHO EN U.S.A.

Printed in the U.S.A.

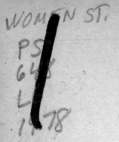

CONTENTS

INTRODUCTION

Red Clay Books is a publishing house run by women. During the last decade work in the office has frequently been impeded by crises in the love lives of the staff and the women writers whom we publish. Confronting this chronic work problem brought us to a realization of how critical in our lives are the affairs of love. To comfort ourselves we speculated that many women are suffering from disorientation and anxiety about attitude changes and new possibilities in love.

We did not at first think of collecting love stories for publication. We thought of checking such a book out of the library, of finding there some support for our own ambivalence and groping. But there was no such book. Surprised, we recognized a need for such stories, an opportunity to share both the dilemma and solutions that a changed consciousness has effected in our love relationships. We assumed that even though we are isolated regionally, we are not alone in our preoccupation, that women would already have written stories about their search for love even though we could not find them published. And we were surprised to realize that we would not have made these assumptions about male writers.

Society has always assumed that women have the greater need and capacity for love. Society depends and even insists upon women fulfilling this role. Woman is, after all, the mother, and the consequence of a mother who does not love is finally more than psychic pain; it is the demise of society's structure.

But women are changing their roles. They are beginning to reject the responsibility of giving succour and the conclusion that their instincts are primarily to couple and procreate. We believe that these changes would be best described in stories about love. We did not know what answers to expect in the stories but we did know what questions were eminent in our own lives. Had our new freedom brought fulfillment or disaster to the most of us?

We wondered if the traditional structures of courtship, marriage and family would prevail if love could be sustained within a conventional marriage. We wondered about sexual freedom, whether it is liberating or a new sort of trap, a circumstance which makes us more available but no less suspect, powerless, and after a certain age, pathetic. We wondered if women are less fearful now of aloneness, if homosexuality and bisexuality are satisfying alternatives for us. We wondered if the release of new sexual vitality is transferable to useful energy in other aspects of our lives. Has woman's realization of her pyschological complexity heightened her anxiety or increased her possibilities?

Having announced our intention to publish this collection, we received over 300 stories from all over America. Reading the stories was an amazing and exciting experience which confirmed our assumption of women's concern with love. We found many women admitting to love as an obsession. Diane Vreul's humorous story about a female window washer who cannot reason herself out of love with a lackadasical man, Lee Smith's characterization of a wife distracted from reality by her love of horses, and Barbara Lovell's passionate and wrenching story of a woman in love with liquor, all testify to love as a sort of madness.

A theme that emerged in many of the stories was that of self discovery, a gradual growth from acceptance of self to a conviction of self worth. This hard won self esteem seems to take many women by surprise. It gives them new insights into their relationships and circumstances. An awakening sense of injustice at traditional male-female relationships produces a range of responses from inertia to violence.

The women who wrote these stories seem to be finding and saying heretofore unspeakable conclusions: that love between women can be an alternative to heterosexuality, that the power struggle involved in games of love is sometimes more interesting than the love object, that sentiment is less necessary to women than it is to men, that sometimes violence is preferable to passivity, that aloneness can be more comfortable than the risks of love.

The stories collected here do not answer all questions but they do give dramatic insights into a wider range of woman's experience and feeling, a conclusion that love is in fact the nucleus of our evolving being.

Charleen Swansea
Barbara Campbell
Editors

THE PEOPLE OF COLOR

Jean Thompson

Behind two sealed panes of glass and screened by the low branches of Norwegian pine, they felt quite safe watching. Not that there was much to see. A U-Haul truck parked in the driveway full of lamps, folded quilts, rugs, cardboard boxes squared away on the back wall.

What did you hope to see, David said. Dildoes? A mummy case?

Very funny.

Firearms? Half a dozen enema bags?

I'm just curious, said Meg. She folded her arms as if they could serve as a barrier to his teasing. She knew he wouldn't stop yet.

Maybe this truck is just a fake and the real stuff, the good stuff, will be smuggled in under cover of darkness.

Yeah. You want the first watch?

But David's amusement was still private. He sat slumped over the table, his neck pouched and foreshortened, elbows dug in. His chin was ragged with black whiskers, each one distinct as a mole.

11

LOVE STORIES

You've got to admit it, he said. You're really nosy. A voyeur. That means...

I know what it means. You need a shave.

At age sixty you and your fellow crones, your crone cronies, will hold long telephone conversations about some poor wretch's laundry hanging on the line.

You also need a haircut.

The last one, she thought, looked like it was done with pinking shears, leaving little tufts and eruptions of hair along his neck. He didn't answer of course, just kept on talking in his voice that was always hoarse yet always projected more than it needed to. A voice that was used to speaking with authority. It was one of the things she accommodated, this insistence on his own humor that left her behind, just as she had resigned herself to his occasional snoring. He was such a clever man, a real original. Everyone said so, and his demonstrable intelligence made one make allowances. He kept talking until the joke was brought to some peak or challenge she no longer followed. He grinned, waiting for her answer. His cheeks were always a bright inflamed red, as if they'd been scoured.

Meg said, All we know is that people of color have furniture just like white folks.

It was not an answer and he had to visibly shift gears. Huh. Yeah, here they are again.

She looked, but the angle of the house obscured them. Two figures in matching army jackets and jeans. Nearly the same height. She couldn't tell which was the man. They all look alike. The joke was stillborn. Wind drove the pine branches down, then they bucked, swung up, like logs riding waves. Through the shifting green she saw them unloading the truck, one, the woman maybe, handing things down to the other until the ground was bright with pillows, record albums, clothes sagging from hangers. Meg looked at her own table, the patterned blue china, graceful even though littered with the remains of their breakfast, the salt and pepper, back to back in their place at the center, the blue glossy field of vinyl tablecloth. She felt a small innocent contentment at the harmony of what she saw, at the thought that her belongings were not scattered on that cold mud.

David was saying something. Beg pardon, she said, raising her eyes.

I said if they eat on their porch we'll be able to exchange plates. He nodded at the enclosed porch, much like their own but not quite parallel, attached to the white frame house some six yards away.

I think life will go on.

I guess. You don't suppose there'll be any ruckus because they're black?

Meg shook her head. The front part of her hair worked itself loose from the rubber band holding it back, two heavy red wings already starting to frizz. No burning crosses. Maybe a little ostracism. I should bake a cake or something, take it over.

That would be liberal of you.

David, I'd bake a cake for anyone, you know. She saw by his grin that he'd tricked her.

Will it be a chocolate or a vanilla cake?

Very funny. She spoke primly, trying not to laugh.

Talk about knee-jerk responses. He stood up, and his unbalanced chair teetered.

Don't you dare. He was standing over her. His loose work shirt made his body seem massive, undefined. His hands were flexed and ready.

David!

She squirmed within the folds of her old green bathrobe. His shoulders dropped until they were level with her head, his hands prying hers loose. Her fingers curled like singed insects. She whooped when he felt for her ribs, then bent double as her laughter came in spasms. Finally he lifted her out of her chair, holding her by her armpits while her heels skidded against his legs.

She couldn't speak for a full minute after he put her down. Her eyelashes were matted, damp. She reached up, kissing him. You big bully.

He blew in her ear. And what will the neighbors think?

She put the breakfast dishes to soak and got out her mixing bowls. It'll be a coffee cake, she called to David, but he must have been in the back of the house. Sprawled on the unmade bed, reading most likely. He had a way of taking up the maximum possible space. You couldn't forget for a minute that he was in the house. He left a trail of clothes, books, overflowing ashtrays; his footsteps made glasses ring on the shelves. A clumsiness, an obtrusiveness she associated with men in general and did not allow herself to nag about. Nagging was for hausfraus, knee-jerk liberals, broads on TV commercials who fretted about waxy build-up. She had promised herself right at the start of her marriage never to submit to such images.

As always she fell into the rhythm of the baking. Her nostrils filled with the smell of sweet dough. The polished blue sky and sun were deceptive. It was only March, and the heat of the oven felt good on her bare legs. If you looked into the heart of the pine tree so that you saw just a corner of sky and fat cloud, then you might fool yourself into thinking the weather was nice.

Meg dressed, squinting at herself in the bathroom mirror. She looked like a war orphan this morning, she thought, pale as the soap in the dish. Even her freckles were faded. She shrugged off the idea of makeup, covered the cake with a clean dishtowel, and walked across the lawn.

She knocked. Blurred noise came from behind the door— heavy feet, the wrench of furniture, thin high music. She knocked louder. The door opened as she raised her hand a third time.

It was a woman. Light skin, beige with an undertone of gold, and short kinked hair worn natural. Yes, she said.

Meg hoped she wouldn't sound too rehearsed. Hi, I'm Meg Macey, and I live next door. I wanted to ask if there was anything I could do to help you get settled, and I brought you a little coffee cake.

Oh, said the woman, surprised and tentative. Meg lifted the dishtowel. Why it looks homemade. Meg nodded. And it's still *warm*. Her voice was soft, breathy. Well that's awful nice of you. Hey come on in.

I don't want to get in your way, began Meg, but the woman had already swung the door open and stepped inside. The music came from a stereo set up in the corner, a bright falsetto soul record. Verg, the woman shouted. Verg, c'mere. A voice answered but all Meg caught was the tone, heavy and irritated. I don't care, the woman called. She turned to Meg and smiled.

THE PEOPLE OF COLOR

He'll be out in a minute. He's havin a fit with the shower curtain. Here, you want to set that plate down. The woman dusted a cardboard box with her shirtsleeves. Oh, I'm Esther. Esther Billups. Did you say Meg? Have a seat. Somewheres.

Esther gestured toward the uneven terrain of the room, the disassembled bookcases and toppling piles of clothes. She produced two vinyl couch cushions and Meg sat, cross-legged. Esther stooped to turn down the music. She was tall, maybe five ten. Long slim legs and narrow waist. In her middle twenties, probably, though Meg always found it hard to tell black people's ages. Esther's eyes were very large, almond shaped. Looking at the strong curves of her cheekbones, her wide forehead and full mouth, Meg realized that despite the old clothes, despite the brown skin that somehow qualified all her perceptions and put them in a separate category, Esther was beautiful.

Esther plumped down on the other cushion. So you live in that house yonder? The one just like ours?

Well they're not quite alike. Our living room's bigger, and you've got an extra bedroom.

That so? They look exaktly alike from the street you know. Like twins.

I guess, said Meg. Secretly she thought her own house, with its evergreens and brick walk, was much nicer. Did you move from out of town? she asked.

Esther shook her head. No, we were living out west but we needed a bigger place. A wadded newspaper in the corner rustled and produced a skinny gray kitten which ran to Esther, butting against her ankles and mewing. Esther picked it up. Cat, what did I ever do to you besides give you a home? Then she twisted her neck around, hearing footsteps behind her. Bout time, she said to the man who appeared in the door frame.

He scowled. Where's the hammer? he asked, not looking at Meg.

Now how would I know. You packed it. Verg, this is Meg . . . Macey.

Meg Macey from next door an she brought us a cake, ain't that nice? This my husband Verg.

Meg could see the man struggling to keep his ill-humor intact. How do, he said. He was darker than Esther, his features

15

bunched too close together. Maybe it was the frown that lowered his forehead. He was wearing a T-shirt, and his bare arms bulged with angular muscles. I need that hammer, he said. No way I'm buyin a new one. He stood for a moment longer, his suppressed anger making him rock a little on his feet, then he turned and disappeared.

Grouch, said Esther without embarrassment, but Meg was already on her feet. I better not keep you from your unpacking, she said, for once glad to use a polite formula. Is there anything you need?

Naw. Just takes time is all. Hey, thanks for the cake, that was sure thoughtful of you. Esther stood up and stretched, her long legs growing taut. The kitten spilled from her lap. Drop on by again, you hear? We can have a beer or somethin.

She's real nice, Meg told David at dinner. He's kind of a character.

David put his milk glass down, swabbed at the smeared moustache it left. A character?

Not very friendly.

Well I guess we don't have to be great buddies. Just not get in each other's way. Hope they don't throw wild parties.

We might get invited.

And have you ogled by a crowd of jive-talking bucks? Uh uh.

You could tie me to your wrist with the clothesline, Meg said, trying to keep her voice mild. This mock protectiveness was somehow irritating.

C'mon Meg, don't sneer.

You sound like a cave man.

What's wrong with that? Rescuing you from a crowd of dusky ravagers. It turns me on. He beamed, thinking of new jokes. Where is that clothesline, go get it, will ya?

Holy shit, Macey, there's cops and niggers all over your front yard.

Meg struggled to sit up in the back seat where she'd been asleep, her body reacting to the words before she was conscious of them. Between David's and Clark's shoulders she saw a wedge of darkness and the mute explosion of red flashing lights. Christ, said David. What did they do, rob a bank?

THE PEOPLE OF COLOR

The car approached, rolling, nearly silent, and the scene resolved itself into components: two policemen getting into a patrol car, backing into the street and racing away even as they watched, two more in the yard standing on each side of Verg Billups, another writing on a clipboard by the light of the streetlamp. Clark pulled into the driveway, and they all got out, uncertain of what to do.

Should we inquire? asked David, turning to Meg. She shivered, the night air penetrating her clothes, and didn't answer. David shrugged and walked away towards the policeman with the clipboard.

How long have they lived here? asked Clark.

Only a week, no, ten days. She was watching Verg, who stood looking at the ground. The red beam cut across his face as it revolved, pulsing every other second, so his features seemed alternately to leap and smolder. But from this distance she couldn't read them.

David jogged back across the frozen grass. Domestic disturbance, he reported, wheezing. He knocked her around some.

Meg breathed cold night air, felt her lungs stop. Esther—how is she?

I dunno, I didn't, hey Honey . . .

But she broke away from his arm before it could encircle her, and trotted across to the policeman. He looked up, his face tinged with blue from the stark light, his voice weary and courteous. Yes ma'am?

Where is Mrs. Billups, will she be all right?

Well, I think so ma'am. She's at the hospital but she seems just bruised, shaken up. No weapons in the assault.

What happens—what happens—She wanted to ask him what would happen to the two of them, Esther and Verg, what would they do? Of course he couldn't tell her, he was waiting patiently for her to realize it.

We'll see if she presses charges. He nodded in Verg's direction; he was being loaded into the back of a patrol car. If she doesn't sign a complaint against him we can't do anything. The man smiled, dismissing her.

She told him good night and walked away. Guess I better

move on, Clark was saying. You folks rest easy. She let David say good night for her, let him lead her into the house. After the darkness the lights seemed too bare, distinct, each object harshly defined and unfamiliar.

I'll be damned, said David. There goes the neighborhood, huh?

Oh don't. Don't joke.

I didn't mean anything, Meg.

I know. She walked across the room, picked up something, a book, put it back down. I would never, she said, her voice surprising both of them, never stay with a man who beat me.

Wow. His laughter stuttered, then failed altogether. Wow, is that a warning? You think I'd ever hit you, you're crazy.

I know. Forget it. She saw him hesitate, then decide to say something casual. You want a drink of something, a nightcap?

Sure, she said, and crossed the room to him, pressing the warm length of her body to him until he put his arms around her.

They had two drinks, stayed up later than they meant to until they felt their earlier fatigue return to them. Still Meg couldn't fall asleep right away. She drew back the covers, knowing she would not disturb his heavy sleep, and crouched at the bedroom window. But the house next door was dark, giving no sign of anyone within the blank walls.

When Meg awoke the memory of the night before was like a sharp edge, something she had to blunt with her morning routine, the familiar actions assuring her that whatever happened could be assimilated, dealt with. Perhaps even forgotten, or turned into an anecdote: Honey, you remember when the neighbors had that fight? But at noon someone knocked on the door. She was not really surprised to see Esther.

Good morning, Meg said, hating the inane brightness of her voice.

Mornin. Hey, can I use your telephone? Mine was sposed to be in yesterday, wouldn't you know. Yeah, thanks, preciate it.

Meg held the door open and showed her where the phone was. Trying not to be obvious, she examined Esther for damage. Nothing she could see. Esther wore a bright purple scarf wrapped sleekly over her head. It made her look like a statue of some Egyptian queen.

Esther spoke into the phone, a few words in her soft voice. Meg stood in the next room, a polite distance that would show she wasn't trying to eavesdrop. When she heard the phone click she returned.

Well, thanks again, said Esther. Hope I didn't put you out none.

Of course not, said Meg. Come over whenever you need to call. Was she imagining it, or was there something constrained, hesitant in the way Esther spoke? Meg let her impulse break loose: Hey, are you all right? After last night I mean?

She was ready for Esther to say it was none of her business. Instead she raised her arms, let them drop heavily to her sides. Yeah. Yeah, I'm OK. Got a sore ass and a headache.

Would you like something, some coffee?

Coffee'd send me into orbit. I'm kinda edgy, you know.

How about some dope then?

They were sitting at the kitchen table surrounded by a comfortable clutter of ashtrays, Pepsi bottles, vanilla wafers, thick rising smoke. We made it up, Esther was saying. She spoke with difficulty, trying to hold the smoke in her lungs. He was pissed I called the cops, I never done that before.

You mean he hit you before? The dope had made Meg hazy, incautious. But it was all right.

Couple times he gave me a punch. Oncet he kicked me upside the head.

Wow. Meg didn't trust herself to say more. But Esther must have caught the disbelief.

Girl, you gotta know I light into him too. Threw a dozen eggs at him one time. Mashed a couple down his shirt.

Yeah, but—Meg shook her head, stopped. There was no way she could say what she felt. That it was the worst degradation to put up with such abuse, and any woman who did had her brain scrambled.

He just gets so mad, said Esther, ignoring the interruption. Her brown eyes slid upwards, remembering. Mm, does he get mad. Allus been like that, we been married a year but I've known him for three. How long you been married?

19

Two years in June. Meg felt oddly embarrassed, as if talking about her marriage, its normalcy and lack of violence, was boasting.

But Esther didn't seem uneasy. A June bride, huh.

Oh sure. The works. Made my folks happy. Meg giggled. We were so cute. Like the little bride and groom they put on the wedding cake. A lu-uvly couple, she drawled.

What's your old man do?

He's a creative consultant for a public relations firm.

Huh. Ole Verg is just public. He drives trucks for the city.

They both laughed. Esther rummaged through the cookie box. Am I ever being a pig. But this is ba-ad weed. It took Meg a minute to figure out that meant good. I didn't know white people had weed like this.

Yeah, it's OK stuff, said Meg. She thought, vaguely, that blacks must know more about whites than vice versa, just because they had to live in a world where whites made the rules. For the same reason women must know more about men than men do about women. Was that right? She'd have to remember it, think about it when she got straight. Her general curiosity triggered a specific question. Esther, she asked, how old are you?

Twenty-four. Twenty-four last November.

Why me too. Except I was born in August.

Huh, I'd a thought you were younger. I dunno why.

The freckles, probably. They make me look like Raggedy Ann.

Hey now, I got freckles too, see? Esther leaned across the table and Meg saw it was true, a cluster of darker brown pigment across the bridge of her nose. I've always been proud of em cause it's real unusual for black people to have freckles. An I'm not even that light.

Well, you're pretty light, said Meg. Was there something indelicate about her mentioning it? A patronizing compliment?

Esther shook her head. The darker the berry the sweeter the juice, that's what some folks say. But my mamma used to say right back, well damn the berry and fuck the juice, mm-mm.

Meg coughed in her Pepsi, couldn't stop laughing. The bubbles flew up her nose, laugh bubbles. It would be wonderful, she thought, to have a mother who said things like that.

When they both calmed down Esther said, Jesus, I got to get home. I must of been here all day.

It was only two-thirty. But Meg felt that they had indeed been there all day, or that they always spent the day like this, something. She staggered a little, her hands swimming as she stood up.

Esther was trying to put her coat on. This thing hasn't got enough sleeves, she complained.

Mine neither. Meg was rooting through the hall closet. Hangers fell in dark rattling piles.

Where you goin?

I have to get some milk before dinner.

Hey, I got milk, plenty of it. Esther seemed pleased to have thought of it. I'll give you some, OK?

They stumbled through the windy sunlight, blinking like owls. Meg was thankful she hadn't tried to go to the store. Esther pushed the front door open. If anything the house was more disordered than the day they'd moved in. Sour piles of clothes lay on the couch. All the shades were drawn, and in the yellow dimness Meg put her foot in a saucer of dark dried cat food.

Esther was peering in the refrigerator, both hands on her knees. How much you need? she called. She held out a quart container, half full.

Thanks, that's plenty. I'm going to the grocery tomorrow, I'll pay you back then.

Don't worry bout it. Esther slammed the refrigerator. Ow, I got work to do. Oughta unbraid my hair, had it up since yesterday. She loosened her scarf. Her head was covered with tight braids, giving her scalp a shaved, naked look.

Why do you braid it?

Strengthens it, explained Esther. Makes it easier to handle. I'm not like these gals with foot-wide fros, they got hair you can bounce a ball off of. She reached up and unbraided a section, then bent toward Meg. Feel.

She expected something wiry, stiff. Esther's hair was soft. Like the fleece of a baby blanket. Yeah, said Meg, laughing a little. It's real fine. Esther raised her head and smiled.

I better stumble home, said Meg. Thanks for the milk. I'll pay you back.

I said don't worry, OK? It's a fair trade for the smoke. No, I think I got a real *deal*.

There was something unreal about being at a police station in the afternoon. The atmosphere of crisis, the humming florescent lights and cold cinderblock walls required darkness to complete their drama. Instead, the room where Meg and Esther sat was filled with calm sunlight. The blue-green swellings at Esther's eye and mouth seemed as garish and melodramatic as stage make-up.

But, Meg thought, nothing had seemed to fit all day. The incongruity of sirens and pale mid-morning TV screen, Esther staggering across the brown marshy lawn, her awkwardness seeming almost comic, Meg running from her own house just as the patrol car pulled up, questions asked at once so the air filled with peaking voices. The trip to the emergency room where the same TV program droned, imperturbable amid the gauze, alcohol, blood. And now the police station where their tension diffused into a series of reports and forms filled out in triplicate.

Esther was not crying. Only at first, when she ran out of the house, had her voice been thick and liquid. She sat, holding an ice pack to her forehead, her eyes closed. Meg too was silent.

The door to the room opened, and Esther's name was called. At the clerk's desk they were told Verg was charged with assault and bail had been set at thirty dollars.

Thirty dollars, said Esther, whispering through cracked lips. He'll be out by dinner time.

Later they sat in Meg's living room. Esther's suitcase was in the corner. She had decided to spend the night with friends, somewhere Verg wouldn't look for her. After that she was unsure.

You have to do something, said Meg. She strained to make her voice firm, as if it alone could change Esther's mind. What are you going to do, wait until he knocks out your teeth instead of just loosening them?

I dunno.

Why not? What's stopping you?

Esther shook her head. It's—hard to decide. I mean, it may sound crazy but I don't want to throw away my whole marriage.

Meg just stared. It was as if she were the one who'd been beaten, humiliated, so intense was her feeling that Verg should be punished. She knew Esther only called the police when it got out of control, she'd said as much herself. How often had she simply endured the violence, or talked her way out of it? Although there was no way Meg could understand such a thing, she realized the extent of the gap between them. When she spoke it was more gently.

You could get a court order saying he couldn't contact you except through your lawyer, what do you call it, a peace bond. It would give things a chance to cool down.

Don't have a lawyer.

Get one.

Don't have no money.

Call Legal Aid. I'll loan you money. Just promise me you'll do something.

Yeah. OK.

Meg heard the gravel in the driveway crush under the wheels of the car. David was home from work. She ran to the kitchen and took the extra house key from its hook. Here, she said, pressing it into Esther's motionless hand. If anything happens you come over here, whether or not we're home. Now, we'll give you a ride to your friend's.

She stood on the front porch watching David slump out of the car, his tired after-work gestures. Why, she wondered, had she not wanted David to know about the key. She had known without thinking about it that he wouldn't approve.

Hi, she said, lifting her face to his. Then, carefully: Could we give Esther a ride?

His ruddy face puckered. What happened?

What do you think happened.

He followed her back inside, said hello to Esther, his voice casual, and carried her suitcase out. Esther walked with her face averted. She gave one quick glance across the lawn and settled into the back seat. None of them talked during the ride, but as Esther was getting out Meg said, Now remember. Call me if there's anything I can do. I will, said Esther. Meg controlled the impulse to wink, like a conspirator.

Jesus, said David as they drove away. Is she all right?

For now she is.

What about him?

Oh he's spending a couple hours in jail. Redneck judges seem to think a man's got a perfect right to beat his wife, especially if he's black.

Now that's not necessarily true, Meg.

It isn't? Do you think that's fair to Esther, turning him loose so he can beat her up worse next time? Meg's voice was spiralling too high.

I didn't say that. Now why are you so damned jumpy?

I'm sorry. This whole day—Meg let air sift through her hands like the words which escaped her.

Yeah. It's rough. But honey, I don't know if you should let yourself get so mixed up in this.

In an instant she was on the attack. Why not? Give me a reason why not.

Why do you think? You might get hurt, Verg might get mad at you for helping Esther.

And then you'd have to do something. You feel responsible for me, right?

She saw his eyebrows tense, saw his hands stiffen on the steering wheel, and knew she was being provocative, unfair. Everything about him grated on her, for no good reason. His too-loud voice, the stale salt odor of his skin. Even his tolerance of her (for she knew he was considering what she'd been through, was making allowances for her mood) irritated her. It smacked of indulgence.

They reached the house. Meg resolved to calm down. But her nerves as she fixed dinner were brittle. David came up behind her, kissed her neck. She tried to respond but some part of her would not relax. Even at dinner when he paid her some over-hearty compliment, transparent in his desire to please, she noticed only the skin of his jaw where the razor had burned and nicked.

Later, soaking in the bathtub, she tried to figure it out. There was no good reason for being mad at David, he hadn't beaten anyone up. He had his moments of insensitivity, of selfishness.

THE PEOPLE OF COLOR

What man didn't, they could all drive you crazy. She shifted her legs and the green scented water swirled. She frowned into the tub at her pale body, disjointed by light. She ought to be worrying about poor Esther, not herself.

For the next few weeks Verg Billups' dark figure remained on the periphery of her vision. She'd twist her head, alarmed, but it would be only a drooping pine branch or a swift cloud blotting the sun.

Sometimes, though, it really was Verg. For he and Esther reconciled, fought, talked it over, promised, threatened, then started the cycle once more. Esther seemed to be always in flight, jamming underwear, a toothbrush into her purse, spending the night on sofas and spare beds, never the same place twice or Verg could find her. A lawyer had been consulted, the court order issued, but Esther hesitated to enforce it. She'd talk about divorce; the next day she'd wonder aloud what to get Verg for Christmas. It was a long inconclusive process which wore on Meg's nerves as well. The grass was new and tender, the trees swayed with birds, and they slept with the window open. But she felt nothing was really changing, just the same endless feud, retreating, then flaring.

Esther had escaped serious injury so far. Perhaps the lawyer had sobered Verg, though Meg thought him incapable of self-control. The police had been called twice. Once Verg found the front door locked and took a tire iron to it. And once Meg watched from her kitchen through a fine silvery rain as Verg carried out armloads of Esther's clothes and heaped them in the gutter. A bored-looking policeman in a rain slicker arrived and made him put them back. When Esther was away Meg fed the kitten; she moved hurriedly through the dark kitchen, always expecting to hear Verg's fists splintering the door.

What do they fight about? David asked her. It was a Sunday morning, and the floor around him was strewn with newspapers, as if they were housebreaking a pet.

Meg shrugged. Everything. Nothing. Sometimes I think they enjoy it. Meg was surprised he mentioned Esther and Verg. His official position had remained that Meg shouldn't get so mixed up in the whole thing. They seldom spoke of it.

No really. What is there that makes him so violent, or is it just Verg's sweet disposition?

Well, she said, frowning, he accuses her of seeing other men. Does she?

Of course not, Meg said. Her voice was a little too heated; she checked it. Not that she wouldn't be justified, putting up with that maniac.

You mean he makes up the whole thing? That's hard to believe.

Why? Give other people credit for having imagination.

He stared at her. She thought this was how he confronted people at work when there was difficulty: eyes level, appraising, his whole body squaring itself. Verg's talents seem to be more in the manual line, he said, although he may have hidden executive potential.

You're making an unfair accusation about Esther.

I'm not accusing her. I simply posited that for so much smoke, there might be a small flame.

Why do you automatically take his side?

If I did, you automatically took hers.

Meg had no answer. She looked down at the floor, where some of the newspaper had wadded under his chair leg. I guess none of it makes much sense.

He agreed. The thing that's really zany is why she puts up with him.

Of course it was what she couldn't understand herself, and what Esther couldn't or wouldn't tell her. How often Meg found herself asking it, as if repetition would succeed where reason failed. One warm afternoon they sat in Meg's backyard, their bare feet ticklish in the mild air, not yet used to exposure.

Feels good, said Esther, arching her back so her shoulder blades nearly touched. Her slow movements were like a continual effortless dance. She had rubbed baby oil into her skin and it gleamed as if sunlight were trapped beneath its surface. She sighed. Wish we was at a beach.

Yeah. Meg closed her eyes. The darkness was veined with red. A beach in California.

Oregon.

Why Oregon?

Sounds like there'd be less people.

OK, Oregon. Behind her eyes Meg saw blue water and pale sand. She and Esther lay in the center of a wide beach. Nothing moved except the white frill of breaking waves. Even their footsteps had been smoothed away. And Meg, for once, did not sunburn, but toasted to an oiled golden brown.

Won't work.

Huh? Meg's eyes pried open.

I keep seein Verg sneak up behind us.

Meg laughed because she could see him too, peering over a cliff. He carried a spear and wore a grass skirt.

Damn, said Esther. He's everywhere. I guess there's no rest for the wicked.

Oh come on. It doesn't have to be like that. As she spoke their old argument hardened in the air. Esther, you could do so much better than him. You've got so much to offer—

Yeah, I got plenty. Just itchin to give it away. She rolled her hips in a mock bump and grind. I'm a real road worker.

You know what I mean, said Meg, annoyed at the evasion. You could do better.

Well, but I didn't.

So try again, you act like you're stuck with Verg til the end of your days.

Listen, said Esther, propping herself up on one elbow. Verg has been my friend, my lover, my husband, and my enemy. That's too much to take lightly.

Meg wanted to say Bullshit, it sounded like such a pat speech, but she didn't. At such times she felt, without knowing why, that their different races lay at the core of the misunderstanding, their differing assumptions. Some obstacle she could throw herself against forever without either of them understanding the other.

Don't David give you shit? Esther demanded.

Sure, sometimes.

Well I don't see you packin your bags.

Well he doesn't come after me with a tire iron, for one thing.

They were silent. Meg thought miserably that they both probably felt they'd proved their points. She tried seeing it Esther's way. Was that the only debate between them, how much shit you should take? Where was the dividing line? What would David have to do before she'd feel the situation was intolerable? When do you lose your pride, your dignity? Then she thought about leaving David and her vision went vast and blank as the beach she'd imagined earlier. She'd never considered it, even when she was angriest at him.

As if they both realized that it was a standoff they sighed. The sun was reddening, and the dampness of the ground seeped through the towels. I got to get moving, Esther said. I'm sposed to meet Verg in town for dinner.

Meg knelt and reached for her shoes, determined not to challenge her, not even to try. She watched Esther stooping over the towel. The slumped line of her back seemed to show more fatigue than Esther's words admitted. Esther, she said, you're my friend. Please don't get hurt.

Esther smiled. She seemed almost shy. Don't you neither.

When it happened it had the inevitability of nightmare. Glass broke over and over again, like a waterfall. The scream might have been her own; it rang, echoed in the dark bedroom, hung there, seemed to assume form. Then the sound she had always known she would hear, the long cracking of a gunshot.

They were both shouting before they were really awake, their arms colliding, beating against the darkness. David was saying, What—what—what—a hoarse monotone, her own voice not yet able to form words. She blinked, suddenly able to see in the dark. David was out of bed, cursing the furniture and struggling with his clothes. She found her robe and waited until he reached the kitchen. She heard the telephone click, heard him stuttering into it, then ran past him to the front door.

Stay in the house, she heard him scream. The heavy door cut him off. She ran, her bare feet sliding in the wet grass. The house next door lurched and tilted in her vision. Before she realized it she was through the door, calling Esther, Esther, her voice shrinking in the sudden silence.

Esther leaned against the refrigerator, her face hidden in her hands. Meg stopped, afraid to come closer. Then Esther lowered her hands and Meg saw her eyes streamed tears, not blood. Esther's lower lip rolled under and she said Aaah. Aaah, almost bleating. Meg looked past her, past the ruined window. In a shallow pool of blood, no larger than a dinner plate, lay the kitten, its fur dark and dripping, mouth drawn back in a rigid grin.

Then David seized her, making her stumble, and behind him the room filled with uniforms, heavy feet. David half dragged her outside, thrust his face in hers. You could have been killed, did you think of that?

She twisted away as far as his grip would let her, then sagged. A policeman emerged, steering Esther before him, trotting towards a car. Get back, a voice shouted, get back, and from behind the house two policemen led Verg Billups, his hands already locked behind him. Meg felt David's hand loosen on her shoulder. She broke free and ran to Verg, her heel sinking hard into his gut, fingers at his face. You fucking nigger, she screamed, fucking nigger, the words scalding her throat. She had never, she realized, spoken more than a dozen words to him. Then she was being pulled away and she struck at all of them, hating her weakness. She knew they were afraid to hurt her, and she took advantage of it, using her lowered head to batter them, until they raised it, and she spat. Then her arms were pinned behind her and she was on the ground.

Squinting through the tears she looked for Esther. She was sitting in the patrol car. Meg tried to call to her but as she did Esther looked up. Again Meg felt her throat burn, but there was nothing she could say. A current of black air seemed to expand, pushing them apart. Then David helped her to stand and they walked away.

Inside he gulped air, trying to slow his breathing before he spoke. I swear I don't know what's got into you.

She did not answer him but noted, with interest, the scrapes and grass stains on her palms, the hot thread of blood running from some cut inside her mouth. She would regard these wounds as badges and as preparations for the next assault.

MAIL

Judith Serin

The mailman walks across the street with an offering. It's not for me. I don't get mail anymore; I took down my mailbox. I wanted to flatten it like an aluminum beercan, one step and it pops. I couldn't. It was perfectly unyielding. I kicked it and stubbed my toe. It clattered down the porch steps, knocking over a jar with an angel-winged begonia I was rooting for my sister. "Oh fuck you," I screamed. My Neighbor Joe came to the doorway of the cottage behind. He's a carpenter. We finished the job with his sledge hammer, and he gave me a glass of root beer with a lemon squeezed in it. He's used to me.

It was easier than I thought. They may have tried to call, but I wasn't answering the phone. A man from the post office finally came by. "Oh she's moved," I explained, trying to look like a healthy young wife. "We're knocking down the partition, making the place into one apartment. For the baby, you know," I smiled complacently; healthy young wives always think having a baby is such an accomplishment. "No, she didn't leave her new address. I think she was moving to Australia."

That last may have been a bit much, but the post office man left. I guess they gave up.

LOVE STORIES

So you can't send me mail. There's no possibility I'll receive a letter with a bomb in it. I could send you one, I guess, but I'm afraid of the authorities. Remember how frightened I was before that flight to Bermuda? You probably thought I was afraid of the airplane. You looked smug, as usual; you love it when I'm scared of things, it makes you feel superior. Well, go ahead, you have little enough to feel superior about. At least you can be proud that you're too dumb for neuroses. Anyway, I wasn't scared of the airplane. I was terrified of the metal detector. All those cops and other officials with guns standing around, the mysterious machine which surely isn't infallible. Suppose it discovers I have silver lungs or a platinum uterus? They'd search my pockets, remove my clothes. They'd have to take me apart. Once accused, I'll confess to anything, you know that. I'd tell them, no matter how irrelevant, about my undeclared income for '71, the bill I never paid when I moved from Vermont, the marijuana I smoke—especially if they have guns or black ties.

You took advantage of this, you really did. When anything went wrong, you blamed me. You knew I believed you, no matter how vigorously I defended myself. You asked me if I read your mail because you knew I can't lie. You can lie, you did it constantly, with such ease I began to believe that you were simple-minded and didn't remember the truth. When I did something wrong, you waited. You knew I'd tell you. I saw your self-satisfied look. "He's waiting for me to tell him," I thought, and did. Then you exploded in simulated hurt surprise.

I'd gladly send you a bomb in a letter, I'd gladly send you a big bomb in a parcel post package, except that I'm afraid of authorities. They'd find me, the cracks in the sidewalk would lead them to me. They'd tape-record my voice and hear the fear in my breath. The color of my eyes would change when they mentioned your name. In them they would see my brain exploding again and again with you at the center.

I won't send you a bomb because police and FBI men can take an airplane across the country or even drive, if they want, gathering evidence along the way in truck stops in all those rectangular states I've never seen. But you can't take an airplane, you could never even take time off for a weekend in

Vermont. And if you could you wouldn't find me with a mailbox and my telephone always off the hook. Or would you come here, walking on the streets, looking for me? You're too dumb to read the cracks in the sidewalk, but you do have good eyes. You don't need glasses, you don't get sick, your blood is too thick for germs to live there, you can hear no messages of pain from your poor body, suffering on the cross of your cruel mind which won't listen to anyone. Still, you might walk on the streets and look for me.

Well I'm not worried. I'm more practical than you think; I can plan. If you come to town, I'll know. I have spies. A black woman walks past my window every morning in a beige raincoat and a blue knit cap, even when it's sunny. That cap knows me; it looks out for you. Some days, I ride on its beak to see if it's efficient. It is. We see everywhere in 360 degrees. We go to the central bus station to ride into the city. All newcomers must pass through there as through a metal detector. We watch for signs of you—the crumpled brown candy wrapper on the aqua linoleum, the balls of dust in the corners of long benches, tumbleweed blown by the wind of your malice.

I have a dog spy, too, a small, dirty one with sharp white teeth that will nip your ankles. All his fleas are watching. He trots around town, he visits every breakfast cafe, waiting by the door for blue-suited businessmen with doughnut crumbs on their lapels. When you come here, bleary from the late flight, a little heavier from all that distance, you will want coffee. No cafe is safe for you. You'll sit down, bending over to sip the first too hot mouthful from the too full cup, heating your hands on it. You'll shuffle your big feet under the table to find a berth for them. Then the teeth, the blood on the ankle, the alarm sounded.

Other spies stalk the town for me. You won't know them. I will tell you only that there are many caterpillars here, and many birds.

When you come we'll take action. The whole town will turn against you. This town is my friend. I know you won't believe me; you think 'I can't make friends, I'm too sensitive, too quiet, why don't I *talk* to people. I don't need to talk to this town. It lets me walk on its streets, buy an ice cream cone in its shops, admire the flowers and sunsets, all with a minimum of words and gestures. It will grow barricades overnight to stop you, huge concrete barrels in a line across the street. The plum trees will drop their fruit on the sidewalks. You'll slip, covering your slick, round-toed shoes in slime, staining your tweed trousers, landing on your ass in a pile of skin and seeds.

You'll walk on the fault and you won't know it's there until the sidewalk rumbles and opens under your feet. On Point Reyes in 1906 a crack opened under a cow, and she fell in. It closed over her, but her tail stuck out. The dogs ate it. This may happen to you. I can't decide which I'd rather leave in the air, your stupid, surprised head, choking with swollen tongue extended, or your slippery heel as you struggle in the suffocating soil, the earthworms and centipedes approaching.

So don't try to come after me because I haven't committed suicide yet. I know you're disappointed; you were so sure I couldn't live without you. You've been getting the Western papers, waiting for a small headline in the lefthand corner of the front page. You won't see it. With you I was always standing on chairs on top of couches reaching for a light bulb a little farther than my arm, always walking on decks on skyscrapers in the wind, my hat blowing away. Subway doors closed between us, the train headed toward Harlem with me on it. There were trapdoors in the long, well-lighted halls without windows. Any word of mine might trigger them. I might condemn myself to death or life imprisonment, asking for a morning glass of orange juice.

Now I stand here with my feet firm on the faulted earth and the hazy sky folds around me. I'm safe, encased in a new metal unknown to Eastern man. But don't think this is forever. Don't believe you'll get away with only a draw, with dropping it, and with time to make us forget until it's a tiny scar on the thumb, a twinge in the bone on rainy days. No. We'll meet again, when I'm ready.

Someday we'll be stranded on a desert island. I'll kill you with a sharp stick, watching the blood drip slowly from your chest. You'll watch it too; you'll die slowly while I dance around you singing songs you hate. I'll eat your flesh, roasting it over a pretty wood fire, seasoning it with leaves and flowers to cover the bitter taste. It will keep me till my ship comes in.

A WOMAN IN LOVE WITH A BOTTLE

Barbara Lovell

Lady wants a story about that, about a woman in love with a bottle. O.K. Once upon a time there was a bottle named vodkascotchcointreauretsinaB&B and cheap Gallo sherry. Woman's name was Barbara. Then you give a little description, a little background stuff, and crank up the plot—girl meets bottle, falls in love with bottle, overcomes a few obstacles to her passion with a bit of suffering; they of course get married, you put the sex parts in here somewhere. How it ends: they get a divorce, this being a modern story, BUT they live happily ever after which is unfashionable and won't sell worth a damn because we all crave that lonely existentialist anguish, right? You want to hear how it goes anyway?

Background stuff: broken home, acne, some confusion about sexual identity, immortal longings in her, artist and all. She cannot live with people, any one person long because screwing gets stale and predictable and so does what he or she says in the morning and when they get home from work at night. The ring around the bathtub isn't worth the trouble. There is also a lot of anger. That gets complex and subtle, part of the immediate plot. Develop as we go along.

LOVE STORIES

Let's do it in the first person and start in the middle. With the sex.

Scene: *Fucking the Vodka.*

I wake up feeling low down and good and excited. Secret. I am in East Orange, New Jersey, I am thirty-eight years old. The September sun is just pearling in. I stare at the wall, the usual first-light, leaf shadow filigree at four a.m. I want it not to dance so sharply from wind through the birch outside this second story window. I want nothing to move. My husband is sleeping; my child is sleeping across the hall; the whole campus is sleeping; there is no traffic.

The bed we sleep in, this man I'm married to and I, is a large wooden platform holding two single foam slab mattresses, constructed so as not to jostle one another as we toss in our nightmares. Clever and particularly satisfactory at this moment as I sit up carefully. Carefully. Because the usual morning evil gets going in the skull the minute the head is lifted from the pillow: the jackhammer, the waves tilting the seasick cochlea, the icepicks puncturing the retina to split a brain full of neurons with no defense. And carefully because it is important to move soundlessly, to make no sudden movement that will wake him. I must not wake anyone, only myself to keep this appointment at dawn. I am a thief in my own house; I move with stealth.

I do not flush the toilet. The stairwell is just outside the bathroom door. The third step down creaks, I have learned, if you step on the side near the bannister. I avoid it automatically.

Illicit love does, after a time, take on its sordid aspects. In the kitchen my breath comes short; I can't get across the room to the cabinet under the sink fast enough, and my hand reaching for the familiar beautiful blue-labeled clear gallon of vodka trembles. My eyes have stopped seeing the setting: grease scummed dishes in the sink, the wilting avocado plant in the window, the dog's water bowl slimy and stale. Sordid. I couldn't care less. I want what I've come for and I want it bad and I'm about to get it. Wanting. All the nerve ends tensely erect, begging, sweetly aching and stretching for contact. A spring coiled tight and coiling tighter every long second somewhere between belly and crotch.

I am skilled at illicit love. Even as I stand there shaking, really

36

shaking with desire, the bottle on the counter now and my fingers tenderly unscrewing the lid, my eye makes instantaneous, careful note of just how far down the label the level is. Not halfway yet, just about at the top of the final "f" in Smirnoff. Sometimes when you're fucking you can't even take time to get undressed, it's too urgent. This is urgent, that spring may snap, and I don't fool with a glass. No foreplay, just the long, sweet release. Bad prose there, same modifier in less than 100 words. But the aching is sweet and the coming is sweeter—no other word for it, it is very, very sweet: that spring finally letting go, the starved nerves getting full and fed and satisfied, relaxing down now, pleasantly limp, sort of purring. In the belly that spreading lifeglow it had been tight for. And warm, so warm. Real good. Jackhammer, icepicks gone. Hand steady. You can walk a straight line and prove it down the linoleum squares. The inner ear feels fine, hums a little in delight. Every cell saying thank you.

I water that sad avocado, but I don't want to think about how it got so sad; I am too happy. I save some of the water in the measuring cup for the blue-labeled gallon, bring the level back up to the "f." Which creates certain problems I'll solve later. Foreshadowing here: hidden bottle bound to arrive on the scene. Right now this bottle and I guard our secret, no one will know.

Back up the stairs, the world still sleeping. I crawl into my side of the bed, into my customary fetal position, my back to this man to whom I have just been unfaithful, and sleep the sleep of a woman who has just been thoroughly and expertly loved.

That takes care of the middle up to the turning point, the—so to speak—climax. Where does the beginning begin, the necessary flashback: courtship, assignations, admissions, the deep sworn vows?

It's such an old story.

Twenty-three years ago. The only undergraduate in a faculty member's living room with six graduate students. Bessie Smith and Jelly Roll Morton on the player. Always, from the first, that funky, low down mood. Everyone drinking martinis, no, Gibsons—it was the smart, in-thing. Everybody except me because in those days drinking was against the honor code for undergraduates. In spite of the blues on the hi-fi and the Gibsons, everybody was feeling pretty miserable. We had gathered at the home of this faculty member, a kind of mentor, to console ourselves for a failure. We, who? Jill the dancer, Anne the painter, Louise the violinist, Helen the playwright, I the poet, and John the Renaissance man, a nineteen year old philosopher and aesthetician who knew all things. It was the first night of Christmas vacation which also happened to be the deadline for entries for the Spring fine arts festival. For weeks we had worked and talked with the total faith and enthusiasm of the young at the age when they believe that they and they alone have seen the light. We had invented, we thought, A New Art Form. It was to be all the arts in one, staged in a new, incredible, perfect harmony. And of course we had not gotten it together. And we had done a lot of talking and made a lot of promises to the whole school, including skeptical professors we were going to prove wrong. So. We could hardly face ourselves, how were we to face the world. Or go home and have a Merry Christmas.

After the second Gibson, Jill, who was six feet tall and all long bones and angles, rose in one motion from her crosslegged position on the parquet floor and began to dance her parody of our tragic plight—clutched brow, moritified slump, quick, static posture of agony, the dying fall. Helen began to giggle and recite *Four Saints, Three Acts: when this you see, remember me.* John and Louise tangled on the sofa, first in a mock fight and then settling down to necking, John still holding his Gibson in his left hand and exploring Louise's blouse front with his right. I watched Louise reach to loosen her ponytail and let her dark hair fall free, something I'd never seen before.

I sat well back in the corner, desolate, furious with them, openly weeping. As far as I was concerned it was the end of the world, life could not go on. Anne, to whom I was closest, Anne who had eyes straight out of Etruscan paintings and which, I thought, saw everything, watched me weep for a while and then said to Claire, our faculty hostess, "For god's sake, give Barbara a drink."

Claire brought me some tomato juice. "Legal." It was the best tomato juice I had ever tasted. The first swallow I felt better. Immediate relief to all that pain and grief and shame. I drank it straight down and felt wonderful. Claire brought me another. That warm glow, that satisfied well-being. The hell with the New Art Form, this was something really worth my time. Got up and mimed our absurdity with Jill, I who had never danced, never used my body to express anything at all. And so fell in love, first kiss, with someone whose name I didn't even know. I was in love, I later learned, with Bloody Mary.

And sang it in the shower for months afterwards: "Bloody Mayree is th' gurl I lo-ove." I was really happy. And kept going back to Claire's every chance I got for more. I got a lot of chances. It was a fine year.

The analogy grows tedious: first blackout, loss of virginity, beginning cocktail hour a little earlier, taking care as I brought them in from the kitchen that the scotch on the rocks in my left hand was mine because it held the extra, secret, generous splash, gradually working it so we had three drinks before dinner instead of one, establishing the nightcap as legal-assignations, stolen moments, whatever. You get the drift, let's drop it.

Scenes from a Bigamy:
Every couple has a formula: let's play house tonight, see you later alligator, with a significant look. Ours was simply, let's try to get to bed early tonight. Goody, put off grading papers (though my cleverness had somehow allowed me to drink wine to get through that onerous task) and make gimlets, drink gimlets, lots of them, nobody counting; prolong "foreplay" for hours and get blissfully numb. Three or four nights a week. And more and more my suggestion. Afterwards one more to go to sleep on (pass out on), celebrate because it had all been so good, we were so skilled, so compatible, so inventive, so free. The lies.

Across the street from us on faculty row lived Cathy: blonde, Scandanavian, a sculptress—metal welding—very good at her work. Not pretty but a good face, reminded me of Clavdia Chauchat in *The Magic Mountain.* Unhappily married like everyone else in the world. And funny. I, over cocktails one noon at the Metropolitan Museum, "Cathy, have you ever been abroad?" She, "Only for thirty-two years." Bright, smart, sensitive. We used to go into the city, gallery hopping and doing the museums. She knew the names and dates of every Kline and deKooning in the Modern. We talked intensely about art and poetry. We talked wittily about bad marriages. She was a jazz freak, too. I liked her. My friendships with women have always been close, too close sometimes. When I was too drunk to drive to the liquor store Cathy would go for me. I liked her so much I gave her my husband. This generosity took care of my guilt and eventually allowed me a separate bedroom and a private bottle right there when I wanted it—which was most of the time. I could stay there for hours; I think it was along in here I switched to sherry for daytime love, for writing my inspired poetry. I, of course, couldn't loosen up to write without a drink. Could anybody? Don't all poets drink?

Quadrangle: him, Cathy, me, Gallo sherry. I liked Cathy so much I very nearly gave her my child. She had none of her own and adored children, especially my nine year old daughter who returned her adoration. Cathy taught her to play the piano, took her to work with her on sets at the college theatre, and would happily come over to my kitchen and fix lunch when Stacy came home from school if I were too drunk to pour the milk or find the pimento cheese. Up to a point, I was grateful.

That point: one fine afternoon in spring I come home from school. (Pattern then: pre-dawn rendezvous with the blue label which, supplemented with spiked orange juice at breakfast, enabled me to function with my classes, home for sherry lunch which got me through in pretty good shape until the early cocktail hour, a few clear hours in the afternoon holding on to the promise of that hour.) That afternoon I had an inspiration. I'd take Stacy to Turtleback Zoo, we'd have a fine time, just the two of us. They had a new acquisition, a small furry beast, a hyrax, but *kin to an elephant*. Which knocked me out. Stacy and I both adored animals, any animals. This was a special thing I could give her.

When I walked in, my husband, Cathy, and Stacy were down

on the green rug in the living room playing poker—a passion he and Cathy shared and Stacy had contracted. Stacy was bright, too; sometimes she won and was noisily triumphant. We all thought it was marvelous.

I, "Hi, gang. Stacy, finish that hand and get your jacket, I've got a big surprise."

Stacy had green eyes, the real thing, like her father. When she looked up at me that afternoon they were cloudy, hidden somehow. What was this? I'd never seen that before. Something in the bottom of my stomach grabbed the answer before it got to my head. She didn't want to go. Playing poker with them was more fun than going anywhere with me. There was embarrassment. Resentment. Even annoyance. I was suddenly an intruder. When this message got to my brain, I scrambled, bribed.

"The zoo, honey, we'll go to Turtleback. They've got something new and really amazing. And we'll get an icey."

She looked down at her cards, raised the ante. She didn't know what to say to me. My husband and Cathy were laughing at her bet. I didn't exist.

"Stacy, the zoo!" Something in my tone reached Cathy.

She, "It's all right, honey, you can go."

I could not believe it. Cathy was giving *my* child *permission* to go out on a spring afternoon with her own mother. Stacy still did not look up. She didn't want permission; she didn't want me.

So now I hated my good friend Cathy. Jealousy is a much more uncomfortable emotion than guilt. She could have my husband, but not my child. I needed a drink. And had one, a long one straight from the bottle an hour and a half before cocktail hour; and another one until something, pain I think, but not the rage, eased. Then upstairs to my room, slamming the door as hard as I could and heading straight for the bottom dresser drawer where the Gallo sherry resided under my sweaters. On the bed fully clothed. The nerves that had been listening for every sound from them, hoping for Stacy's steps coming up the stairs, gradually began not to give a damn, and I let the sherry seduce me into blankness. Just not think, turn off. Pass out.

I don't yet know what they said, how they got dinner, got to bed. The next morning Stacy brought me coffee in bed and hugged me. Neither of us said anything. I knew, in some way, it was only that she had been having fun. And then, too, I *had* been gone from her in one way or another a long time. But Cathy. Terror began to rise. I reached for the Gallo which tasted terrible. Cancelled classes and stayed in bed until time for Stacy to come home from school. For a couple of days I coped. We never did go to the zoo.

Repeat this scene any number of times. Except that when Cathy came over I went upstairs. And the coping got foggier. And the terror more intense.

I guess that's the climax. Or this: one morning that summer lying on the couch caught in the terror cycle. Staring into a cold fireplace, the winter ashes still not taken out. Stacy was just outside the door to the left of the fireplace on the screened porch teaching herself magic card tricks. I could see from the window across the room Cathy weeding the flower bed along her front walk. My husband was at the college teaching in summer session. I had a salty dog, very little grapefruit juice, propped on my chest. I was trying to break the terror cycle so that I could walk. I wasn't drunk. Just frozen. I wanted to go out to the backyard and cut the old-fashioned tea roses—one bush was actually orange—we had inherited from some flower loving faculty member at least twenty years back. I wanted to put them in a certain blue-grey salt glaze vase we'd gotten in Nashville, Tennessee, before Stacy was born. She loved flowers, I did too. We all did. This was the first year I hadn't helped her plant her own flower garden, her zinnias and nastursiums. I really *wanted* those roses on the teakwood table before lunch. But I couldn't move. The terror cycle is awful. It had grown familiar, become a daily battle. It's hard to describe. There's the ice in the belly. Then something rising up, constricting the throat, invading the brain, actually impairing eyesight. Rationality departs, you cannot think, the heart thuds, knees weaken. It's worse than that. It is, I suppose, a kind of reverse of that satisfying warm and soothing feeling of liquor going down the gullet to the belly, that hot *yes* that then spreads to the nerves, the head, and the consequent illusion of being unusually clear-headed, in control and at ease. It's a cycle because liquor helps immediately, thaws the ice and you can breathe. It must be like an adrenalin injection when you're choking with asthma, nitroglycerin for angina, morphine for the junkie—I don't know. It's a cycle because it doesn't last. The liquor wears off more and more quickly as the months pass, terror returns, even worse, requires more liquor. And so on. This morning I drained the salty dog and nothing happened. The ice was still right there. The gin bottle was on the rug beside me, I filled the glass, hands shaking so badly I splashed as much on the rug as into the glass, and drained it—nothing, no help, just out of my mind terrified. I threw the glass shattering it into the fireplace and screamed, not from the brain, but from the ice in the belly and in a voice I couldn't recognize as mine, "Oh, god, I want to die!" I meant it.

Stacy came running in and there was *my* terror in *her* green eyes, "Mother, mother, don't curl your fingers like that. Mother please!"

I looked at the catatonic claws that were my hands still in the motion of throwing that glass. I looked at her terrified face. "Go get Cathy."

Denouement. More of the same cycle, but not the screaming. Stacy having nightmares, clearly uneasy when her father wasn't around. Psychiatrists, marriage counselors, even one comic, idiotic scene when my husband was in a committee meeting and Stacy was over at Cathy's, with two over-rouged evangelical women from A.A. I thought they were cheap and contemptible. I still do.

I struggled to an understanding of my hang-ups from a broken-home childhood, my anger and resentment at being married to a man much brighter than I was and, more important, a better writer, my anger at myself for having given that man my mind, the humiliation when a colleague would ask what I thought about some fairly elementary literary matter and my complete loss: I have to go home and ask my husband what I think about Pound's contribution to Eliot's development as a poet. Anger at having given away the child I worshipped. Anger at having failed to do the writing I had always believed I had to do and wanted to do. A lot of anger. A lot of understanding. No good. Terror. And liquor the only help.

One week that summer my husband took Stacy to visit his parents. I was in no shape to go and didn't want to and even knew, dimly and reluctantly and heartbreakingly, Stacy's need to be away from me for a while. I, of course, promised him not to drink, that I'd get straightened out, etc., both of us knowing I was lying. The dog stayed with me.

For about an hour after the car pulled away from the curb, I felt a great calm. No fear. This is nice. I'll feed the dog. Dog bowl by kitchen cabinet containing blue-labeled vodka bottle, as you remember. So have a drink, a nice normal unterrified drink. Then do something pleasant, take a walk, pick the roses. Yeah.

Well, something new: the liquor triggered the terror. For three days I lived on valium from the first psychiatrist, thorazine from the second, and vodka. I forgot to feed the dog. Didn't eat myself, most of the time just plain forgetting to. When I remembered, I got nauseated. I remember noticing a white crinkled scum of mold on the surface of a pot of Scotch Barley soup on the stove, and vomiting in the kitchen sink.

I was afraid to sleep in my own bed. I slept in Stacy's which kept her own special sweet odor, trying, I think, to make some kind of hopeless contact with her. For some reason I read Graham Greene's *Complaisant Lover* over and over, the print blurring, not remembering when I got to the end what I had read and so compulsively reading it over again. I must have read it twenty-five times.

Wandering the empty rooms, driving back roads, bottle in the passenger seat, getting lost and too scared to cry. For days I had been having convulsive stomach spasms and flushing of face and chest; it had happened from time to time before, and the doctors had never been able to explain it, but now it was constant. One night spasming on the couch, in the dark, staring at the spot where I knew the fireplace was, I had this sudden, kinesthetic, claustrophobic feeling: I cannot inhabit my own skin anymore, I've got to get out. How do you get out of your own skin? A drink to get to the telephone. "Cathy, can you come?" A drink while I waited. The last one.

The medical doctor, the specialist in alcoholism who'd been working with me, met us at the hospital. He was a big, fatherly, gentle, reassuring man. He put his arms around me, and I had the illusion, like that peaceful moment when my husband and child had driven away, that it was going to be o.k. My dignity was somewhat salvaged by the admitting diagnosis, acute gastritis. In the wheelchair, up the elevator, sitting limply on a chair by the door while nurses moved around doing something efficient. Cathy left. Dr. Berlan left. I needed a drink. Badly. My roommate was the typical fascinated-with-illness, tactless, fake commiserative type, "What's wrong with you, my dear?"

"I'm a goddamned alcoholic." Silence.

In bed, hooked up to the I.V., shot full of some kind of tranquilizer that's supposed to help. The silent disapproving resident leaves. The nurses leave. The roomie goes to sleep. The panic returns in a rush, as bad as it's ever been. Worse. I jerk the I.V. needle from the vein, ring the bell. I've got to get out of here. I've got to get to Stacy. To the nurse when she comes, "This is a mistake, I have to get out of here." She takes one look, wheels around, and I hear them paging the resident. Another nurse comes in. We fight. I want out of that bed and she holds me down. I've *got* to get to Stacy. The woman in the next bed is praying for me. The resident comes in a hurry. He is very angry and very rough. Informs me I could easily have died, have been very stupid, there are people really sick in this hospital, he will not tolerate such nonsense.

Something strange happens to time at this point. All at once I notice that there is an awful lot of blood on the sheets they are changing, that he is Philippino, that the needle has been reinserted, my arm strapped to a board, my feet tied to the foot of the bed, my cigarettes gone, the side rails up, and the roomie is moaning of pain and interrupted sleep while they jab a needle into my right buttock. I want a drink.

I must have slept. It is light. Dr. Berlan stands over me, a hand on my shoulder. He informs me gently that today will be the worst, that he'll give me shots for the withdrawal symptoms. He's right. The day is agony. The slightest movement on my part, the nurses', the roomie's scrapes, flays every raw nerve and they're all raw. I try now to think of some neat literary simile and fail. If the whole body and brain were a skinned knee and they poured on iodine, it wouldn't even come close. But the worst is the I.V. The eternity between each drop and I am hypnotized, have to watch, wait, beg that hanging drop to fall. Trying to force the level in the bottle to go down but can't perceive it, the way you can't perceive the hour hand on a clock move. I beg for shots, and the nurses get angry, and I'm beyond caring.

This goes on for three days. When my husband and Stacy come to get me, she brings me huge red and blue Mexican paper flowers. When Dr. Berlan dismisses me he explains about the metabolic process of the liver and antabuse, how I won't drink anymore now because I'm intelligent and understand that this will make me very, very ill, I'll feel absolutely lousy.

He's wrong. What woman in love ever was rational, when did intelligence ever win over desire? He was right about the antabuse. You feel like hell. You think you're going to die.

Repeat the above scene, omitting the part about jerking the needle out, three times. Lovers are slow learners.

Then one day it's over. All over. The analogy applies. You just aren't in love anymore. It's gone flat, magic fled, the thrill is gone—all the sentimental pop songs are right. No will power involved at all. No strength of character. It's just all over, no magnetism there, nothing.

So that's the denouement. Of course I left my husband, left Stacy with him where she belongs. Some years have passed. She visits me and we have a good time. She's my best friend. I have a new dog. I go to drinking parties, me and my diet cola, and it's great fun. I'm in love again. With myself. With this pen on this page. With a poet I see from time to time, another writer better than I, but that's somehow irrelevant now. In love with my students. With this good life. I wake up feeling good, secret, excited. Who knows, this may be the day I write something good. I can't wait.

Lady wanted a story about a woman in love with a bottle. Wonder if this is it?

HORSES

Lee Smith

How the Indian Got the Horse

Once I turned the television on and here came a weary Indian, walking across the plains. The plains stretched in every direction as far as the eye could see. From one corner of the plains a horse came galloping, tossing his mane. He was not tired at all. The Indian was weary and footsore. The horse came galloping across the plains. The Indian had an idea! He snapped his fingers. He quickly gathered a handful of something horses love. He held it out toward the horse. The horse came galloping across the plains, jerked it from the Indian's hand, and ate it all up. Then he galloped away. The Indian stomped his foot. Then he gathered some more. This scene was repeated several times. At last the Indian grabbed the horse's pure white mane, swung up, clamped himself around the horse, and they went galloping across the plains. This did not last long. The horse began to rear and snort. He tossed the Indian far up into the clouds. He whinnied and galloped away. The Indian lay on the ground and wept. He got up and looked around, but the plains were empty and stretched in every direction as far as the eye could see. The

Indian sighed. It was night. The Indian ate some jerky and went to sleep. There was a commercial. Did the Indian dream of horses?

It was early morning. A white, ghostly mist drifted across the plains. Out of this mist galloped the horse, tossing his white mane, straight up to where the Indian slept on the ground. It bent down and nuzzled him. The Indian leaped up. He patted the horse. The horse nuzzled him and pushed at him with its nose. There was some horseplay. Then the Indian sprang up on the horse's back and they galloped away through the fine white mist together across the plains, flying, the horse's hooves above strange vegetation, fennel and artichokes and larkspur, together over the unimaginable plains.

My Actual Experience with Horses

My actual experience with horses has been slight. When I was small I was sent every year to a camp, although I was homesick and scared of bugs. At the camp we had a Wish Day. On Wish Day we could do anything that we had not signed up for. My specialty at that point was the making of lanyards.

On Wish Day I stopped making lanyards and walked up the hill to the riding ring. It was hot there and the riding counselors had circles of sweat beneath their arms in their Oxford cloth shirts. They were chewing gum.

We went on a trail ride. My horse was named Martini. He kicked, they said, and so they put me at the end of the line. We entered the woods where it was even hotter and the leaves were a dark, dusty green and they brushed our faces as we went past at a Walk. Crossing a clearing, we attempted the Trot. The Trot was bouncy. We became exhilarated. The counselors passed it back to Walk again.

Once when someone fell off her horse we all stopped and the horses began to eat the leaves. I looked around. Then I thought: I will remember this for the rest of my life. I have, too. Yet it is a completely unremarkable memory: how hot it was, the way the leaves looked, the green fly buzzing around Martini's black neck as he leaned forward, eating the leaves.

The next year, on Wish Day, I took Dramatics.

HORSES

I am married to John of John's Body Shops, otherwise known as the King of Rock and Roll. He is becoming rich. He owns six Body Shops, two in the city and four in outlying areas. The Body Shops sell records and clothes. The Body Shops have mirrored walls, black light, incense and periodic art shows. Before my father died, he said, "Martha, your husband is a dingbat." I am not sure this is true. To work, John wears jeans, boots, a vest and a serape. John has a pony tail. To relax, he sometimes wears a tie. John is 38.

The Horse Family Includes the Horse, the Ass, and the Zebra

The horse family (Equidae) is now represented by one genus only (Equus), which includes the horse, the ass, and the zebra. The Quagga, of this genus, became extinct in 1872. The horse family, the rhinoceros family and the tapir family are believed to be descended from a common ancestor with five toes on each foot and with the middle toe in line with the axis of the leg. In the horse genus, the other toes have disappeared or have become vestigial, the foot being now what was once the middle one of five toes. The horse's hoof corresponds to the nail of man's big finger or third toe. The horse genus is descended from the Eohippus genus of the Eocene epoch, about 45,000,000 years ago. The Eohippus (GR: dawn horse) was about eleven inches high, or about the size of a fox. It had four toes on each front foot and three toes on each hind foot. Its home was the region that is now the Great Plains of North America. Similar animals of the horse family lived in the Old World at the same time. These became extinct.

The Horses in Our House

We had three children in a row. When they were small, it was difficult to eat dinner. Whenever we sat down to eat dinner, a catastrophe occured. At last I worked out a solution. Johnny was 4; Libby was 3; the baby was very small. I put the baby in her carriage and wheeled it into the dining room. I put the two rocking horses in the dining room. We ate by candlelight. At the edge of the candlelight we could see their faces, back and forth or up and down, and the creaking of the springs put the baby to sleep.

I think that is the only real solution I have ever made. Unfortunately, it did not last.

The Olive Versus the Horse

The city of Athens, having as yet no name, held a contest. The city would take the name of the god or goddess who gave it the most valuable gift. Poseidon struck a stone with his trident and out popped a horse. The people cheered. The goddess Athena came bearing a shrub. "What is that shrub you've got there?" they asked. "This is no shrub! This is an olive tree," explained Athena. "It will make you rich." The people cheered even louder. Athena won the contest and the olive tree took root.

My Mother's Friend

When my mother was young, she lived on the Eastern Shore of Maryland. My mother's best girl friend's name was Lydia. Lydia's family raised trotters and one of the trotters, Dan Cord, won many races and became famous all over the Eastern Shore. Lydia was famous too, later on. But when they were young girls, my mother and Lydia and Lydia's father took a load of bricks on a boat somewhere and were becalmed for three days. Later, Lydia became incredibly beautiful. She was Miss Maryland. She was so beautiful that a total stranger came to the gate of her house on the Eastern Shore and shot himself dead beside the mailbox. He left her a note inside the mailbox. "I think you are very pretty," the note said.

Who Has Horses?

1. The Four Horsemen of the Apocalypse.
2. Helios, whose horses pull the sun. These included Amethea (no loiterer) and Erythreos (red producer).

3. The Pale Rider.
4. Pluto. One of his horses is named Abaster (away from the stars).
5. O'Donohue, whose horses are white waves which come on a windy day, topped with foam. Every seventh year on May Day, O'Donohue himself reappears and can be glimpsed gliding, to beautiful but wild music, over the lakes of Killarney on his own white horse. Fairies with flowers precede him.

The Steeplechase

A long time ago I was in love with a crazy boy, not John, who is dead now. Once we went to a Steeplechase. We had a box. There were three couples in this box. The girls wore corsages and light wool spring suits. I had a pink suit. Ann had a green suit. Mary Louise had a yellow suit. A friend of ours was riding in the race. He was very thin. He looked big from the front of his jodphurs and very thin from the side when he went by on his horse, up out of the saddle, leaning forward.

I had been to the drugstore that day and the druggist had given me three free samples of a new banana perfume. I took the samples out of my purse, and Mary Louise, Ann, and I put on the perfume. It was terrible. People in the neighboring boxes turned around. We were all laughing. Our friend won the big race, the Iroquois. His horse finished lengths and lengths ahead of other horses. When he won, I wanted very much to kiss him. Instead I kissed the boy I was in love with, banana perfume and all.

On weekdays I get John off to his Body Shops, my children off to school, and go back to bed for an indeterminate length of time. Sometimes I go out to the branch library for a good look at back issues of *The Chronicle of the Horse*. I am most apt to cry in the afternoon. At dinner, I am competent and cheerful.

Mint Juleps

Our friend Carter had a mint julep party outdoors for her 100 most intimate friends. One of the guests was the Arab psychiatrist, Paul Fuad. I pulled him into a corner of the porch and made him listen.

"Do you want an appointment?" he said.

"No."

"Social work?" he said.

"My motives could not be worse."

He kept inching away.

"Tell me what to do!"

"I think," Paul Fuad said, sipping his drink, "that the thing to do is free your mind of horses."

I became indignant. "Horses are as good as anything else!" I snapped.

He stared at me inscrutably over the mint in his glass, beads of water beading up the picture of Citation winning the Derby on his Kentucky Derby glass.

I began to laugh.

"Why are you laughing now?" he asked.

I let him go. Arabs are not ironic.

Katherine the Great

We all know how Katherine the Great met her end. I think we know. Actually I am afraid to look her up at the branch library for fear it is not so. I think Katherine the Great was an insatiable nymphomaniac. I think no man could ever satisfy her. I think she took a fancy to a great white stallion in her stables and had him rigged up with an intricate system of pulleys to satisfy her insatiable lust. I think the experience was beyond her wildest dreams. Unfortunately, the system of pulleys failed. The great white stallion crashed down and crushed her there on the stable floor.

The End

I Dream of Horses

In my dreams I am walking through deep green grass which has no texture or weight; formless, it swirls in widening concentric circles about my dissappearing feet. There are tall black tropical trees like thunder-clouds which toss in the wind at the edge of the dream. I know they are over there. I am on a Stallion Hunt. I carry a stallion trap baited with olives and something horses love.

I set the trap. I place it in the center of the clearing where it disappears immediately into the swirling grass. I move back but keep clear of the trees. I know they are over there. I look at my watch. The stallions should be coming now. It is time for the stallions to show up. This place is supposed to be a favorite haunt of stallions. Where are they? I am dismayed and anxious.

Suddenly from the edge of the dream comes the tiny Eohippus or dawn horse, cantering gaily. He is eleven inches high. He canters along through the grass, going straight toward my trap. I stand; I am screaming at him; I am running to stop him. Running is hard in this kind of grass. He has reached the trap. I reach him with my hand outstretched. Luckily, the trap has disappeared.

The tiny Eohippus stands perfectly still but quivering all over. He stares up at me with his big dark eyes. I kneel beside him in the moving grass. I touch him. He steps forward, hesitates, backs off. The trees are over there. He steps forward again and nuzzles me with his warm nose. I look down. This unusual Eohippus has tiny perfect hooves already, each hoof corresponding to the nail of my big finger or third toe.

The Rose
In The Snow

Kathryn Kramer

There was a northern woman in the north, a southern woman in the south, but their thoughts were elsewhere.

The northern woman was blonde-haired and blue-eyed and had a clear skin of rosy complexion; she was pure, quiet, dispassionate, reserved, cold. The southern woman's hair was as dark as a room without light and her face pale as the verge of passion; she loved indiscriminately, was the adored of the earth, of men hastening to plunge back into it before their natural deaths.

The northern woman sat in her parlor, boots buttoned up above the ankles, hands in her lap, watching the snowflakes pile up in inexorable delicacy around the house. Upstairs, counterpanes stretched neatly; dark posts decreed the air observe the indecipherable message of the bed. In the attic, in locked trunks, were stored all her possible lives.

The tears of the northern woman were shed one at a time into tiny glass vials which stood on the upper edges of the windows; it was so cold there that the tears had no time to splay but froze pear-shaped as they fell. When the southern woman relaxed her vigilance, the lemon-colored sun coalested in the gray northern sky, and the tears refracted the light into the four primary colors which danced over the woman's pale hands and allowed her to flex her fingers, stretch her stiff feet, and exhale.

In the south, the woman yawned and caressed poppies. She pricked her finger with the thorn of a rose and tasted the blood with eager tongue. She embraced the willow and the cottonwood, sniffed their fallen balls of dust, sneezed. She cast her anxious limbs into the unmown rye, nostrils quivering as bees lit to suck pollen from her red lips.

Moon, she cried, you are a poor relation! You hover over the tall house in the north—go ahead, starve! And you, Sun! Even you are but the pampered patriarch of my house. When I inhale, the stars pull into formation. Light, she cried, I am illumination! And, mouth open wide, she drew the fat sun into her mouth. Sucking hard, she elongated it into an oval, then into the shape of a gourd. She opened her throat, sucked with her lungs, her stomach, her thighs, her calves until the molten pear and all of its rays pulsed inside of her.

In the north, the woman sighed as the shadows lengthened, and the pitiful moon tried in its roundness to impersonate the sun in her window. She chafed her cold hands and knelt to blow the embers of the fire into flame. She continued to kneel, her legs as shamelessly unarranged under her long woolen skirt as under bedcovers, while the red and orange tongues lapped at the absence of everyone she had ever known and everyone she never would know.

What's the MATTER? breathed the dark-haired woman, curls falling into her eyes. The woman in the north stared at the moon and wondered if it were responsible. Matter? Was something the matter?

The doorbell pealed—great rich tones scampering through the house—and the butler brought calling cards—hundreds of them. The southern woman laughed and blew on the ebullient red of her fingernails. She held up the cards with her toes, while outside oleander climbed the white columns, poppies sprouted in cracks on the floor of the veranda, huge turquoise blossoms snowed on the roof and smothered the chimney. The southern woman gasped and ran to the fireplace as petals the color of an azure sea neither of the women had ever seen wafted into her drawing room.

I knew it! she cried. Oh, I knew it!

The butler asked, What do you intend to do now, Madam?

Do? she laughed at him, splashing into the azure petals which drifted into piles like leaves. Do? She tossed them into the air where they turned into birds, who sang with a sweetness so rich that the fish in the pond lay their heads on the waterlilies to listen.

In the north, the kneeling woman continued to imagine elsewhere, while the farmhand stomped the snow from his boots and said, I've never seen it last like this. It's drifted up over the roof of the shed—you can no longer tell where the fields dip; the wind fills up all the gullies. Somebody must be mad. If the tunnel to the barn caves in, the cows will starve before I can get back.

The woman looked at the letters stuffed into cracks in the plaster, stuffed around the door and window edges to keep the draughts out. She rose from her crouching and told the farmhand to stay in the barn with the animals until the snow let up. There is scarcely any cruelty to equal the cruelty to animals, she said, and sat back in her chair to continue her passionate waiting.

No lovers will be able to penetrate the snow to reach your chill fortress, the southern woman scoffed.

You have so many lovers, they dishevel you; better to remain pure...

Frozen, you mean.

Which way is the population moving?

The envy, hatred, and adoration of the southern woman for the northern woman and of the northern woman for the southern woman were not limited by time and space, only by the bounds of their imaginations. Their passions ordered the vegetation of the world, its weather, the tides of the great oceans, the architecture of centuries, the sun and the moon.

They were not certain, however, of their geography. For the butler's benefit, the southern woman referred to northerners as gaunt, hard, thin-lipped; the northern woman assured her hired man she could easily go south if she wanted. But the northern woman didn't know any longer whether she acted as she did because she wanted to or because the southern woman forced her, or whether her picture of the southern woman included the southern woman's picture of her, or whether either of them were any less changeable than the shifting currents moving up and down the continent, or whether they were on the map. It was not clear, in other words, whether or not they existed.

The southern woman began to wonder if she were not a bit harsh in her judgment of the northern woman. Might not the northern woman, for instance, on a warm day, put on her snowshoes and revel in the winter woods in the very way the northern woman imagined the southern woman writhing in humid ecstasy in the magnolia forest? The northern woman thought she might be a little silly—certainly the southern woman must at times feel despondent, and the southern sky sometimes cloud over, and the southern woman have to ring petulantly for a butler not trained in the art of fire building (as is my hired man, thought the northern woman with satisfaction).

The uncertainty, however, was more unbearable than war in a country without maps, so they renewed their bickering.

You steal all my lovers.

That's impossible, they were never yours.

Your intensity will drive them in my direction.

At least I have them to lose.

The southern woman hurled burning stars at the northern woman, but by the time they reached her hemisphere, they had cooled and twinkled lamely against the endless snow, the frozen rivers and ponds. The northern woman watched and did not try to stop the southern woman from devouring fields of ripe grain, quenching her thirst with slow rivers, jarring the keystones of arches of great cathedrals neither of them had ever seen, and resting, replete, among the massive, fluted columns that stood still for her.

The northern woman rose to ascertain that all the doors to the outhouse were shut. Damn that hired man, she thought, damn his ill tidings and country predictions, but she could not reassure herself that his forecasts were unfounded, so she wrapped her shawl more tightly about her shoulders while the southern woman rolled onto her back on a muddy, sun-drenched riverbank, while alligators tickled her feet with their snouts and watersnakes brought her sprigs of wild mint in their tight mouths to cool her forehead.

Some say the forces are moving north, some say they are moving south. One or the other of you must be wrong, Madam, stated the butler.

You can't both be right, smirked the hired man, in his barn.

Oh, what do you know about it? the women shouted in unison. And they laughed. But without that unifying force of opposition, they drifted apart again, and peasants in countries the women had no time to imagine stopped working—what is it all for? they wondered—and wiped their damp brows with their shirtsleeves. The southern woman fanned herself drearily with a torn fan, and thought of the northern woman taking out a pearl-stemmed pen and trying once again to explain in her elegant, measured script to all her lovers why it could not work out.

They are moving north! shouted the southern woman. They are buttoning up coats and waiting for a fire to allow them to be giddy.

They are moving south, the northern woman contradicted, sucking lemon drops and smiling indiscriminately.

Are you certain, inquired the hired help, that there is movement in either direction?

The northern woman's fingers were turning blue, and her toes were numb as she shoved the last few logs onto the fire. She thought of the southern woman, rolling off the brocade chaise lounge into the arms of her afternoon lover.

My heart has changed, pleaded the southern woman. Let me breathe on your frozen tears and melt them. She moved toward the window.

I can't let you do that. I can't.

How exasperating you are! If you fear my influence, at least set the vials on the mantle and let the tears melt by themselves.

What use would I have for them once they melted?

You could pour them together . . .

And then?

The southern woman threw her arms around the northern woman. Then empty the vials into a cup, one of your fragile china cups with violets or pansies on it, and I will drink them. I will drink all of them! Then you will not be sad anymore.

I am not sad! the northern woman insisted. I am merely cautious.

Do you know the century? screamed the blood-red mouth.

My stillness is more passionate than all your shouting.

Who will know?

The southern woman swung petulantly in her hammock while her fury tortured the frozen tears into hideous shapes. When the slender, pale woman buttoned on her gray silk robe and came downstairs in the morning to blow on the fire, she gasped in horror at the wizened, gnarled forms that looked like roots and dried leaves, like the carcasses of starved deer lying frozen in the woods.

I did not weep those! she shouted. Those are not my precious sorrows, my tenderly preserved grief. How I despise your clumsy passion! she shouted. Look closely, sun witch! Huge ants crawl up your skirt, but you cannot separate their hungry red bodies from the red of your dress until they bite you. I despise you now. Could you not consider my only exhibition with charity?

But this is life! declaimed the southern woman.

The keystone cracked, the arch quivered; stained glass shattered in pieces across the nave. In return, miles of tropical vines tightened around the white mansion.

It's not a greenhouse.

You pervert my meaning. Neither is it a cathedral. No one will absolve you, say, Now, my child, you may go forth into the sunlight and sin. There is no sin.

Yes, there is the sin of not seeing others as they see themselves.

Your words would confuse the sun and the moon. What are you afraid of? Why do you stiffen in my embrace, why do you turn your head so my lips will meet not your lips but your cheek, why?

It is impossible to love everyone, and it is impossible to differentiate. But that does not mean I don't love you.

You go on talking.

It is you who keep the flowers from growing back in my

flowerbeds, you who will not let the snow stop falling, is it not?

I am not the one responsible.

Someone must be.

You are the one who is cold.

Your passions make more noise, that is all.

There is a solution.

That is forbidden.

Why is it forbidden? Who forbids it?

It is forbidden because then there would be no more seasons; there would be a staid sky and a few solemn flowers, a river of unvarying speed, a land of uniform elevation, an ocean without waves.

You think you know so much. But those forces are ourselves.

That is why we must not admit aloud their existence, said the northern woman, why we must be very quiet beside fires though our fingers and hearts freeze from inaction. People must be allowed to go on thinking that weather is outside.

Those are only reasons, said the southern woman. You are a coward and revolt me. I give up. I'm leaving!

But, while they had been arguing, the snow had piled up so high around the house that it was impossible to go out. There was no way of telling how long they would have to dig before getting through the drifts. The northern woman smiled, prepared now to be generous. You see?

The southern woman stamped her foot and snorted. You'll see! she shouted. She began to blow furiously against the windows, filling her lungs as full as possible. But, instead of the fierce sunlight she'd anticipated, she blew out a bright red tulip, and then a rose, and then a purple lilac. Each time she exhaled, another flower fell from her lips. You did this! she cried. Damn you to ice forever, she cried. In exasperation she held her breath, but, when she finally had to release it, such a profusion of blossoms showered from her mouth that she was astonished. I did not realize, she said . . .

I suppose, the northern woman relented, that if I hadn't sent him away, the hired man could have dug a path for us to the world outside.

Yes, the southern woman agreed, magnolias and hibiscus tumbling from her lips, it is my fault as well, for refusing to come in the carriage.

Well, we shall have to make the best of it, the northern woman said. She began to gather the flowers and stand them in jars. (See how pretty they look against the icicles?) But there were so many of them, it soon became ridiculous, so she carried them in the coal shovel to the unused rooms, piled them on the trunks in the attic, on the neat counterpanes in the bedroom, twined them around the balustrade of the stairs. But soon the attic was filled, and then the bedrooms, and the stairs covered, and soon the dining room, the library, the pantry, and the kitchen were filled, and still it snowed.

Which thought the other? This was not clear. But it wouldn't be long before—under either petals or snowflakes—they suffocated.

Mother Courage
At The O'Hare Airport

Laurel Speer

The plane touched down at O'Hare Airport at six a.m. She shook her head to make herself wake up. Rod would be waiting for her, and she'd been sitting up all night, sleeping fitfully. It had been four months since they'd seen each other, and she was dreading this confrontation because he was going to be ready and waiting to assert all his marital rights, and she wasn't sure she was up to any of it.

One year was a long time to be without a husband, even after being married for fifteen years. She'd gotten used to it too quickly. She liked it too much. He'd left the July before to take another year of post-doctoral training, an unparalleled opportunity, one he couldn't pass up. They'd talked about making the move with the three children for the year and finally had come to the conclusion that they couldn't possibly afford it. She would stay at home, take care of the house and the kids. He would fly home for the kids' birthdays and Christmas. She agreed a little too readily, even for herself. The time away from her husband looked good. She could relax the rigors of attention and care. The kids were in school. She might be able

63

to get some reading done, take up some projects that had been nesting in the back of her mind for years.

"Are you sure it's all right?"

"Of course, I do fine by myself."

She had a fleeting moment when she wished the plane would crash as it came down. Dramatic ending to a non-beginning.

"Get hold of yourself," she thought. "You've got to get back to the grind," and then laughed at her own allusion and gripped her legs together in the cramped seat. She was slim, medium-tall, brown eyes, brown hair, medium everything. No beauty, just turned thirty-five and beginning to show a few white hairs. Nothing remarkable, she thought. Nothing particularly going for her outside marriage and kids. The thought of going to work was boring to her. When she had free time, she sat and read. She'd always sat and read since she'd been a kid. This year, she'd taken up the piano for the first time, but after applying herself as hard as she could, she knew she was never going to be anything but mediocre.

Her husband was very talented at what he did. He was a specialist in surgery of the bowel and this year had been a year of further training in pediatric surgery of the bowel. He loved his family; he loved his work; he was tall and good-looking in a boyish way, quiet, self-contained and very rational in all his undertakings. In fact, though, he wasn't very exciting for her, and looking back on it, she now knew he hadn't been for years. Marriage had become a routine. He made love to her two or three times a week when he wasn't too busy with night cases or preparation of talks or journal reading, and he seemed to enjoy it and her. He was a good lover, she supposed, as men went. He was the only man she'd ever had, so she had no basis for comparison; but she'd been responsive to him in the beginning, and as they continued to live together, she was still responsive, only it had become just physical. Her emotions were less and less engaged. In fact she hadn't really thought about missing sex in the year he'd been gone. It got so she really didn't think about him, either, between his phone calls and letters and quick visits home.

But now she had to get back into it full time, and the thought made her feel weary and duty-bound. She had to come up to it, of course. Rod had planned a vacation around her flying out to meet him and then driving back with him to bring his car home. He'd been waiting for four months; he'd saved his money; he'd made the reservations, starting with a lakefront hotel up in Wisconsin. She glanced at the fat, distracted businessman in the seat next to her. No reason even to speak to him. But she was married to Rod. She had to come up to his expectations.

The plane touched down smoothly. So much for the expectation of a dramatic crash. She gathered herself. "The face to meet the face," she thought. But not right away. Rod had a funny habit of holding off at meetings in airports. He'd never rush up or signal to her if he saw her and she didn't see him. She would walk down the ramp and look all over for him and not see him.

She had a moment of panic. What if she looked right at him and didn't know him? But she had to know him. You don't live with someone for fifteen years and not remember what he looks like. Tall, rather massively built, cool gray eyes, gray hair, big hands, straight teeth, boyish smile, fully curved mouth. She'd know him, she'd have to know him. But he'd hold off. He'd be standing off in a corner somewhere and be looking right at her, but not let her see him. Then he'd start toward her and come right up to her while she was searching the crowd, and he would control the moment when their eyes met. She always felt surprised by him and secretly observed. It gave her a flash of annoyance and nakedness under his scrutiny.

She stood up and took her cosmetics case in one hand. Not very heavy. She had a clear, olive complexion and wore no make-up. She carried just lotion and toothpaste, a toothbrush, deodorant, brush and comb and some perfume in the case, along with two paperbacks.

She walked down the ramp and took a deep breath. She was wearing a short, green cotton dress and sandals. He'd prefer that she were more dressed up. He liked to see her make an effort for him, but it was all so uninteresting, she must have lost the incentive. She really didn't care anymore how she looked, as long as she felt neat and clean.

She stood at the end of the ramp and swept her eyes over the crowd of people waiting at the terminal. No Rod. Maybe he'd missed his connections. She lowered her eyes and then raised them again to see him striding toward her, his biggest smile on his face. He took her arm, bumping her purse off her shoulder onto her elbow and drew her aside and kissed her. His tongue went inside her mouth, pushing up against her palate, which made her want to draw back. It was so big and pushy, like a penis inside her mouth.

He pulled away and beamed down at her. She smiled back and felt wooden in her response. This was going to be harder than she thought.

"Never thought this day would get here," he said. "Never had a week go by so slowly. Come on." He took her arm and directed her to the baggage claim area. They walked quickly. Both of them were athletic and well-exercised. They liked to swim and play tennis. That was something they could still do. At least that didn't require intimacy.

They stood, waiting for the bags to come down and he talked of his last week of work at the hospital and the morning traffic and how he'd had a helluva time getting the landlord to give him his deposit back.

"Are you all checked out of your apartment, then?"

"Ready to go. I slept on the floor the last two nights because the furniture place took back the stuff I rented on Monday." She listened and didn't listen. None of this required very close attention. He squeezed her arm again. "Been doing a lot of thinking about you."

"Have you now." She smiled back. Get it up, she thought. Make him feel loved and wanted. Do the wife thing. Don't disappoint him.

"There's your bag." He grabbed it off the moving line and they moved quickly out the door, showing her stub to the uniformed attendant.

Now we're going to walk to the car, she thought, and get in and drive to our hotel.

"Have much trouble parking?"

"No, they've got these underground things here. I got pretty close to the terminal."

They walked more rapidly now.

He can't wait, she thought. He's got a hard on in his pants just thinking about it, and I'm dry as a bone.

His car gave her a familiar jolt. A whole year with just her station wagon in the carport and Rod's Karmann Ghia in Chicago.

"I had a helluva time getting even this much stuff in the Ghia," he said.

"It looks nice. You must've gotten it washed."

"And tuned and new brakes."

"Your child."

"How are the kids?"

"Fine. I left them with Grandma yesterday afternoon. They're looking forward to having Daddy home."

"God, I can't wait to get back together as a family. I'm so tired of living in a goddamn studio apartment."

She said nothing. One of the aspects of the year that she liked was release from family things. She didn't have to go on camping trips, she didn't have to go on half day picnics, prepare big family dinners, go on Sunday drives. She cleaned house on Sunday now and let the kids find their activities with their friends.

"We're going to have to get back into the social thing, too, you know," he said.

Neither of them liked the round of parties they had to go to, but they were good for Rod politically, so they'd always gone, for years. She hated them. They were so boring and repetitious. That was another thing she loved about the year. With Rod gone, her command performances had been minimized to nothing and she reveled in the free time to do just what she wanted with herself.

The car started smoothly and they pulled out into the traffic heading for the freeway that would take them to Wisconsin.

He took her hand and squeezed it. She had forgotten how big his hand was. A paw, with a huge palm and long spatulate fingers. She wondered how he could get such a big hand into the intricate insides of some of the smallest of his pediatric patients.

"How's the research going?"

"OK. I'm going to try and carry it on when I get back. If they don't have too many patients waiting for me."

"When do you have to get back to work?"

"Oh I don't know. Sometime the second week of July. They said I could take a week or ten days getting back home."

"Really?"

"Well, it's been a whole year."

"But usually they're not so generous."

"Look, I just told them I wanted to be with my wife."

She winced. If they spent a week getting home, what would they talk about? How could she stand being closed up in a car like this for a whole week. A year was too long. She was spoiled for the marriage thing now. How could anyone have a whole year of freedom from everything except the routine duties of house and kids and expect to get right back into a close intimacy? The thing was getting worse and worse and she'd just begun the vacation.

"Hey, I almost forgot. I got something for you."

She smiled as he reached into the back seat and pulled out a box with a ribbon on it marked I. Magnin's.

"Hey, I. Magnin's. You're getting pretty fancy."

"Nothing too good for my wife."

She pulled the ribbon off and took the lid off and then pulled open the tissue paper. It was a brown shorty nightgown with beige trim with the briefest of bikini panties and a cutaway top that would leave her stomach and breasts exposed when she put it on.

"You can see I've been thinking a lot about you." He reached over and pinched her nipple, and she winced again. He was always right on target with that maneuver, like finding the point of entry in a surgical field.

She held the nightgown up and thought how ridiculous for her, not her at all. She liked zany patterned, medium-length nightgowns that hung loosely from her shoulders and required no underwear.

"Like it?"

"It's really nice," she said and packed it carefully back in the box.

They drove in silence for a while. Rod was really a very quiet person. He never made too many demands on her conversationally, at least he never had. He was content to think his own thoughts about his work and other things private to him. She was happy to let him. When he did talk, it was less a conversation than telling her something that was on his mind. She'd found out very early in their marriage that he wasn't very interested in listening to her talk, and that when she did try to convey to him something that was on her mind, he'd often take a mental walk. She'd discovered this by trailing off and then waiting for him to ask her to go on. But he never did. So she'd gotten used to keeping her thoughts to herself. She really talked to nobody.

The country was becoming rolling and green and sparsely populated.

"It's not bad out here," she said.

"Really, you get away from downtown Chicago and it's almost rural. I met some people this year who live this far out and keep horses."

"How far is this place?"

"Couple of hours. You want to stop sooner?"

"No, that's all right."

"You had breakfast?"

"No, but I'm not particularly hungry."

"I know something that's going to raise your appetite." She was quiet then and looked out the window at the passing countryside. They'd be there soon and go through the ritual of lovemaking. That was the first thing they'd do. And then Rod would want to lie in bed for a while and then do her again. She squeezed her legs together in anticipation of the feel of him pushing inside of her. She hadn't had sex in a long time, and it was going to make her sore. She'd never complained about soreness before, so he wasn't going to understand when she didn't want it as often as he did. It had taken her a week to recover every time he came home during the year. She got so she began to dread the thought of having him come roaring in on her like a bull. She began to invent things to do with the kids to keep them up late at night or ask to go places and encourage him to drink and eat a lot. None of it worked. In three months time, he worked up a head of steam that made him want to climb on her constantly. Importunate lover. Tolerant wife. What if she said no? She found herself imagining them walking into their hotel room, dropping their bags, having him reach for her to undress her and pushing him gently away. "No, Rod," she'd say, "I don't want to have sex with you right now."

She smiled at the incredibility of it. She never said no. She must've said no a total of three or four times in their whole married life. It just wasn't her personality. She acquiesced. He needed it. She could afford to be generous.

"I wanted to stay two nights at this place," said Rod, "but we have to go back to Chicago tomorrow night to have dinner with the head of service and his wife. Sorry to lay that one on you, but it's a political necessity."

"OK, I guess I can stand one night, if it doesn't happen too often."

"There was just no way to get out of it."

"Doesn't matter."

"See what you think about him. He's really an interesting person."

He started talking about the background, academics and personal interdynamics of the chief of service.

"His wife died five years ago and he just remarried after living a rather swinging bachelor life."

"Sounds like a dirty old man to me. How old's his new wife?"

"Thirty or so."

"And he?"

"Fifty."

"Why'd she marry him, aside from the fact that he's probably well fixed. Is he good looking?"

"Not at all. As a matter of fact, he's remarkably ugly. No, I think she married him because she'd been married before and has a seven year old boy by that marriage and had been out in the cold long enough."

"So he bought himself a wife. Is she accomplished?"

"Very."

"An excellent hostess?"

"Well-dressed, makeup, etc."

"And travels with him everywhere, getting babysitters for the boy?"

"Right."

"I'm going to hate the evening."

"Well just don't show it. He has to think well of us."

"Questions about why you left your wife at home?"

"Some."

"So we have to appear the perfect couple."

"He's very sharp and appearances are important to him."

"Do my best. I brought the white dress you gave me for my birthday last year."

"Perfect."

She sat back and wondered at the easy familiarity of their talk. As if they'd been talking to each other for years and knew exactly the direction their thoughts would take. But of course they had. A year away from each other didn't change the habitual responses.

When they got to THE HIDEAWAY it was only a quarter to nine, and they had to wait for their room to be prepared. She could tell Rod was annoyed. His jaw tightened and his eyes narrowed at the dyed blond, heavily made-up clerk behind the desk, but his voice was polite. She always knew he was very annoyed when his voice tightened but remained polite. Seeing him standing at the desk in a tensed posture of irritation reminded her of all the times she'd irritated him, when he'd modulated his voice with an effort and only indicated his feelings by a tightness around his eyes and mouth. She sat down on the blue vinyl couch across from the desk and waited. They'd left their bags in the car. Rod never made a definitive move until everything was ready for him.

"What's the matter?" she said as he walked over to the couch and sat down beside her.

"Room's not ready."

"How long will it take?"

"Who knows. I called them twice from Chicago to make sure they knew we'd be here early and sent them a deposit for a night's rent."

"Did they forget?"

"She claims they never knew anything about it. I pushed them a little bit. She said a half hour, that she'd get the housekeeping crew right on it."

"That means an hour."

"Or more. It pisses me off to arrange for something and then have the cretins in the system foul it up."

This was like his response to a nurse who failed to follow a post-op order. She glanced over at him and smiled, but he was distracted and far away. She settled back to wait and wished idly that she could reach into her cosmetics case and take out a book. But she didn't know whether Rod was up to that from her yet. He'd probably forgotten all the ways she'd developed for passing the hours between happenings between them. Better to sit and wait and make conversation if he wanted it.

"Their check-out time isn't until two. They probably thought we were coming in after that."

"Goddammit, I called them. Twice," he added and lapsed into silence.

"Nice place."

"It's supposed to be the best place within easy driving distance from Chicago. Some of the residents told me about it."

"Looks expensive, too."

"Well, we earned a vacation."

After fifteen minutes, she got up and wandered over to a big picture window that looked down on an indoor pool with an attached whirlpool and suana. Big tropical plants reached all the way to the window. The pool winked invitingly, a deep blue, but no one was swimming at this hour, not even the kids in the hotel. "Fancy, very fancy," she thought.

Then she went into the giftshop and browsed, noting that all the prices were triple what she would expect to pay. Signs in the lobby pointed to places in the hotel where they could get a meal. THE HIDEAWAY DELUXE, gourmet dinners, coat and tie, please. At the back of the hotel was a wide expanse of brilliant green lawn banking a large lake. Sailboats and motorboats made their way sluggishly in and out of the harbor. "They'd have tennis courts, too," she thought, "and an outdoor pool. Probably a golf course. Everything a happy couple could want."

At ten o'clock, Rod got up and went to the desk again and came back triumphantly waving two keys. She smiled back as hard as she could. "Well here it comes," she thought.

"Got them."

"Not bad. Only forty-five minutes."

"Come on, we have to drive around to the back."

They walked rapidly out of the lobby, wedged themselves in the car and then sat while Rod consulted a map of the grounds to find their room number. Behind her and to the left, she could see the tennis courts, three of them, all empty, but her legs felt heavy at the thought of putting on her tennis dress and forcing a run for a shot across those courts. After they made love, Rod would expect her to jump right out of bed and gallop off to the courts. But the air was humid and that made her logy. Maybe he'd let her sleep a little before she had to run, cutting through the damp air and sweating. After all, he'd been here a year, he was acclimated. Right now she didn't feel like doing anything except lying down in air-conditioned comfort and sleeping away her night's travel.

"Here it is. The east side."

Rod, the perfect navigator. He could consult a map and pinpoint exactly where they were and where they needed to go. Those one dimensional flat plans always looked like a maze to her. Her mind turned off to the challenge of finding themselves in the puzzle.

They pulled up outside Room 167, an outside room, downstairs.

"Here we are," said Rod and jumped out of the car expecting her to do the same on her side. Then he opened the trunk and pulled out her bag and his own.

"This will be enough for now. You carry your case?"

"Sure. You want your tennis shoes and racquet?"

"Not now," he said and smiled at her.

The key turned in the lock and they found themselves inside a deluxe motel room, thick drapes, cold air conditioning, shower over the tub, two wash basins, two king-sized beds with firm mattresses, chairs, a desk, ice bucket, glasses in their sterile containers on the sink, an overview of the lake and a porch outside their room.

"This is nice," she said, putting her case down on the open luggage rack.

"Should be at the price we're paying."

"Do you think we can afford it?"

"I've been saving up. Remember this is our vacation. Don't worry about the money. Let's just enjoy ourselves." He was pulling the heavy drapes, cutting out the blue lake water as he talked.

"Here it comes," she thought. She opened her bag and started hanging up her dresses. He double locked the door with the bolt and chain after putting out the DO NOT DISTURB sign and then came up behind her and put both his arms around her waist, bringing his hands up to take hold of her breasts.

"I've got an idea."

"What's that?"

"Why don't you unpack later."

"All right." She turned to him and let him kiss her. Rod never fumbled with his clothes when he undressed, not even when he wanted her urgently. He carefully undid his belt buckle and unzipped his pants, dropping them onto the floor, then pulled off his shirt, while she dropped her dress and underwear and slipped out of her sandals. His eyes were closed. He was nuzzling her with his face and leading her to the bed, laying her down and kissing her on the mouth, on the breasts, all over her body. He was going through the routine though he wanted to take her immediately, and she was grateful at his perfunctory consideration because it gave her some chance to get ready for him. He touched her to see if she was wet and drew back a little. She knew that she was dry and tense.

"It's been a long time," she whispered.

He went down and put his mouth against her and that made her feel awkward, like clamping her legs together because she knew he really just wanted to get inside of her.

He began pushing against her and she could feel herself giving a little. "All right, if you can get in, it'll be all right," she thought, "then all the old responses will take over from there."

When he entered her it was almost like a surprise and her eyes widened at the insistence of his body. She positioned and lifted herself as he thrust in and out, but she was completely detached, outside of herself. Somebody else was getting done and she was helping her. She worked him with her hips. She wanted him to come quickly, to have him love it. She thought of the short nightgown nesting in its box. He bought that for her, he probably paid fifty dollars for it. She owed him something. He made all these arrangements, he went to all this trouble, how could she tell him, Look Rod, I don't want this, I just want to lie down and sleep very quietly for about five hours and then get in

74

the car and go back to O'Hare and go home. I don't want to spend a week in a car alone with you. I don't even know you anymore. I don't know myself, either. I can't possibly get it up and keep it up for one whole week with anybody. I'm doing well to make five minutes of conversation with the check out girl at the market. He was getting ready to come now. She opened and lifted herself to meet him. He grabbed on to her and shuddered against her and she held him while he came and came, four months worth of come. Then he lay quiet, resting. Rod never said anything after lovemaking. He was very quiet, very rested, very content. And then, if it were the end of a long day, he'd turn over and go to sleep and she'd be grateful for his fatigue. She angled her arm up over his back and looked at her watch. But it was only ten-thirty. They had the whole day ahead of them. He wasn't tired. He'd want to do her again and again. Even now, she could feel him stirring inside of her, getting hard again. He started to move and she felt her nose wrinkle.

"Puke," she thought "I've got to get up."

She pushed at him to get him off.

"Hey," he said "wait a minute," as she got up off the bed.

"I have to go wash," she said.

She reached down and took hold of herself so she wouldn't run on the rug. Strong, sweet, thick male smell that would stay on her hands when she touched herself and all the washrags in the room. One time, she'd accidentally taken a washrag she'd used on herself after lovemaking and washed her face with it. Pukey, dried come smell. She went to the bathroom and wiped as much of it out as she could with toilet paper, then ran warm water on a rag and washed herself. She had five, maybe seven minutes in the bathroom and then she'd have to go back. He'd be lying on his back on the bed waiting for her. He wouldn't even want to wash himself before he climbed on her again. Maybe she could hold him to two and then sleep. Then he'd want to do her again before she could get him out on the tennis courts, then again before they went swimming. She touched herself carefully after she washed and could feel the soreness where he'd rammed home and then worked her up and down with the hard shaft of his penis. She had a fantasy of flight, of grabbing her bags and running away from the hotel. "Two more minutes," she thought and leaned against the sink. She didn't look at herself in the mirror. She didn't want to see her flushed face and tousled hair.

"Hey, what're you doing in there?" He was lying on his back on the bed, calling to her.

She opened the door. He was ready again.

"Come here," he said beckoning to her with his hand. "I want to make love to you. I won't be so quick this time."

She paused only for a minute before she moved toward his hand, but she didn't look up as she did it, only at the bright red, unpatterned rug.

LEARNING TO MEDITATE

Helen Barolini

Blackness. A train speeds out of a long tunnel and its black
wake diminishes in classic perspective recalling Mantegna...
Italy. Beautiful but irrelevant. But nothing is irrelevant in
meditation, they say.

Thoughts sweep in, then out with the whoosh of the
speeding train. The train carries the word...catch it and
repeat, repeat. Let it slip into the mind—no not the mind. Forget
the mind. Being is enough.

"What a mess if we had to worry about thoughts not being
right in meditation," our leader said when I had worried that
mine weren't exalted, were a kind of mental garbage. "Garbage
is real, too. Everything is being."

The mantra comes back. And with it the words of Dr.
Ferber, the gynecologist I saw last week: "What about sexual
activity?"

"I'm a widow."

"But you also told me you were having sex—pretty
regularly." He says this chidingly, as if I've duped him.

"That was at last year's visit. Now it's over."

"No sex life at all?" he chides again.

"No."

"Well, you're an attractive woman," he says, "you shouldn't be giving up sex."

"I'm not giving *it* up, it's given up *me!*" And so I accommodate him by offering an explanation. He insists on knowing more. Don't I have a chance to meet men? Is it because I still have a child home, and I'm not able to go out? Can't I have "visits" at home while Jane's at school?

Can't he shut up?

Can't they all shut up? Like friends who say, "Look, you're still young, you should get married again. It's not good for you to be alone."

And Dr. Woolf, the analyst. In his forties, handsome, arrogant, he says: "You have to be more primitive, more instinctive. It's useless to think of meditation unless you've worked yourself out of the karma that still needs to be expressed in your life. And your tennis playing," he laughs, lighting up his pipe, "is just avoiding the issue."

All of them scolding at my aloneness. They are telling me to get a man so that I can become visible and acceptable again. I have to belong as they do: paired up. It's as if I'm a starving beggar pressing my face against the window of a restaurant, watching everyone eat while they scream at me to stop starving to death.

And with whom should I be having sex? Frank, that boring old maid of an English professor who takes me out to dinner and a concert once or twice a season and is too unsuave to even hold my arm when we cross a street? Or the accented man in the theatre lobby who offered to accompany me to the play because I was alone? Or the balding, bespectacled writer who sort of grabs me intellectually and with whom it's pleasant to spend an evening but who when it comes down to bed or not, the answer is no. I should be having sex just for the sake of getting full points from doctors Ferber and Woolf that I'm a woman? But then being a woman would be poles apart from being a person and the male part of the population is right in considering us poor cows.

But no, there's more. I know there's more and when old Woolf won't hear out my suspicions and illuminations, that's when I quit. Then alone I panic and relapse: I'll just put ads for a companion in upper-crust literary journals; I'll invite some of my older students over for dinner and get them boozed and bedded; I'll put my name and earnings in a machine and let it mate me to something similar. I'll take in a male lodger to give Janey a father figure and me someone to play with. And then I wonder.

After all, I've had lovers. I had Ben. I had the best.

Again the holy word in waves, softly and soothingly, a lapping that carries into darkness. Repeat, repeat . . . soft, deep nothing.

Janey turns on the television and it mingles with the mantra. The TV reminds me of the communications instructor who came up to me after the faculty meeting at the beginning of the semester.

"How's your love life?" he greets me. Flip, aggressive, young, and hostile. And me? I panic and split the scene mumbling about having to be back early for Janey.

That's where it all is. They all want to know if I've got a man because my aloneness is a bother; everyone dines bachelors but not female singles. Doctor Ferber adds that without copulation I'll run down, run out, turn to ashes and rue. And psychically, says Dr. Woolf, I'm hiding, dodging the working out of my base drives, getting sicker.

They aren't wrong. I miss a man. I miss lovemaking. I'm forty-seven and I miss it. But sex isn't all there is. I know for sure, now and forever, that it isn't all. (In our marriage, what did John used to say? Sex in itself isn't so bad, but it's all that wriggling that makes it ridiculous.) Irrelevant.

But I don't want to be a sexual port; I want to be a whole person. And that's something I have to do alone.

Joy in work, advises Frank who's been divorced and going through his own hell. For three years I've been working as a man does to support a family, pay the taxes and mortgage, put the girls through college. Three years since John died. Three years of making my way and I'm doing it. At least it looks that way. But if I'm truthful (and why not?) a good deal of my survival, maybe all of it (no! not *all*) was because Ben was there. Ben carried me through. Then he left.

Why?

79

Because, says Dr. Woolf, I'm a nest-builder and it scared Ben. He could see me absorbing his life into mine. If that's how he saw me, then it's because I'm not free. When I'm free I won't have to absorb other lives. I'll have mine.

The last evening Ben and I went out together, I wanted him to come back to bed with me because Janey was away at a friend's. Ben said no, that I had to get over all the lovemaking business—we could still be friends and see each other occasionally, but all the lovemaking was unnecessary. He was punishing me for having asserted myself. He was also pulling out of a situation that made too many demands on him without John there to balance it.

And in a second I saw how little we had if we didn't have sex. Nothing. Ben wasn't the companion, the generous friend John had been. Ben was my beautiful, formidable lover, my sun-king, my center; but he was husband to his own wife and father to his children, not mine. He had his life and the way it ran suited him; I was on the side.

No one who values freedom wants to depend for long on outside support says Maharishi.

Yes, I value freedom. I want my freedom more than sex, I swear it. More than my child who will leave me anyway as her sisters have. More than the resurrection of John, or Ben's return. All through the loneliness of night I know that I want freedom more than anything else. I would like it shared—sharing separate and equal freedoms with a companion. A companion who would be with me where I now am alone—on trips, walks, at the theatre, or home.

Come back sweet mantra. They can't force psychic suttee on me because I've lost my man—my men. I know something different. If only I can connect, I know that my aloneness is not a sore, but sacred. I know I can be alone and connected to the large stream.

"But am I doing it right?" I ask the leader anxiously. "Should I be having such trivial thoughts? Shouldn't they at least be higher?"

"Higher? What's higher?" the leader says. "Everything and anything is right. Your thoughts are stresses that have to be worked out, absorbed, deflated of their tension. Let them come—don't block them. It all works out. You'll see."

"But with all those distractions how will I know when I reach that level of consciousness you call Being?"

"You'll know."

"But when does it come?"

"There's no hurry. It will come when it's the right time to come."

I'm not young. Not old. It's an age my friends know, too, and we cling to one another for some sense of security, because our looks are going, our figures are going, our kids are grown, our husbands are dead or "dating," our lovers are gone.

"You're a pretty woman, Em," friends say.

Yes, still pretty. I can still wear a Bikini. And I could still love a man.

The bottom came not with John's death, but after, with Ben. From one day to the next. No more calls, nothing. As if he had died, too, but was even more dead than John. As if I had died. And I had—that part of me that could ever again attach unconditionally to a man.

Now I'm choosing another way. And I'm doing it . . . with relapses, but still doing it. Ben as a hurt and John as a loss are receding. Or I'm advancing. I can almost feel myself, at times, growing in a physical, palpable way.

I still have my thoughts but they're becoming like old familiar movies on the late show—I look at them from a distance. I'm not playing in them any longer.

"Whoever gets you for keeps will have nothing but treasure," Ben my lover had said.

Only connect! Only connect! My eyes, my fingers, my lips, my legs entwined with his would plead. But he never did.

John connected. John connected me to his life with gossamer strands of love made of total incomprehension. "You shall be the queen of my home and family," he told me when I was twenty. He was too many years older. And he thought he gave me everything when he gave me his love and proved that I couldn't exist without him, away from his protection and care. I lived in that silken captivity as if in a shell, a husk, for years. I'd cry for no reason, dream of going off alone to Santa Fe, Bermuda, Australia. Then Ben appeared and put the first semblance of a person back into me.

* * *

The paradox: Ben is not only the instrument of my present aloneness, he was also the instrument of my first growth.

He taught me to value myself, to form my own personality independent of husband and family. He compelled me to start working, to stop living through others. Then he left and that was right, too. And it's right I don't call him back.

With what timidities I reach towards myself! Me who was the queen of the home, who could only cook, shop, mend, cart, drudge, type and proof John's things. But Ben insisted: "Nothing," he said, "is impossible, improbable, or everlasting."

All the men in my life had their great sayings.

I am learning that no man, no person, is a center. The past is going. It still comes and seeps into the meditation but it bothers me less. It recedes. Into the black tunnel.

The sound of the mantra. Now I am alone, but not all alone. I am connecting. I haven't reached where I'm going, but I'm going. I'm connecting.

First I grow, then I connect.

If it's given, then, that I'm still attractive and, in principle, accessible to men, why is there no contact? What veil is there between me and a man? If the attraction were working and my willingness to be joined also working, there would be contact with someone—some one of all those I see or know or talk with.

But something hinders. Some part of me must have put that veil between myself and others in order to establish inviolate privacy with myself first.

What is there that can make muddy water clear? But if allowed to remain still it will gradually become clear of itself. Who is there who can secure a state of absolute repose? But let time go on, and the state of repose comes. Practice inaction, and there is nothing which cannot be done.

Practice inaction, let me occupy myself with doing nothing.

Leave all things to take their natural course, and do not interfere.

Cheer in adversity . . . this cheerfulness is that stability which is stronger than fate . . . in adversity be strong within and sparing of words. Do not lean on thorns and thistles.

Remember that life is generous.

THE ARM OF HER CHAIR

Ann Taylor

It is late summer 1953. I am in love with a woman I have never met. She has been a Methodist missionary in China; she was run out by the Reds; she will teach me to eat cherries with chop sticks and pump her black portable organ while she plays hymns. She is my next year's teacher, Mrs. Humphrey. I am about to enter the second grade; my mother is president of the PTA; Mrs. Humphrey is coming to visit. She is going into the homes of all her students to see how they live and meet their mothers. Mother wants to make a good impression. We polish the silver and make little crustless cream cheese sandwiches on special thin white bread from the bakery. We live in Oklahoma City; it is about ninety-five degrees; the sandwiches melt under a damp tea towel while Mother and I dress.

I am going to wear my very favorite dress. My grandmother and I bought it at the Dixie dry goods store in Chichasha for my birthday during the week I spent with her and Granddaddy on the farm. My mother hates the dress; it is pale aqua with an elasticized smocked bodice and eyelet ruffle around the neck. I'm chubby; Mother likes to hide me in navy blue. When I want a cuddly white synthetic fur coat, she buys a camel hair polo coat with a matching tam. She also dislikes gathered cotton skirts fluffed out with layers of stiff-net petticoats, but I've made a deal with my best friend, and each morning before school we meet in the washroom and she finds me some of her crinolines to pull up under my tailored dress. I want to be glamorous and love to lower the ruffle of my aqua dress over my shoulders. In my black ballet shoes, no socks, I am a Spanish dancer, a gypsy, a cancan girl, a star.

I sit in the bathtub for over an hour, shaving my legs with the sharpened edge of a thin, almost used up bar of soap. My mother is already dressed and anxious when I unlock the bathroom door. My dawdling exasperates her; sometimes she sits in the car ready to leave and honks the horn again and again until I come out of the house. Today she is careful not to get angry; Mrs. Humphrey might come to the door at any minute. She asks me softly to please hurry, but I take my time dressing. If she sees me before my teacher arrives, she will make me change. I wait until the doorbell rings before I come into the living room. My mother glares at me, but what can she do? We are charming at the door. I curtsy, lowering my right knee almost to the floor.

We sit in the living room. Mrs. Humphrey takes the easy chair, Mother the sofa, and I pull a footstool around to the side of my teacher's chair, sit on the stool and lift my feet up on one arm of the chair. I am the height of sophistication. I am beautiful, as beautiful as the crippled blond princess who rides in her wheelchair through my fantasies. My darling feet in their marvelous ballet slippers are raised as high as my delicious shoulders nestling in their exquisite aqua ruffle. I am totally desirable. I am offering myself to the woman I love.

ODE TO YOUR COCK

Sara Rose

I marvel at your mysterious organ, the banner of your maleness.
The barometer of your desire. Part of you, yet not subject to
your conscious command.

I wonder at the way it maintains its independence. You
cannot, by the usual chain of command from brain to muscle,
move it as you would your arm and leg. You cannot say, "Be
still, be unobtrusive," with the confidence that, inflamed by
passion, it will not rise up and embarrass you. You cannot say,
"Rise up and harden to your fullest," with the confidence that,
betrayed by anxiety, it will not retreat and shame you.

It often knows what your mind doesn't know. It knows when
you are filled with a fierce wanting for me—or for someone
else—even before you may know it yourself. It knows when you
are weary or angry or fearful—even when you try to hide these
feelings from yourself. Insistently, it tells you, "This is how you
feel."

Years and years ago, days before I was to be married, I
walked into my mother's kitchen as she was laughing with a
friend. "A man's business...so funny-looking...ugly, with

everything hanging down and sticking out that way . . . how can they look in the mirror without wanting to die of embarrassment?"

She looked up, embarrassed herself to see me standing there. She shrugged and said, "Well, you'll see it soon enough for yourself. Just don't be too disappointed at what you see. It feels better than it looks."

I had already seen all of you—and felt all of you—by then, and had wondered at the beauty of your body, its lines and patterns and textures so different from my own. I wondered whether I'd ever come to consider any part of you ugly.

Now I am almost the age that she was then. You and I are twenty years older. Your belly is a little rounder now, your waist a little thicker, the hair on your chest a lot grayer. But your ass is still small and tight, your shoulders still strong and muscular, your chest still broad and manly. The beauty of your body remains undiminished.

I chortle with pleasure as I watch you go through your exercises in the morning, your naked body stronger and more muscular than those of many men half your age. The only loose part of you is your cock as it waves wildly up and down through your jumping, your twisting, your bending. I wonder that it doesn't fall off.

Such an interesting decoration. If I were designing a man, would I ever think of such a thing? Ever think of topping you off with a cock that forms a fancy furbelow for your birthday suit?

Occasionally I come upon you as you are peeing. I realize that you are holding your organ absentmindedly, thinking of problems at the office or what you want for breakfast or a million other things that have nothing to do with that handful of flesh. I am amazed that you can ignore it so, when I am so fascinated by it.

Oh, the fickle phallus! Oh, how the chameleon cock changes in shape, in size, in direction, in feel—and yes, even in color! I love to look at it in all its manifestations. Pointing in front of you as you climb out of bed in the morning, still groggy with sleep. Stretched out between your fingers as you pee. Hanging small and limp before you as you step into your briefs, your thoughts on the day ahead.

ODE TO YOUR COCK

And yes, of course, hard and high and bursting with its purple veins as we make love. I love it when you come to me already hard, engorged with your passion for me. And I love it when first we come together and you are still soft, and I am the one who makes you hard.

I take it in my hands and feel it spongy and squishy and formless under my fingers. I stroke it lovingly in the way you've shown me, the way that feels the best to you. I am grateful for your tutelage. Never having had a cock myself, I cannot imagine what one can feel like.

"What feels best?" I used to ask, eager to please my loving mentor, eager to be teacher's pet.

Gently yet firmly, you would take my hand and make a circle of my thumb and middle finger, and you would put your thick, strong hand over my small one. It was as if we were dancing and you were leading. Only this time the only space I'd be traveling would be the few inches along your shaft, as I would encircle it and move up and down, up and down, up and down.

I feel the ridges of the veins that traverse your cock emerge under my touch. I feel the surge of hardness as you respond to the constant, steady movement of my hand.

"Faster?" I murmur, immersed in my activity and your pleasure.

You groan in assent. Faster and faster I go, all the while feeling your cock grow and pulsate, feeling your body writhe in ecstasy. Finally your passion explodes and I see the creamy spurts shoot out at me. You come and come and come. I put my hand in the pools of semen on my arm and on your belly, and I smear it on my own belly, on my breasts, on my face. I drink deeply of the smell of you, the aroma of your lusty delight. Outside I am wet with your ardor. Inside I am wet with my own.

I want you so badly. You see how much I want you. You rouse yourself from your utter relaxation and move toward me. I feel your fingers skirting my secret place, just as mysterious to you as your cock is to me.

You barely touch the little button of my clitoris and my body leaps inside me. I am as hard inside as you were outside only moments before. Your fingers—which I have taught as painstakingly and lovingly as you have taught mine—are sure as they seek out my hidden folds and crevices.

Back and forth you go, the soft pads of your fingers slowly moving along the wet cushiony walls of my cunt, coming back each time to tingle along the guardian of my desire, my clitoris. You have learned to be slow with me as I have learned to be fast with you.

Shiver after shiver runs through me. I am up, up, up. I feel as if I will never come down again. I could be in ecstasy like this forever.

Without warning, the explosion comes. The sharp tingle goes through my whole body, along all my limbs, to emerge as a fiery burning in the tips of my fingers, the ends of my toes. I can almost see the lightning flashing through me. My body convulses. I cannot remain still. But then it becomes too much. I cannot bear any more. Roughly I push your hand away. I need to sag, to sink into the cool sheets and the cradling mattress, to come back to myself from wherever I have been. Your hand rests lightly on my belly, my hand covering yours. I am grateful for your hand. You see, I love more than your cock.

Yes, I love *you*. Not just the parts of you. I know how you jealously compare your cock to those of other men. Whose is longer, fatter, straighter, higher? Whose works harder? Whose has more fun? Whose gives more fun? Is there a man who doesn't? I hope that this paean to your penis doesn't stir up even more anxieties. Because there's so much more of you to love. But this is such a delicious, special part of you that it needs a love song all to itself.

You stand before me, your cock pointing straight ahead, your mouth set in a smile, pleased with yourself, pleased to be with me. I'm smiling, too. We have such fun together. Swiftly I sink to my knees in front of you and I take your hard cock into my mouth. Suddenly I don't feel like your wife of twenty years, the mother of your children, your best friend, a person I know you love and respect. I feel like a whore who loves her work, who loves to make her man happy. I want to give you the best blow job you've ever had in your life. Oh yes, I've become skilled over the years. I've learned from your cues. I've read one book after another. I've talked technique with my women friends.

ODE TO YOUR COCK

Now you will reap the fruits of my labors.

I can feel the velvety softness of your clean, smooth, dry glans as I run my tongue lightly over its tip. I love to take you into my mouth so that I can experience you more closely than I can with either fingers or cunt. Nothing senses you more acutely than my caring tongue. The organ that speaks to you of love with words also speaks to you of love with movement.

I know that there are women who will not take their men into their mouths—even the men they love, even the husbands they are bonded to. I cannot imagine the revulsion they feel. I cannot imagine being revolted by any part of you. You are all you, all part of the man I love. I feel such joy as I give you pleasure.

As you fall back against the bed we share, I stay on my knees before you. I move my mouth over your cock, drawing it deep inside me, as far as it will go. I run my hands inside and around your thighs, down your legs, up your sides, feeling the smooth stretches between the forests of your chest and your back.

I am all movement. My tongue moves around and around, quicker and quicker, feeling the rim that girdles your glans. It moves up and down the sensitive, tender inner shaft, lightly tracing the lines of the swollen veins. My sharp little teeth come down ever so gently over the rim, just enough to let you know they are there, not enough to make you anxious. My hands move all over you. My body rises and falls, my ass dancing circles in the air. Even my toes curl.

I feel your hands tightening on my shoulders, I feel your body tightening under my hands, I feel your hot, smooth cock bounding within my mouth. It pulsates—and I taste the salty essence of you. "More, more!" I shout inside my head. "Keep coming! Release more of you into me!" I want to cry out. I cannot speak, for my mouth is still closed firmly around you. I keep moving my tongue around, keeping time to your throbbing rhythms. Hungrily, greedily, I swallow the syrupy nectar of your passion. I feel filled by your joy. And eager for my own.

You draw me toward you on the bed, look over at me, and smile. No longer contorted by passion, your face is smooth, relaxed, content. I am content to have made the miracle happen for you once again. Part of my contentment rests on my secure knowledge that you will make it happen for me before long.

LOVE STORIES

I love to experience your cock in so many ways. To see it, to touch it, to taste it. To feel it rise against my body as we move dreamily across a dance floor. And oh, to feel it enter me, making our two bodies one! Whether or not I come each time, I always thrill to a special feeling when I hold you inside me.

Sometimes you kiss me or fondle me to arouse my desire. Sometimes I come to you already wet with wanting. Either way, I yearn to welcome you into me. With my hand I guide you inside, into the very center of my being. Since I am slick and slippery, you make your way in easily and quickly.

It is so elegant, the way we fit together, the way this fitting together gives us both such joy. You move your body inside me, thrusting and withdrawing. I move my body around you, enclosing and releasing. We gyrate, we rock, we swing, we come closer, we pull apart.

You are above me, your weight comforting and comfortable on my body. My legs are wrapped tightly around your back, my arms clasping your shoulders. Or my legs stretch out straight and wild, pointing to the corners of the room. Or they fold back in front of your chest till I am jackknifed beneath you. Or I sit astride you. Or lean down, facing you, our chests and bellies meeting and moving together. Or, on my knees, I present myself to you as you mount me like a dog in the streets, ramming your cock against the womb where our babies grew. Or I sink down flat under you, my ass rising high against your belly.

However we couple, it is our union that counts. The sense that I don't know where I leave off and you begin. That when I am running my hands over your body, my flesh tingles as if I am caressing myself. That I smile when you come, feeling your fervor.

We mean so much to each other and are connected in so many ways that the unity of our bodies seems part of some grand plan. I'm so glad that plan includes your magical, mystical, mercurial, magnificent, miraculous member. The cock I love.

LULLABY

Lee Sokol

She had been sitting on the porch for a long time watching the
storm come. The clear honey green of the summer evening sky
had changed quickly from a mirror of the bright earth to smoky
black and fast moving grey vapor like ragged wisps from a
chimney. The edges of the trees turned a dull purple, and all
across the sky ran a deep shuddering mumble of thunder. Emily
was imagining what it would be like to have Charles beside her,
and she even spoke out loud to him—to his empty chair—
without looking at it, pretending he was there.

Everyone has had someone they can't quite imagine being
without. Someone who is so much a part of one's life it is as
natural to expect them to be there as expecting a light to turn on
when the switch is flicked; and to have that person in your heart
is as natural and filling as the blood. If you lose that person; if
that person steps out of your life, is suddenly gone, runs away,
or dies unexpectedly and unreasonably; if you are left behind by
the hook that life throws in what seems to be so casual a manner
(look around, everything goes on but you) you will feel as cold
and alone, as sad as Emily when Charles died.

But death is a different loss than any other. Especially after seeing the body, watching it lowered into a hole (what else can one do?), touching its face, hoping (praying, begging, pleading) for a life to light again in the eyes, for the mouth to speak, for the heart to beat ("Please, please don't be dead, please, for me, for me!") until you want to scream because talking to the body of the person you love the most is like talking to a dead person. Emily screamed until her throat hurt, and her eyes were swollen shut from the contortions of the face in enormous sorrow, and screamed and screamed until nothing came out when she saw Charles dead.

For all this time her mind had been hashing and rehashing through the 'if only's' that come and can't be stopped. When death seems avoidable, as Charles' death seemed to Emily, all one can think about are the very simple ways it could have not happened. "I should have done this; if only the car had not been there, or if he had been detained a minute or two longer; if only he hadn't been detained, if only, if only," if only on into the nights and days that pass and drag and follow and parade by until she had somehow lived for two weeks trying to learn that the person she loved the most was dead.

Emily sat on the porch still wondering why and how and what it meant. How could she relate to a grave? There is nothing there, it is only a grave, a piece of earth. She had thought of planting a tree above the spot where Charles was, something she could watch grow, something that would make more sense than the forest of tombstones at the cemetery. But she knew she did not ever want to go there, that Charles was not really there at all.

She had wondered endlessly about what it would be like to be dead. Even in her dreams Charles would come to her. Sometimes from out of the ground. Once he appeared in her yard as she watered the garden they had started and tended together. In her dream she thought Charles so clever for finding his way out of the grave. But wasn't it so like Charles to find a way out of the most difficult of situations. In her dream she laughed. If anyone could come back, it was Charles.

In another dream she saw him, only briefly. There he was, alive and dark and happy sad Charles. He had stood before her, smiling with a clear joy on his face, and then he turned and ran away. He had loved to run so much. She had awakened from this dream happy with the vision of Charles, big and bright and alive as a full moon, and she told herself that her sorrow was selfish. After all, didn't the dream tell her how happy Charles was, and shouldn't she be happy for that? But no matter how many times she told herself "He is all right. He is probably happier than he ever was on this earth," she was still as sad as a crumb.

There had been a sadness about Charles that she could hardly understand: a look, the way he sometimes approached her, the way he slept, sadness that she wished to God were never there. Especially now she could not bear the thought of Charles being sad or uncomfortable or in pain. She was grateful that his death had come instantly, a consolation indeed when she thought of how it might have been.

She remembered how she would sometimes look at Charles and say quietly to herself, "Please always be with me, and I will always be with you." Now she would come home to the house they had lived in together just two weeks ago, a month ago, a year ago, and would hear a noise inside and for an instant would think, "Charles is home" as naturally and casually as before. Or a car would pass by and she would forget he was dead and be ready to run to the door to greet him. To run to the empty door.

For weeks before Charles' death, Emily had been sad herself. She had had visions of taking her own life. She would find herself sitting blankly, painfully alive in her yard near the garden, "What am I doing? I am nothing." Thoughts flowed into her mind that she could not understand or stop. Now here she was, close to the death she had longed for through the death of the person she loved most. "Is my loss so dreadful? Did so much of me rely on Charles?"

They had spent most of their time apart, busy with their own talents and jobs and friends. She was sure that was why they loved one another so much, why their time together was so precious. In four years of marriage they had never fought. But there was a part of herself she had never shown to Charles, a part of herself she would never show to anyone, and being with Charles would almost always render that part of her inactive.

With Charles she was always vital and there was so much to do. It was only sometimes that her darkness—that part of her that she wanted to kill or to die—would come out. She tried to hide it, but sometimes, sometimes she would think, "He knows; he knows, and still he loves me." And there was a part of Charles that she could sense but not understand. She simply knew it was there, like water underground. A look across the room would send her running into his big arms to bury her face in his chest, to try to get closer to his pain, to smother it along with her own.

Once Emily cried all night at the thought of Charles dying hungry. He was killed just before dinner on his way home, "to me, it's my fault" and then feeling absurd, "what does it matter, hunger or death?" But still she cried, cried all night.

What could she do but try not to talk or think about it when she was with friends? "I've got to stop this. I must quit thinking about it," she would say to herself. "Life goes on."

Emily had never had anyone to turn to in her life until Charles. She had never had anyone whom she trusted enough to let them know she needed them. She knew she looked strong to her friends. She had spent so much time separating her sorrow from them, she didn't know how to ask them to help her confront her pain. She had strived to be there for the people she cared about when they needed her, yet she had never been able to cry in front of anyone.

She trusted Charles. He had opened himself to her and always let her know that he cared. She knew that he had often wished she would not be so quiet and precious with her fears. It kept them apart. He was big and kind and patient and she had learned so much about loving and being loved. Now he was dead and all she could think about was if only he were there to talk to.

She lit her cigarette and smoked it as if she were Garbo, as if she knew no fear; as if what she was—her reality—was as distant and unreal as a film made in the thirties, and she could cast her crude feeling into the raindrops.

The night before, while standing at her kitchen sink, she had taken pleasure, mean and cruel pleasure, in the slow killing of three cockroaches. Even while she did it she was appalled; she had always believed that every living thing had a right to life. But that night she did not. She ran the water in the sink as they swirled and struggled around and around until they went down the drain at last. Except for one. The fourth one. It was undrainable, alive, and although she became more and more intent on killing it, it managed to crawl up the plastic basket in the sink over and over again. The whirlpool in the drain could not suck it down. Each time, just as she thought it was finished, it sprang back with inexhaustible energy and genius, or luck. She knew she could have killed it easily enough by crushing it. But she could not bring herself to that. "Is life so cheap that I have come to enjoy watching and causing the struggle of cockroaches?" This last roach, the undying one, the one she could have killed if she had employed more passion, she scooped out of the water with a spoon and set it on the dry porcelain to run back to the cracks it lived between. She was angry at the roach for not dying, for fighting and claiming its life from her. She felt spineless and angry that she did not want to live as much as the cockroach. "I should be covered in walking cockroaches. They might come to my ear to tell me something, how to live, how to want to live, even if it is in filth and crumbs, in glue and garbage. They would leave their sticky footprints on my body and chew my eyelashes with purpose. I try to kill them with no reason." She whispered, "Why life? Why death?"

The rain had stopped and the night took on a falseness as the July heat set in. Emily got up from her chair on the porch and went into the bathroom to splash water on her face. When she turned on the tap the water was almost hot and she had to wait a few seconds before it was cool enough to drink and soothe her face and neck.

She thought of his fingers and felt them running down her neck, lightly playing the chords of her body, her soul. She closed her eyes and heard the force of the running water as a waterfall. She looked at herself in the mirror. Her skin was dripping and beaded with water. Emily had always been desperately aware of her face. Now she wanted to banish all mirrors and cameras. She clicked a mental picture to take with her into the next room. She needed it to exist at all.

The bed with its twisted sheet had hollows where their

bodies had stuck and pushed. She lay down and closed her eyes.

There is a raft that they float on as the water laps over the sides. Their feet are always wet. They rise and sink as their bodies change shape. It is slippery and it feels good to wrap her legs around him.

The telephone rings and she does not move. "It is probably him." The ringing stops. She does not receive him but instead rolls over and off the raft into the dark water. "There are hills to map and climb if I reach the bottom," she thinks. "If I could see through the salty blackness." The water is thick ink and spreads before her as she sweeps her arms. There is no direction, no destination that will make any difference, only a peaceful vastness. She sways in smooth movements and then slows to see if the water of her wake will rock her.

She knows she will never reach an end. The water is cool and she feels the full moon and the stars falling and dissolving like snow. There is a tingle when they touch her skin.

There is fear. Not of snakes and sharks. That is sensible. There is fear of the desire to go deeper, to go further into the blackness until her body loses shape and becomes the blackness itself. She feels she could swim forever. The raft has disappeared. She wonders if he is still on it or if he too has slipped into the water.

She lets her body go limp at the surface and it floats and bobs. At last she doesn't have to support herself and the moon will pull her blood through her fingers into the sky if her heart stops.

If her heart would only stop.

From

SCARS ON THE BODY POLITIC, a novel in progress

Deena Metzger

As if Eve then, when she was older, when she had not looked on the face of Cain for years, should meet him at the edge of the field, at the furthest point that was permitted to him, if she should wander there on the borders of his exile in order to catch sight of him as he passed by looking at his wheat and the apples and ripe figs on the trees which he had planted; if she had offered him an orange perhaps, or water, then seeing the brand upon his forehead, how it twisted the skin and framed the eyes manically; if she had seen him in the agony of his loneliness, had noticed the scar where God had touched him, the scar which told her that he was now God's, God had marked him, he was bent under God's finger, doing God's work, God's darling, His whore... what then, Eve?

"The man in the waiting room, the German, did you see him?"

"Whom?" he asks.

"The madman, the Nazi, surely you noticed him."

"No, I didn't. A Nazi? Of course there were so many people, I could not keep track of you."

LOVE STORIES

They get the last stateroom with barely space for both of them to stand simultaneously. The old ship has been carried over the mountains to the world's highest lake. At the table they drink Chilean wine and go to sleep early in order to awaken and watch the Bolivian dawn. Above them assigned a couch on the lower deck the German types through the night. He works while they eat, and in the morning just before dawn she comes up the stairs and glimpses him at his post. His eyes are a bit red perhaps, but otherwise he seems unaltered. He does not pay attention to the approaching morning.

Perhaps she is oversensitive, sensing always that she is endangered while he does not have the mentality of the refugee. I took in fear with my mother's milk, she thinks. Now it comes to her, that furtive quality in her mother's eyes, that restless aspect of the dim grey eyes, which rarely focused, it seemed to her as a child, on anything long enough to see it, eyes which lacked concentration, intensity, depth, were always looking, waiting for the return of an enemy that had come once in the night in Poland, had pulled the blankets off her as she slept in the bed above the stove, but in the faint light had happily mistaken the short cropped hair and smooth chest as evidence of a young boy. She had not spoken; she had placed her small palms between her legs, covering herself, hoping the breastless chest (at fifteen—it had been her shame) would be convincing.

And what did her father do then? What was he doing while the men in boots pulled the covers from his youngest daughter? What could he do? What could a poor Jew do? Silently, I ask her; very silently I whisper to her, "What does your father do when the Germans stand over you seeing if you are a ripe young girl for their pleasure?" Her eyes dart around the room looking for soldiers, listening for noises at the door to astonish her in the middle of the night, listening for boots pounding in formation down the locked city streets. What can an old Jew do but stand in the corner, moaning and bowing, praying in a humble ecstasy, in a ritual defense of self-abnegation to the God who howls in the corner of the sky. The old Jew prays to the God who is laughing as his darlings parade through the broken streets.

Dare you Momma, I ask you, dare you ask whether he was a

good father to you? "Papa," you say . . . "This is Papa's glass" or "This is Papa's chair," or "Look at this photo of Papa. Wasn't he straight, even when he was old? Wasn't he handsome? My Papa." But do you dare, Momma, ask whether he was a good father to you? What was he thinking when the soldier whose hand he knew was bloody, moved toward you on the bed he had made himself for you that night above the stove, hoping that the embers of the fire would keep the littlest daughter warm during the bitter Polish night?

It is so bitter, this story, so bitter, and I do not know the place which is the source of so much bitterness within me. It is as if once broken into, once opened, once woman, there is no end to grief.

What was he thinking? Don't you hear me Momma? Why don't you answer me? I know what you were thinking as you held yourself with your little hand hoping that your shame would be your salvation and that no one would see the secret under your palm.

Dare we think that he forgot you in a moment, that from his depths a lustful thought accosted him, distracted him, because it was the first time in years, wasn't it, that he had seen you naked? And in penance he threw himself into an orgy of prayer. It was a convenient rhythm wasn't it, moving back and forth, up and down, intensely distracted. But you had seen that rhythm before hadn't you, Momma, not only in prayer, not only in the synagogue, not only in the minyan, the comraderie of men, but at night when you couldn't sleep in the corner; you had seen that same rhythm acted out upon your mother, hadn't you?

What did he do, this father of yours, my grandfather, when they pulled the blankets from you? Did he close his eyes in prayer with the image of your buttocks engraved upon his mind; did he see your soft skin as he closed his eyes to pray to God?

When will you ask yourself whether he was a good father to you, this Papa, who, when the men came into the house with their bloody boots, opened the door to them? Do you remember, they knocked and your father opened the door? And then what? He recognized them; they were men; they were the same breed. Remotely they were his brothers; he knew what they were after, what plunder they dreamed in their eyes. And your mother sat in the corner with her gray eyes darting just like yours dart now, looking from the soldiers to your father to your older brother and back again, the eyes restless, waiting for a signal, but there was none.

It was familiar to him; he had stood in a circle of men before; he had told the story of Abraham; he had told it with respect and with honor. "Abraham is our first father. Honor him." He taught you to call Abraham "Papa," Papa of the Jews, and how Abraham had taken his son and put him on the stone on the altar in the synagogue and had lifted a knife to his chest and was about to thrust it into his heart when God, laughingly, stopped him, and said, "Wait. There's time. There'll be another time."

It was to test him, Abraham said. It was to test him? And so now when the men come into the house, it is to test *him*, Papa thinks. It is to test *him* that Papa lets them pull the blanket from your frail little body which has never questioned anything. And you? Does he wonder what you are thinking? Did Abraham ask Isaac what he thought at that moment? Or was the action shut between them forever?

At the end she held you in her arms while your father continued to pray to God thanking him that he was spared. Remember, your mother held you till your father cried out from his prayers, "Make a glass of tea, Gita; thank God we are spared."

When he had opened the door, when he stood at the door, and for a moment there was flicker of recognition, of knowledge in his eyes, was that the moment in which he invited them in; was it that he knew them by the mark upon their brow?

We watch the sun come up across the Lake Titicaca, the highest lake in the world they say. It is rimmed with mountains, with peaks, as if it were a crater on the moon filled with water. And across these rough steeples, the punctured sun breaks into violent oranges and yellows which run across the blue sky.

You do not notice that we do not stand together but wander from each other, now to this side of the ferry, now to the other, to watch the morning star fading, to catch the moon as it descends pale before the explosion of light upon the sky.

He is continuing to type below. And above deck you and I seem to stand near each other but actually move in opposite directions like magnets with a similar charge; we send each other across the deck. I remember that you went to bring me coffee and could not find me before it was cold. The dawn is very cold. The lake is winter blue. And the sunrise astonishes us, but somehow we cannot touch our hands to share it together.

Where are we now? We have been crossing from Peru into Bolivia, but I do not know the point where one country changes into another, where the Peruvian Sol loses its color into the icy tin of Bolivia where the landscape becomes cold and ominous. I do not know the moment when the man who is relentlessly typing has come home.

And last night do you remember, how we crept into separate bunks and I invited you to share the narrow bed, which was of course too narrow for two, but wide enough for two who were afraid. In the rocking of the ship I wanted to make love, one rhythm imposed upon another, but you were already so far away; the speed of the ship gave you impetus to travel.

Do you remember how I invited you to be with me, asked you as best I could, but you were already traveling. The boat gave you encouragement, your eyes fixed upon the porthole and stretching beyond; it is the circle through which you can abandon me.

As in the train, remember, but you know now that I always need to make love when we are traveling. How far the train and boat take you each time and I am unable to run so far or so fast to remain with you. And how we lie during those times, one body in demand and the other in retreat, running.

The lightning streaks across the Mexican sky; they shuttle across the land in an iron car, on an iron bed, in an iron room; she pushes against his body for warmth, but he pushes her away, oh so gently, no one watching would notice the barest retreat of the groin, the slightest shuffle of the muscle for comfort, so that her body does not quite press against him. This is his territory, his metaphor: flight.

And when she tells him finally that she cannot sleep, and tosses with her heart pounding, waiting for the knock upon the door which he can stop by coming to her, when she asks him for the last time to join her, his hand raises from the bottom bunk, gently, tentatively, to her. It is all that he can give her at the moment, not a condescending gift, but a disembodied arm nevertheless, a detached gesture from a body which is so far away it does not recognize the continent where she is sleeping, a hand which reaches out in distraction, like a father who pats a crying child's head as he continues the conversation he has embarked upon; he reaches out to her and it is as if he hears her, but she knows from the absent-minded gesture, from the fingers which are cold and which swing with the rhythm of the ship out of her reach and back, that it is with the same distraction, the same preoccupation, that he does not quite notice the tone with which the men at the door announce themselves. But preoccupied, he stumbles out of bed and still half asleep grapples with his robe and worries about belts and slippers; he gropes also for the door, because it is true, isn't it, that when the door is knocked upon it must be opened, and therefore, opens it wide, doesn't he and then . . . what?

Does he let them in? . . .

His voice, the voice of the one she loves, breaks out of absolute silence. It is night. Another night perhaps. Somewhere else. The silence of two people lying in bed reading. Each pillow is a territory. Then the lights are turned out. And they whisper to each other. Travel talk. Preparations. Geography lessons. Population figures, square miles, landmarks, government, novelists, artists, industries, prisons, poverty figures. "The gross national product of Chile is equal to the budget of the University of California," he is saying.

Things he wants her to remember. Information sought, absorbed, filed. The dark wraps itself about the words and separates them from each other. His voice goes on and when she tries to interrupt it or deflect it, he deftly moves aside and continues. She pulls the darkness closer, interjecting her own thoughts, her own visions. Then there are two voices hovering in the dark looking for a place to land. Evading each other. Two voices expelled like light beams into the void traveling without impediment and therefore without return. No impact. No rebound. Two lights. And the darkness increases. Grows heavier.

From: SCARS ON THE BODY POLITIC

The imprint of a man upon a woman. That is familiar. She has always known that. The body retreating under the weight of the man as he sags upon her after orgasm. The body which tension sustained, suddenly limp upon her. The mutual tensions no longer a dialogue, they were no longer two ends of a string pulling tautly against each other, but one end, released earlier, and the entire shape altered as one hand relaxes. And her own body, softened, edging around his, trying to maintain tension despite his erratic twitches or probings for the last bit of pleasure, licking the spoon clean, sticking the tongue into the crevices for the hidden bits of flavor. And she retreating or advancing, holding what she can for herself, requiring maintenance to produce the release within herself.

If he was with her at all, he has left her, she is out of breath having chased him so far, hunted him down, miles away, abandoning her again. "I was miles away," he says. She pulls him in. "We are going to fight it out on this terrain, right here," she says. "On this geography. Old tired earth. No new lands to conquer. No strangers. Here in the belly of the familiar."

"Do you mind," he says. "I was miles away. I forgot you existed." And asking, "Where were you?" she knows she will not get an answer. Even he does not know. To escape the prescient, as well as the pressure of the immediate, the agony of the touch, the undeniable ordinary fact of two sweating out of *sync* bodies touching.

"I don't mind." He knows she is lying; she knows she is lying.

There isn't anyplace else to go, she insists silently. Relentlessly and even with malice pulling him in. This *is* it! Not imagination but the archetypal situation. It may as well be with him that she works it out because he isn't any different from anyone else. And she isn't different either except that she knows what it is about.

So they were thrown out of the womb in such different directions. An explosive birth ejected each of them in opposite directions. She is East and he West. Running after the sun, chasing it, trying to prevent the recognition of night, thinking he can run fast enough to preserve constant daylight. "How fast would I have to fly," he says, "to keep up with the sun?"

"How high are you?" she asks.

"Yes!" he says. "That too will make a difference. And what is the circumference of the earth? How many thousand miles? What if I walked? How quickly would I have to walk to cover the circumference in 24 hours?"

She pretends to calculate. But she is standing still when he begins running. He gathers speed, sheds his shoes, runs barefoot, regresses, is Greek perhaps, the torch in his hand, to get it where without its going out? Is he the bull dancer announcing the beginning of the game?

Where are you running, she wonders. At the end of your chase you will be back before the cave and it's with my thread, this very same crooked cord with a twist where every knot was tied, (every time we come together, we get knotted in) it is along these scars, these unremovable twists, that you will travel into that darkness, and it's along this cord that you will return if I continue to hold, if I continue to maintain the tension, if I am loyal, if I remain standing here, faithfully. And if I don't, then you remain inside. There is only one way out: across my fingers.

He thinks he's running across the belly of the earth, cutting the jungle heat with his bare feet, or miraculously, another fake Christ, running over the water, walking on water, crossing the sea. It is in his mind. There isn't anywhere to go but here. There isn't any other country, any other war but this. He is running. They are splitting apart, he thinks, like the universe dividing.

It's your image, the expanding universe. The center doesn't hold, you say. The stars, the planets drift apart. Everything is separating. Even the milky way thins, you say. The milk is watered. The lights float away from each other...

"The center doesn't hold," he yells in agony and falls back into the dream.

"I was a million miles away," repeated after a silence. Long silences.

You hurl yourself into the same capsule with the space men. But the dead moon isn't far enough away. Dare she say these things to him. Of course, you don't take me with you. You don't take women. You dare not. Saying, "I was a million miles away, weightless, alone with a machine which recorded my every breath. I and a machine. Records of myself. I was in a capsule of mirrors."

But the moon isn't far enough away. And it is dead. I'm not

surprised. I was a virgin and now I am alive. But you are always virgin; you haven't been penetrated yet. Piercing your ear was a tame initiation, and it's all the penetration you have managed up until now.

On to Mars, then. She throws her arm across the bed and they both turn. Into the solar system, to Pluto, to the ass end of the universe following every comet and then out and beyond.

"How fast do I have to run," he muses, "how fast do I have to be shot into space in order to keep up with the universe which is running away from me?"

"It's your image," she insists. The center holds in her mind. She lets him out on a thin thread, on a web which maintains the universe, and then she pulls him in. Not all the way. He isn't ready.

When you're not flying, you're looking for another woman. Perhaps he is asleep. She hears his regular soft breathing and the weight of his body on the mattress. But her silent conversation continues. We pass you from hand to hand. You create differences desperately looking at every blond head because I am dark. I don't understand the fantasy at all.

"I'm a million miles away," he announces from what he thinks is the periphery of the known universe. He's standing on Mars ready to jump off into the heat of the sun. She does admire his mind, its protean desperation. The broken mirrors he manages. It is fertile in its odd way. Time and space are wonderful cunundrums which he postulates. A million hours away. And centuries postulated also.

Lost without his watch. And very careful about his hiking shoes.

Once setting off, on snow shoes, skimming the surface of the snow, he stopped, puzzled. "Where should we hike to?" Frowning.

"What difference does it make?" she asks. "Let's go this way." She plunges ahead with the sun in her face because she wants to keep the warmth in front of her.

"We've gone there," he says.

"Where is there?"

"To the lookout!"

"Well, then why not go again? Or why not go half way..."

"Or walk around the tree in a circle? One doesn't just walk around in a circle. One doesn't just walk around one's garden," he says. "One doesn't just take a hike in one's garden. One doesn't just walk up and down the block," he says. "One doesn't just traverse the road ten times, one doesn't circle the city endlessly, one doesn't drive continually on the same freeway, one doesn't loop the tape recorder, one doesn't see the same movie three times, one doesn't repeat the same words in the same paragraph. One doesn't use the same adjectives. One doesn't write the same book again. One doesn't continue to love the same woman. One goes somewhere. One goes where one has never been before."

"Does one?" she asks, amazed at all his intensity. If she squints she can see the images he's throwing up on the fog.

She's waiting for him to get out of breath, but he runs twenty minutes every day, needed or not, just to keep in shape.

And she whispers in his ear. There isn't any place to go. We've found the center, the single spot, where everything combines. It's fear, she knows, that prevents him from seeing either the bone or the rib. And his bone withers in terror and withdraws. He tries fusion only for a moment. She waits.

They're going to work it out here, fight it out, the last battle, without the accompaniment of cannons, or thousands of cavalry, or movie projectors. No press. No newspapers. No glory. It's the last battle.

"What am I going to gain from this?"

"Gain? You won't gain anything," she answers. "You'll lose."

"What's the point then?"

"Why, there isn't any point!" she says.

He exercises a lot, afraid that maybe the chest muscles which are hard will sag just a bit and look like breasts, the resignation of old men who cannot support such distinctions. She isn't as afraid of the joke of old age that sets everything right before death. Exercises lots, he does, and when he thinks of the breast, of her fingers finding a breast on his chest, he experiences terror. Finding it, he or she now with his hands, he's always talking about his and hers. He invented a language which distinguishes each from each: the house is hers; the car is his; cheese sun his; meat earth hers. Everything marked, every property line precisely demarcated and entered in the book in a clear fine hand and then reprinted and stored on microfilm and in libraries so nobody forgets which piece of property belongs to whom—where you begin and I end. He invented science to know everything precisely. To divide the universe into the most precise portions he coined wealth; he invented equivalents—so many stones for so many grains of wheat, and counted everything. Such fine distinctions were finally so necessary that not even the electronic microscope was enough or the telescope on Mt. Palomar. Nothing was sufficient to keep the breast from his chest, to keep his beard long, to keep his body hard—tennis and swimming and boxing and breaking the universe with a ball, batting stones with trees—to keep those muscles hard and most important to keep his legs in condition for running.

There is stubble above her upper lip. See when she smiles what you think is just a shadow is actually fine black hairs which darken as she ages. He runs. There is a girl next door; she is younger; she does not have that stubble yet.

"I am beginning to know where you begin and I end," she admits to him.

"I was a million miles away," he offers his answer from another planet. "I didn't know you existed. I forgot you existed. I can't see you in the dark. Sometimes you are Carol; sometimes you are a dark black woman; sometimes you are Balinese. You are the stranger. When I touch you, I am happy not to know your name."

When he startles awake she asks him to name his horrors. "Tell me a nightmare."

"Last night," even now his voice trembles a little, "I dreamed—it was unbearable—Siamese twins, joined at the groin and at the heart . . ."

"And at the base of the brain," she finishes the sentence for him. An old habit.

"Yes, there too."

"The dream came from far away. I could feel the memory pressing up through the mud. I was standing on a plain of wet, dark, soft sand and could feel my feet slipping into it, not quickly as into quicksand, but with the same terror that if I picked up a foot, the mud would stick to it; it had the horror of honey, something from which I could not get free, and if I managed somehow to clean one foot off, where was I to put it while I cleaned the other? Ooze. The dream came at me from somewhere deep in that primeval ooze. Even as I was dreaming it, I thought to myself, don't worry, this is just an atavistic memory; you're dreaming; you will wake up; you will emerge from this dream sleek and shining as a baby, clean as chrome, polished, safe. And bubbling up from this ooze, maybe even the sulphur smell was in my mind, bubbling up, was the dream, from deep down, at the soles of my feet, and this form expanded out of me like a shadow that became flesh and could not be detached from my feet, a cunt from which my penis could not be dislodged, caught at every moment, a heart that took half my oxygen—tied together, two awkward tripping racers in a sack race our feet tied together. Damn, I couldn't make a step without carrying this burden with me, tried to kick it off, but found somehow I couldn't even finish a sentence without the other voice interrupting just before the verb. Taking the words right out of my mouth. Couldn't get free. Like a man caught in a trap which has fallen from between the trees, and the vines growing faster about my thighs than I could cut them. And then finally I was scared to cut them because they were blue and red vines, one carrying the blood from my heart and the other carrying it back. Trapped. Damnit. I wanted you to see how I was tossing and turning. And why didn't you wake me? Why didn't you tap me on the shoulder and tell me I was dreaming? But you didn't, damn you.

Jonah in the fucking whale—it's so damn dark—and no way out but past those teeth that don't open but swallow a man whole—a Venus Fly Trap—Venus so alluring—"Oh my, what big thighs you have"—or the big mother spider sitting there on those eight spindly legs, weaving, damn her, weaving and waiting till I get close to her. "I have a little thread here for you," she whispers—"just the very thin thread you need—a little thread, hold on to it, that's it, little one, take the little thread so you won't fall and follow it—it's so easy—just hold on, and don't let go. Now you can close your eyes and walk along without looking, feeling safe even if you are the blind man. The little thread will take you where you want to go. And so you follow it because you know you must, and you go down that hole wandering around blindly in the dark—and it doesn't matter if you have eyes or not because you can't see there anyway—holding on to the little thread just like mommy told you to—big spider mommy with eight arms and legs that straddle you at every point—obeying mommy, holding on to the least for dear life and not even breathing without it—It's your fucking life you know and it's your death line too—going down into that stinking hole full of soft stalactites and stalagmites made to look pretty, limestones breathing on you, soft porous desert rocks which are going to grow around you which extend and harden as you pass and even reach out—but you think you're safe because you've got this little thread which led you in and you think it's going to lead you out—so go down—seeing yourself as little warrior—with a $2.00 plastic sword, which bends like soft grey rubber, pretending, going to kill that monster bull down there— "go fight the monster, dear, but don't be late for supper." Hearing spider mommy whine in ear, "don't be late for supper"—what a thin irritating voice she has for you—nasal and insistent and mocking. You are going to play a little with the bull calf. Be careful. Don't fall and hurt yourself and don't forget, don't let go of the string, or you won't know the way back and will have to wait for mommy to stick her hands into the cave to pull you out and mommy's busy, you know. So you go down because you don't have any choice, and you find the bull calf which is half dead anyway and made of styrofoam and cotton stuffing, and you poke at it a little till it jerks its head, and then you tap it three times at the back of the head, and it drops its neck accommodatingly and then you rub a little dirt on your boots and some red mud on your forehead, pretending you've been wounded. But you've won. You strut out of the cave, holding the thread which cuts your hand like spun glass in your fingers and just when you think you're out and ready to let go, breathing the clean air and out of those wet stinking trees which look just like hairs stinking wet with urine, she, spider mommy drops the web on you.

"Why didn't you wake me up?"

THE GRANNY

Pamolu Oldham

Ellen poked another spoonful of vanilla pudding into her granny's mouth.

"Now when you finish, we can get started. Come on now, swallow it."

She watched the cord of muscles in her granny's throat ride up and down.

"O.K. now, let's start with just holding the spoon."

She pulled the granny's left hand from under the covers.

"Hey, what hand are you?" she asked.

The granny's dark brown eyes stared out of her body as if it were a cave she had fallen into.

"Yeah, you're probably right. Most people are."

"Now hold this. Wait, let me wipe it off."

Ellen walked to the bathinette in the corner of her granny's bedroom and pulled a yellow kleenex out of the box. She wiped the extra pudding off the spoon and dropped the kleenex into the wastebasket. Ellen still wore her schoolclothes: a bright red and kelly green kilt with matching green sweater and knee socks. She swallowed as she neared her granny's bed. She had

111

never had a human patient before, only chickens orphaned by poultry trucks when they drove through town. The last one she'd given a total of 32 stitches, 10 in the upper part of its wing and 22 in its tail end. And then there was the toad whose legs she'd injected with Vick's Cough Syrup. Ellen wanted to be a doctor.

"Now hold this." She clasped the granny's soft fingers around the spoon handle. She pulled her own hand away and the spoon dropped to the covers. The granny looked at her. Ellen picked up the spoon again.

"Now I'm going to put this spoon in your hand," she said a little louder this time. She said each word so slowly she seemed to be counting seconds. The granny watched her hand inside Ellen's. Ellen took her hand away. The spoon fell.

"O.K. now, one more time." She picked up the spoon and reached for the granny's hand. The granny dropped open her jaw, "UNNNNNNNNNNNNNNN."

Ellen stepped back from the bed.

"UNNNNNNNNNNNNNNNNNNNNNN," she cried as she stared at the door.

Ellen stuck the spoon back in the pudding cup and wiped her hands against the back of her kilt. Her mother and Aunt Orene were in the next room.

"I'll go get momma," Ellen said.

"UNNNNNNNNNNNNN. UNNNNNNNNNNN." She sounded like a car stuck in sand.

Before Ellen had made it out of the room her mother and Orene met her at the door.

"She must need a change." Orene said walking to the bed.

"Roll over momma." She pushed on the granny's left hip. "Madge, get me a diaper."

The granny's hospital gown—they had bought a half dozen—had separated like stage curtains, leaving her flat white fanny fully exposed.

"And bring a washcloth."

"UNNNNNNNNNNN," the granny cried into the wall.

"Madge, in the hall closet," Orene yelled.

Ellen stood back against the wall. Her eyes moved down the granny's yellow crack to the mud pile on the diaper.

"Shew," Orene said as if she'd developed a leak. She dabbed at the granny's fanny and then folded the diaper.

"Ellen, reach me that baby powder here," Orene said.

A shadow of rash had spread from the granny's anal area across the curve of her buttocks.

"Get me that petroleum jelly too, please," she asked.

Orene bent over and rubbed down in the crack with the colorless goo. Ellen remembered putting petroleum jelly on her horse Pandora to get the hair to grow back over a scar.

Avoiding the area already glazed with the petroleum jelly, Orene sprinkled the sweet baby powder on the rest of the granny's bottom. Then she laid her hand on the granny's stomach and pulled her back over.

II

After a year had passed, the doctor said the funniest thing had happened, that the granny's heart instead of weakening had gradually strengthened itself. "She could live several years in this condition," he said.

Each of the women stared blankly at the celery green carpet of their mother's living room. Orene swung her right foot. Madge raised her index finger to her mouth, running the nail between two of her bottom teeth. No one had believed Granny Perkins would last two months and then six months. Now a year had passed. Madge's eyes swelled with tears. She made a visor over her eyes with her left hand. Orene shook her foot faster.

"So far her kidneys have held up and her skin. That's one thing with a patient who's laid in bed long as your mother."

"Could you stay till Roy gets here?" Madge asked. "He's coming to get momma up, and I'd like him to hear this."

"I can stay a few more minutes," he answered.

Dr. Foster leaned forward, his elbows on his thighs. You have got that good girl from down in the country now. I know that's taken a lot of the strain from just you two."

He patted Madge on the knee. She made no response. With the right people it was said Dr. Foster could get out of hand.

He leaned back on the sofa and crossed his legs. A thin band of white leg showed above his yellow socks. Dr. Foster always wore loafers and bright socks. His wife, Inez, sometimes filled in at Orene's bridge club.

"Ida Rae's been a godsend but I don't know how long we can keep her up here," Orene said raising the corners of her mouth in a pretense of optimism.

She and Madge joked about how clean and chipper Ida Rae was when she left them on Friday afternoon when Roy came, a bright red or blue bow in the middle of her fuzzy hair, only to return bowless, unwashed and generally worn out on Sunday night.

"Is she good, I mean with your momma?" Orene's partner had asked as the cards were being dealt.

"She's a jewel. One day I came up through the back where momma's window is, and there was Ida Rae singing to momma and dancing to beat the band. Momma just loves her. On the week ends momma cries till she gets back. Lord, she comes in on Sunday night and we just point her to the bathroom," Orene said to end the conversation on a humorous note.

"Orene? Magdalene?"

"In here Roy," Orene said.

III

The granny slumped forward in her wheelchair toward the t.v. as if invisible strings attached to her forehead kept her in strict alignment with the screen. Roy sat on the couch, eating a piece of lemon meringue pie from a saucer on the coffee table.

"Hello Roy."

"Magdalene," he answered. She had been named Mary Magdalene which she had changed to Madge when she got married.

"You all right today?" she asked.

Madge walked across the room to her mother and straightened the gown that had slid down on her shoulder.

"Ellen, why don't you brush granny's hair for her."

Ellen walked out of the room. She knew her mother liked symbolic acts. The last time the family had hiked to the Indian dam that spanned a river they owned land on, Madge had insisted that she and Ellen should squat on the rocks and wash each other's hair. Ellen had wanted to feel the flow of ancestry through her mother, but she remembered most the water moccasin that slithered onto a rock next to them. Her brother had screamed at them and smashed it with a rock. Babies leaked out of the moccasin's fat, brown body and floated downstream.

She returned with a lavender hairbrush. Roy was still eating his pie. Madge sat next to him, ready to watch Ellen.

She pulled the twistie off the granny's braid and ran her right index finger down the middle to separate the hair. She began with several strokes from her forehead over her scalp all the way to the end of her hair. Next she bent the granny's head slightly to the left and held it with her left hand while she made one long sweep down from her temple. She brushed in slow motion. On the t.v. Perry Mason and Hamilton Berger "approached the bench." Ellen bent the granny's head to the right and did the same as she had done on the left. She had saved the best part for last. The granny's eyes nearly blinked shut as she felt the gentle scratch of the brush on her neck. Ellen brushed until the granny sagged forward, her gaze aimed at the floor.

"We better put momma back down," Madge said.

Roy stood up, brushed the crumbs from his pants and walked toward the granny's bedroom. Madge grabbed the handles of the wheelchair and rolled the granny away.

Ellen cleaned the granny's hair from the brush and threw the hair into the fireplace.

"Hold her head up, Magdalene," Ellen heard her uncle say.

"You be good now Miz Perkins while I's gone now," Ida Rae said.

"UNNNNNNNNNNNNNNNN," the granny strained from deep inside.

"I'm going go now Miz Perkins but I be back," Ida Rae said, already working into her teasing, week end voice.

Ida Rae followed Roy. She carried a paper bag with her things for the week end.

"We'll see you on Sunday then Ida Rae," Madge said.

IV

They shared the same bed that night. Ida Rae was gone for
the week end. It was Madge's week end to stay. They fitted
together as perfectly as plastic-bottomed school chairs. Ellen
always slept in jockey position, her knees bent and her
shoulders forward in galloping position. As if lower on the stack,
Madge fitted the top of her thighs against the bottomside of her
daughter. Her arm lay across Ellen's arm.

They always started out that way—Ellen breathing slowly
not to show her restlessness, Madge always cupped behind her,
smelling of Ivory Soap and the Vaseline Intensive Care she used
to oil her feet. "Always take care of your feet," she said.

Soon her mother would turn over and stick one of her size 10
feet from under the covers. She said she couldn't breathe unless
her foot was out. Ellen shared her habit.

When the granny started, it was two a.m. by the clock on the
bedside table. Ellen turned and grasped the spread to her chin.
She pulled her foot in and listened. The moon shining through
the window highlighted the jumper she'd worn to school that
day. She lay stiff beneath the sheets, listening for the next cry,
but all she heard was the steady suck of her mother at the bed's
other edge.

And then she heard the granny again, only this time higher in
pitch and more urgent. She clenched her teeth and heard the
jerk in her mother's breathing that meant she was awake.
Madge rolled on her back and with her eyes still closed waited
for the next cry. The moonlight made her face creamy. Ellen
shut her eyes and relaxed her jaw. Madge looked at Ellen and
was glad the cries had not awakened her. At the onset of the
next cry, Madge gently slipped her feet to the floor and walked
to the door.

Ellen opened her eyes and waited for her mother's whispers.

"O.K. momma." The bed creaked as the granny was turned
to her side.

"Stay over now."

Ellen could see her mother's left hand on the flat white hip of
her granny, holding her on her side until she could slip the soiled
diaper out and lay another in its place.

116

The floor creaked as her mother walked to the bathroom. The toilet flushed. Water splashed in the sink. The plastic top of the hamper scraped as she stuck the wet diaper into it. When the water made a steady sound, Ellen knew she was washing her hands.

From the bathroom Madge walked back to the granny's room. This time there were no voices only the click of the light switch. Past the bathroom and back into the bedroom she creaked across the hardwood floor. Her shadow moved against the wall.

Madge sat down on the edge of the bed and then pulled in her large solid feet. Ellen had taught her how to get into a car properly, rear end first, then feet. Now her mother practiced the new skill almost unconsciously.

Madge sighed. The covers rustled as her foot tunnelled to air. She pressed her back against Ellen who had turned on her side. When Ellen felt her mother's breath go shallow, she pulled away silently as an unmoored boat. She had dreams of her own.

V

Madge turned from the bed and walked past Orene. Pretending she'd seen nothing, Ida Rae stared toward the floor, her hands a wad in front of her. They had spent half the night swabbing phlegm from the granny's throat. Orene talks about it now, not specifics, just how "the sun shone out so bright when the life slipped from momma. She'd been sick 26 months."

The service was held at the funeral home. Somehow a church didn't seem the proper place, as if she'd been divorced and marriage before a pulpit was out of order. Madge and Orene picked out a pale blue dress with tiny tucks at the neck and a pine casket like their daddy's.

Ellen didn't go to the funeral. She also stopped tampering with frogs and chickens.

LEAVING

Margaret Gibson

In the fantasy of the man returning, the man always returns, and there is pleasure. There is no recrimination or indifference, no struggle. There is laughter. There is trust. There is generosity. In the fantasy of the man returning, you open the door of your apartment and there he is. He doesn't have a bouquet of roses, but sooner than you think, afterwards in bed, you realize you are the rose. Or you are in the kitchen making a sandwich for dinner and, in the fantasy of the man returning, he comes quietly out of the icebox or the broom closet—he has been there all along—and without your hearing a footstep or his breathing, he is behind you, around you, his hands on your breasts.

This is your fantasy because you grew up with the story of the man returning, and there were differences. They thought you would be eager to see him. But when the man in the brown uniform, back from Britain or Germany and the war, opened the door, you stood behind your mother and would not go to him. Your younger sister said the syllables that mean father, although she had never seen him and you had. You said,

"Who's that man, Mamma?" and would not budge.

And yours is the fantasy of the man returning because you are unwilling to admit that you are the one who leaves.

You turn the key and the door opens easily because it is in fact unlocked. That means he will have come early and will have made himself a Bloody Mary. He will be sitting on the blue sofa, faintly annoyed. You will open the door into the kitchen, which, because it is shaped like a traincar, always seems to be moving under your feet.

But he is in the kitchen leaning on the sink, eating a cup of yogurt. He has not even turned on the lights or taken off his baggy raincoat. Spoon half-way to his mouth, he looks at you and says nothing. Immediately you begin the chatter of excuses.

This is an affair. He is married, has children. You, once married, are living alone for the first lengthy time. He comes on Mondays, Wednesdays, and Fridays for three hours, between his teaching and tennis. You free-lance and during the evening occupy yourself with books, records, wine, other men. You consider yourself as faithful as he is, the man eating yogurt who is thinking, who is now saying, "This is the first time you've ever been late. You're always here first," thinking but not saying, not yet, "What's wrong?"

In the fantasy of perfect communication, the two of you sit quietly in a room of sunlight and green plants. Each of you is thinking silently. Neither of you touches the other. You turn to him and begin to speak. Without needing explanation, he understands, responds. You also understand his thoughts without his speaking them. This is what it means to be transparent.

But the fantasy of perfect communication always ends with a hesitation in the voice, yours, followed by a sound so faint and distant it could be the sound of glass just before it breaks, that strain, that warning.

Later in the summer you construct a fantasy of what you should have done if you'd been smarter. Because you've been driving around unwilling to admit that you want more than you're getting, or less, you don't arrive late. You're there on time and when his key turns the lock, you're already saying, "I thought I'd be late, because I stopped at the Deli. But you are." You will be teasing, of course.

He comes into the kitchen and cuddles your breasts while you make his roastbeef and horseradish on rye. When you pull out the sardines and begin to slice an onion, he protests. You know, you say, but you had a craving. While he's wondering what that means, you say, "I knew you wouldn't mind." He makes an offhand remark about kicking old Stuart around, but is teasing, of course.

You, however, take him seriously and you leave the sandwiches in the kitchen, fix Bloody Marys, and talk. You tell him exactly how fixed, how limited, how stifled you feel. You tell him that the relationship works only on his terms. He says, "Give me the summer, at least." But you say no, and he leaves. In the fantasy you know he will be back after he's walked down to the parking lot, seen the alternatives, opened then shut his car door quickly, his hand unsure. So you go to the kitchen and, leaning against the sink, you begin to eat his roastbeef on rye as his key turns in the door and it opens.

He says, "Give me the summer, at least," and you, no fantasy now, nod yes, guiltily. You have explained yourself badly. You know he is not, as he says he is, baffled. But you do know he's hurt, and that frightens you. For a while you hold each other without moving. You do not let him see your face because you're relieved that he won't be leaving, afraid he'll stay. You'll give him the summer, then you'll leave. About that you are clear, conscious. You are sure that you love him.

In the fantasy that you love best what you must leave before long, you always love. That summer the repetition, the schedule of your affair is precious to you. You tap out its basso continuo on your fingertips, delighting in the pattern of recurrence and return. It is not an affair by Pachelbel or Bach, because you miss the variations and inversions in the upper melodies, but you tap out the base rhythm anyway, dreading any change in key or tempo.

LOVE STORIES

One out of three days a week you have lunch together at a small obscure place—good pizza, dry omlettes, country western on the jukebox, beer. These lunches satisfy the illusion you both need—that you can risk being together safely some place besides the apartment. These lunches also satisfy a need to talk. You face each other across the table in a narrow booth. You look directly at him, he looks directly at you. There is no refuge in sex or in the confusion of gin. You tell him you've never felt closer than now but the coming separation interests you; you wonder how or if you'll grow. He says, "We're cut out of the same cloth." And you agree, wondering if that means he too will feel objective and steady when the time comes, if he too will be lost and shaken, if he too will have confused his strengths and weaknesses. You punch "Sunday Morning Coming Down" on the jukebox and think of loneliness, rain, Sunday sidewalks. You take refuge in romance. In the fantasy that you love best what you must leave, you construct conclusions which permit you to stay.

In the fantasy of the terrible accident, his wife is killed instantly, the children are at home with a baby sitter, he gets off with a broken arm and guilt. Even then you wonder if you'd want him. In the fantasy of the terrible accident, there is not enough choice.

But choice is fearful, too. Over the phone he says, "Even with the best of settlements, we'd be stuck in an efficiency." Inwardly you sense a faint sneer at material comfort struggle to take shape, struggle to fade. That night, past midnight, you drive yourself into his darkened neighborhood, down the shaded street, the summer smell of crepe myrtle, throbs of cicada, past his darkened house, bikes in the driveway, stationwagon, hedges, the settled life of shrubbery, ivy and pachysandra, flagstones.

You know clearly you'd never want that life, separating it from yours with a contempt fainter and easier than Stuart's contempt for his own choices. Back in your apartment, you turn on every light and play music until daybreak. Even though you do not drink, the night goes quickly, too quickly. You have changed, but you have the same name. You have asked yourself all night what you want, what you really want, but the summer night has rolled over so quickly that now it is noon, you hear Stuart's key turn in the door, and what you want is a question you forget to ask.

"There's nothing explicit," you reply to your friend's question about a lover. Later you overhear her tell her husband that you're terribly masked. Another woman, a more maternal friend from whom it is useless to conceal anything, suggests that you examine your feelings for your father. So you begin to construct theories, intricate diminutive worlds of cause and effect. In your dreams of these worlds, they appear as spiders' webs suspended invisibly in lanes of garden boxbush, massive *sempervirens* centuries old. In your dreams, the webs suspended across the paths break across your face and stick.

Occasionally you and your lover find yourselves invited to the same party. He comes with his wife, you with a friend or alone. Because you are careful of each other at the party, because you never speak to each other at length, you are wary of everyone. You are too reserved, too careful. Around you others knock against tables, tip the hors d'oeuvre trays, talk loudly. You are too cool. You suspect that the pool of light and water about you has turned to ice, that your secrets dazzle.

After one party a friend of Stuart's takes you home, you drink a bottle of wine with him, you tell him. He is surprised. Gratified, you tell him how the affair nears a chosen conclusion. You are calm, rational. During the summer weeks, you see this gentle man for dinner, for a swim, for a walk. Although you plan a trip south with him in the fall, the future is unreal, disembodied.

Your world is circumferenced by the apartment walls. It is real three days a week. On these days you treat yourself to small splendors—avocado, red caviar—and listen obsessively to certain string concerti by Shubert and Beethoven, to country western ballads. Somehow the music seems more real than his hands on your body, your hands on his. You think you understand why, for in the future, you will still have the music and in it, whenever you listen, there will be pools of light, dim questions, avocados, his hands and yours. The music, as you listen to it in summer, isn't going anywhere, but you are.

In the fantasy of passion undimmed by time, there is time, you realize, for love to continue, for love to create a spotlight around you and your lover in the darkened room. Because the spots of time you have are recurrent and circumscribed, love takes longer to conclude. Because it is brief, it is long.

You feel his side of the bed lighten, the mattress shift. The sheet he disturbs as he gets up in the early morning light is pulled off one of your breasts. The morning air is just cool enough. You watch in the faint light your nipple rise and tighten. You hear him dressing, footsteps on wood, a click of the door.

This is your final week together. His family, a week ahead of him at the beach, waits for him. This is the grande finale, but during the week, each night, he gets up at four, drives home and sleeps another four hours. At daybreak all the neighbors are given the reassurance of his car in the driveway. Stuart returns at noon. This is your final week together.

You want him to leave quickly. You want him never to leave. "It is all right," you tell yourself. "I have left already. This is theatre."

The last night you make love roughly on the floor, again more gently in bed. If you sleep at all, you sleep the faint, hazy, confused dream of not being able to sleep. You believe the bed is a window and that you stand at it, as you did sometimes in the afternoons when Stuart would leave, waving. You believe that the bed is an open window, and you start, catching yourself just as you believe you're falling through.

You feel his side of the bed lighten, the mattress eased of his weight. Your face is wet, you must be crying, and there is a quiet freedom in it. Don't, he says, mistaking it. And you don't. You sit on the side of the bed watching him dress. You are numb. You wish you could say something. Footsteps on wood.

You sit on the bed, sheets tangled, your arms and hands limp in your lap, your back hunched. Before you have a chance to pick yourself out of the posture of dejection, you realize he has come back to the bedroom door and stands there, a bulky shadow watching you. He has come for a final look, objective and steady. You look at his looking, unashamed. But at precisely that moment you begin to hate him; at precisely that moment you know that it is hatred you will have to struggle with, after whichever one of you, by refusing to look any longer, leaves.

FUSION

Carole Rosenthal

The couple upstairs is fighting again. Or moving furniture.

"No, they're not! They're fucking." Arnie pulls his lower lip up to hide a grin, and yanks me down onto the bed next to him, grabbing at my toes and trapping them between his legs. Just correcting me gives him an erection. You can imagine how much he gets off on his students when he's teaching. In fact, we met when he was the Teaching Assistant in my advanced zoology lab. Years ago.

Not five minutes has passed since he told me he was too tired even to talk. He'd been working on laboratory slides all day, peering into microscopes, couldn't I understand how exhausted he was, why was I trying to have a serious discussion with him? He covers my face with slippery snail tracks of affection.

"How do you know what they're doing?" I ask. "They're so noisy."

"Would they move furniture every single night? You think we have interior decorators in this tenement?"

Later, when I'm in the bathtub, a watery trickle of blood falls through a crack in the ceiling onto the white tile floor. "Help!" I yell to Arnie. "Call the police, they're killing each other!"

"Rust," he says, slipping his fingers into the redness and sniffing. His voice is crisp and factual as he bends over, the Voice of Science. But my panic excites him.

He carries me into the bedroom on his back, fireman-style—though I'd like it better front ways (like Rhett took Scarlett, like King Kong took Fay Wray)—and he levers me off his shoulder like a backpack. I fall spread-eagled below him and pretend to be asleep.

"Do you like what I'm doing?" he asks me, his head bobbing upward from my belly and pushing next to my cheek on the pillow. "You should tell me, I want to know."

"Yes," I nod against him. His skin feels loose, a size too large. It scares me. Since his thirty-fourth birthday last month I worry a lot about his mortality, about how fragile our connection is, about blue veins forking helplessly beneath his surface and lying thick and passive above his thighs and along his cock, throbbing susceptibly in his temples. What if he leaves me? What if he has a heart attack?

I've got to stop feeding him eggs for breakfast. All that cholesterol. I lick the shallow cavity between his ribs and worry.

"What're you thinking?" He turns off the light, stretching, then smiling and issuing instructions. "Why don't you talk to me? Talk dirty." He tells me what he wants to hear and how to say it. "Use your legs like calipers," he urges. "But gently, gently."

His mouth comes over my face like a hollow tube. A laboratory siphon. My head begins to spin, separating my thoughts from the feelings. My eyes shut.

I'm fixating on light patterns behind the lids, the colors are shooting into my head and I feel myself being rolled over and pressed down beneath his moist body weight. He checks to make sure that my diaphragm is inserted correctly and then begins kneading me like yeasted dough beneath his fingers, pulling at my flesh. I am growing bigger, budding, rising. Growing right up against the corners of the room.

"I want a baby," I tell him, but he's not listening. He's sleeping. I'm sitting four flights up with my nose pressed against the cold morning windowpane, the sunlight reflecting into my eyes from the steel building across the way.

I don't like being alone in the morning. It makes me nervous.

"Wake up, Arnie, it's already half-past ten. Get up, I want to talk with you."

Even though we tangled close for sleep last night, we weren't touching this morning. He sleeps with one arm cupped, protected, between his thighs. There's something inviolable about him even in sleep. The curl of his lip, or maybe the color of his hair which is filing-cabinet gray against the sheets.

When he opens his eyes he can't understand why I'm bothering him, why not let him curl into his Sunday morning dreams like other members of the zoology department?

"Fill in crosswords! Amuse yourself with funnies from the *Daily News*, Judy!"

"This is my weekend, Judy. I let you do what you want, why can't you leave me alone?"

"I want a baby," I say. "I'm almost thirty years old. We're both getting older."

He simulates a snore.

We've had this discussion—a fight really—a hundred times before, a billion times it feels like. What does a baby represent, he wants to know, talking about finances and responsibility. I talk about love. The form is so ritualized I hardly know how much I mean what I claim.

"You're not even paying attention to me," I say. And finally, I begin to cry. His jaw, marked with shadows, juts out.

I picture my ovaries: a tin of open caviar that has been sitting too long in the refrigerator, the little black eggs getting harder and tinier, until finally they have to be scraped with a spoon and flushed away.

Abruptly he sits up, not looking at me. "Oh, for the love of it, stop feeling sorry for yourself! I don't know why we have to plan the future of mankind before you even get me breakfast."

"You used to say we'd decide as soon as they put you in charge of the laboratory."

"Sure," he says, folding his arms across his chest and pulling into himself, his knees close together, so tight the air around him is a vacuum suction. "Do you really want a baby?"

"Really, yes."

"And not a new job? Or plants, or tropical fish? How about a Burmese kitten, or a collie puppy, you'd probably like that." Then: "Just teasing. You know."

"I want you to take me seriously. I want a permanent connection between us, something created by—"

"Crap! Do you think you can send a kid across the street to pick up a carton of milk for its breakfast? How'll we pay for it, who's going to change the diapers and get up in the night? I've got a 9 a.m. lecture to give, so? Try worrying about a kid instead of about me or yourself and it's going to be twice as painful, you'll see. That's a lot of responsibility you're talking so cheap."

"But I'm prepared. I wasn't a few years ago, but I am now. Besides," I touch the tip of my nose with my finger, a sign of honesty from my childhood, "you said when we were first together that we could have a baby. You promised!"

His lips pull in against his teeth, tight, flattened until puffs of laughter push them out. He shakes his head, rocking forward, and squints his eyes like he's sizing me up. "You," he says. "You want to be a child, not to have a child."

Tilting his head, as if he's studying me. Dissecting me with his distance, peeling my skin back, cutting me down smaller and smaller until I almost disappear. Turning, bracing myself on the glass, I stare into the sun above the roofs. Maybe I don't need him after all.

Back in the room, I see a tall silhouette edging off the bed—he could be anybody, no one special—he is all angles reaching a gray hand out to me. "Don't be upset. Do you really want a baby? I'm only kidding, we can talk about it..."

He begins stroking me with dark fingers, there are sunbursts in my eyes, scintillae disintegrate from him as he leads me to the bed. My breath is methane gas around him, my body, cooling, a foreign planet. Unreceptive. How does he survive? There is no life here. Slowly, I grow swampy.

"We could make a beautiful baby," he says, teasing, taking little sucks out of the back of my neck, sponging the tears on my cheek with his brow. "Do you really think I'm serious? I've just been waiting for the right time."

"You're making fun of me."

FUSION

"No," he promises, spreading his legs against the sheet and lowering himself slowly, his vertebrae uncurling, serpentine from Air Force exercises each morning. "I really mean it." He's not smiling, he's almost crooning. "If you want to have a baby, we can have one but you have to be the one who takes care of it during the day."

I think it over while stars shoot around the room and burst open, while he pulls me down onto his body and prongs his penis into my mouth.

"Do I have to take care of it all by myself?"

"I'm in the laboratory, working all day." He strokes my face with his penis. There are oceans on my body, crusts form, resistant but not unyielding. "You have to watch the baby during the daytime."

"What if I break it?" My voice sounds foolish, high and slender.

"I'll make you a new one. And if you want to give it away, we'll sell it. Do you like that idea?" But his voice suddenly stops coaxing, his Science voice again. "As a matter of fact, Judy, that's not so ridiculous. It's extremely difficult to get white babies anymore, did you know that? We could probably trade a child—a high I.Q. child—for five or six thousand, and maybe more." Then slow-voiced again, steering me to his prick. "So come on, just pretend it's an ice cream cone and you can have whatever you want."

"A baby!" I cry.

"Yes, baby," he says as my lips fit over him and he begins to growl back in his throat like a canine, his eyes uplifted and rolling. "Oh, come on baby, that's the way I like it, yes, give me some tongue."

His finger is sticking into me, splitting me in two. This is the beginning of mitosis, cell division; he saws me with his finger. I don't need his sperm to come into me, to fertilize me, I am simpler than that. I don't need him at all. I am an amoeba, I split and have my children, I fuse and have my sex. My own child, my own parent, creating myself endlessly.

"Baby," he is arching backward, he looks as if he is creating the universe, crowding inside me, thronging life into my mouth, proud. I swallow. I am all hollow stomach.

I open my mouth, breathe deeply, fill myself with air. Blow up, evolve. Damn him, I am not so simple as that! Not just an amoeba, a harmless blob. Does he think I'll take any shape I'm pushed into? Let him leave me if he wants!

No, I am bright blue, purple, phylum *coelenterata*, traveling up the evolutionary ladder. I'm a Portuguese Man o' War leaking enzymes, devouring, eddying in the air inside our bedroom. Alternating: sexual, asexual.

"Did you mean that about the baby?" I say. "Why did you come in my mouth then?"

I'm getting bigger, thrusting outward, aggressive, pink-crested with anger, caught up by a riptide that catches the long knots trailing from me, poisonous, stinging nematocysts. They paralyze. He doesn't move.

"You just said that to get me to do what you wanted, didn't you?"

But he flexes himself away from me onto the mattress, then pushes me down, spreading his arms wide and lying on top of me full weight.

"Roll over," he says.

"You're squishing me," I call, but it's as if he's buoyed up on my body and hardly hears me; he begins pressing the air out of me, pumping me down. Flattening. I'm diminishing. And then, almost gratefully, I realize that I'm a planaria, flat and cute with crossed over eye spots. I can barely feel anything, my nerves are fused into a small knot, primitive ganglia.

Then, as he enters me, finding somewhere an opening, I begin to roll into shape, a round worm, a *nematode*, I'm churning the earth, writhing up, up, taking different forms. And now I am changing again, hanging on him with pincers, then scuttling, silent, away from him as he rearranges himself above. To watch him I turn my skinny stalk eyes, phylum *arthropoda*, a lobster, curling my body upwards as the tension mounts. He mounts me, I'm almost a *chordate*, I can feel my bones, sharp, sticking into my flesh, a sun-mottled carp . . .

"Are you wearing your diaphragm?" he asks. Usually he checks me with his finger before we start. He doesn't trust me. But this time when I nod my head he doesn't stop to find out that I am lying about the rubber stopper, the cap, the plug in the earth. His body presses into me. I hear the sound of wings, a flapping, class *aves*. Almost human . . .

"I'm coming," he says, releasing life into me, premature amphibians, tadpoles, thousands, millions of baby froggies, black and swimming, no legs—like the ones he poured down the sink of his laboratory—into me. They're swimming like crazy, flagellating, they want to live, they want to join with the caviar eggs inside me. I'm not going to stop them.

"I'm coming," he whispers into my ear, beginning to moan, pressing against me, his teeth against my mammalian nipple, a man thrusting his life and history into my core.

"Oh, baby, I'm coming . . ."

Strange. Even unhappy. I don't know how to stop him.

LOSING HEART

Tirza Latimer

Beatrix considered that she had a veteran heart. She rarely gave its heaviness or lightness a thought anymore, assuming that come what may, her heart at least held no surprises for her. And so, when the woman to whom she had given her heart gave it back, her heart did pretty much what she expected. It sank. When her gorge rose, her senses receded, her nerves twitched, and her mind went blank, she was not genuinely shocked.

She had seen the Northern Lights. She had seen the cactus in bloom. She had seen two total solar eclipses and a total eclipse of the moon. She had seen five Grey Whales pass not two hundred yards from the promontory on which she stood. She had seen a double rainbow, a tornado, a flash flood, and an avalanche. But nothing had ever taken her breath quite so completely as the sight of her lover Cora's naked body, wet from swimming, caught in the late afternoon sunlight, or lying smooth and asleep beside her.

She did not know how not to love Cora. In the beginning she had loved her too much. "I'm offering you all I've got," she would say frequently and Cora would say either, "That's not very much," or "I find that hard to believe."

LOVE STORIES

In the middle she had loved her too little and Cora would say, "So this is what you were offering. I was right. It isn't very much." And Beatrix, surly, would answer, "Maybe if you didn't ask so much you might get more."

One night she hit Cora on the nose with a bottle. The next day she decided to take a trip. Go away for a couple of months and let the air clear. She hadn't returned for over a year.

In the end she loved Cora more than her own loneliness, but Cora was tired of the whole thing. Cora slept with her back to Beatrix and took to saying, "Maybe if you didn't ask so much you might get more."

Beatrix tried repeating, "I do not love her. I do not love her." In the middle of the night she would wake up thinking she felt her lover's caress along her bare shoulders.

"A space is either empty or it is not," she told herself. Nevertheless, the empty space beside her at night was a presence to be contended with. Each morning she woke up hoping not to notice the empty space. Not to feel the same. If she drank enough coffee she could sometimes fool herself until almost noon.

She tried to develop new interests but lost her old ones instead. Distractions no longer distracted her. She had considered, briefly, Religion, EST, or drinking herself to death. They had worked for other people.

She tried to indulge in a new love but her heart was not in it. "How do I do this," she wondered looking across the formica table at Rose. Rose was not a witty speed freak. She was serene. Bovine even. Beatrix found this refreshing. "It's been so long I forget what to say," she thought, "Or maybe I never knew what to say. It's been so long I forget that too." She began to talk in vague concentric circles about "Trust" and "Affinity."

Uncannily, whenever Beatrix was about to use the word "Attraction" conversations around her stopped in midstream leaving her with her mouth hanging open. Finally she blurted out, "It's just that I feel so comfortable with you." She reached across to touch Rose's hand tenderly and knocked an ashtray off the table. They bent over simultaneously to retrieve it and bumped heads.

"I feel comfortable with you too," Rose had said.

Beatrix concluded that romance was out of the question and did not pursue the subject further.

Beatrix packed to leave. "I'm going to take things as they come. If I'm happy, I'll be happy. If I'm depressed, I'll be depressed. I'm not going to worry about what comes next."

Cora looked out the window at the roof of the house next door. She counted the light spots where shingles were missing.

"To hell with yesterday and to hell with tomorrow," Beatrix said. She rolled a bunch of odd socks into pairs and stuffed them into her pack.

Cora got up and slapped Beatrix on the ass. "I love you anyway," and she left the room.

Beatrix was heading North. Having already headed East, South, and West in the not too distant past. She was resorting to distance. As much as she could afford. And time. As much as she could stand.

She pulled up her collar and slid to the far end of the high-backed bench. Something Cora had said to her came to mind: "I want more for you than a series of painful relationships which you can write about in beautiful prose." Or had it been "beautiful relationships and painful prose."

She hoped she did not look as defenseless as she felt. Defenselessness attracts attack, and there is no place to hide in a bus station save the bathroom. If she hid in the bathroom she would miss her bus.

An adolescent girl sat down on the bench beside her, having first, for no apparent reason, wiped the seat with her sleeve. "Name's Lorraine," she said, "what's yours?"

"Sirus," Beatrix answered.

"Serious," the girl said, "You gotta be kidding."

"Sirus," Beatrix repeated, "for the dog star."

"Going home," said Lorraine, "Where you going?"

"Home," Beatrix echoed rather than answered. She hoped the conversation was over.

Cora had contended that Beatrix was one of those individuals people "Just told things to." She had been born that way, Cora said, as surely as she had been born with brown eyes. Beatrix herself felt that she had heard enough confidences. She kept an eye on Lorraine, but sidelong. As if insights would not reach her obliquely.

"I escaped," Lorraine stated.

"Oh, no," Beatrix said, thinking of how to escape herself.

"Ripped my pants on the fence. Hurt my leg. Supposed to be there voluntarily. Supposed to be able to walk out the gate."

Beatrix's heart clenched. But it was too late.

"Under age," Lorraine continued. "Got pregnant. My father." Beatrix took a good look at Lorraine for the first time. Her pants were ripped, and her leg had been bleeding. She was indeed pregnant. And her face, perhaps her whole body, was covered with sores. Bad diet, bad nerves, parasites? Her eyes looked out of focus.

"When it started to show Mama didn't know what to do. Made me wear a girdle. Too young to leave school without a reason." Lorraine showed no sign of letting up. She talked fast. "So she told them I had a nervous condition. Put me in that place in the city. Just until it's over she said."

"I tell the doctor I'm going to have a baby. My father . . . The doctor thinks I'm lying or maybe crazy. But he finds out I'm right."

"I tell the doctor why don't you do something. He says, 'I can't do anything, I'm a psychiatrist.'"

"I say, 'What if I'm crazy. Then can you do something?'"

"He says, 'Spell table tops backwards leaving out the middle letter.'"

"I say, 'You do it.'"

"He says, 'I don't have to, I'm the psychiatrist.'"

"I get mad. I say, 'S·P·O·T·L·B·A·T.'"

"He says, 'You're not crazy.'"

"If he won't do anything about it why should I stay. Go home, I figure."

"Why home?" Beatrix asked in spite of herself.

Lorraine answered, "I don't know how to get anywhere else."

They sat together in silence for a while. Lorraine seemed calmer. When she got up to leave she said, "I like you, Sirus. You have a nice name."

*   *   *

Beatrix relaized that she had not thought about the woman she loved for the better part of an hour. Had not brooded about the perpetual strain of imbalance which had pulled them both below their level of tolerance for each other. Not that thinking about Lorraine was any less depressing. "Scratch variety and you get the same old thing," she complained to herself.

Expanse of black highway broken by unfamiliar cities, old friends, odd jobs, new seasons, drunken scenes, random encounters with other passers-by. She was getting nowhere.

She got up and stood in line again at the ticket counter. She could trade in her ticket and go home. Try to start over. The man behind her in line was eating ice cream. He stepped on her heel. She ignored it. The second time he stepped on her heel he stepped harder. "You're stepping on my heel," she said.

"And I'm going to piss on your head. I've already pissed ten times today," he said, "I can make it eleven." He was serious. "Get out of my way or I'll shove ice cream in your face," he added.

"Hostile," the ticket agent said shaking her head. "Some of them are like that."

THE SELLER OF WATCHES

Diane Vreuls

I was talking to Rose about Tolstoy. About how we read him at twenty and try again every ten years. She was in her third attempt and not doing well. "There's two things to a story," she said, "finding out something you didn't know and keeping the characters straight." Rose couldn't keep the characters straight. She'd tried several methods. Wrote family trees on an index card she used as a bookmark ("No good, there's too many hangers-on"). Wrote a running synopsis with each name in a different colored pen ("Got as long as the novel"). Renamed the characters after acquaintances ("Works for the women but not the men"). Gave up. "It isn't so bad to figure them out at first, you get lots of clues. Trouble is, they reappear. After fifteen years, who can remember? It would be bad enough if my own friends showed up after all that time. And an author that's good knows they've changed and a lot of things have happened, why keep up?" Well, I've thought about it and decided the only solution for her is a story where all the characters appear only once. Give or take one or two. She's never been to Toronto, so that's where I'll start.

LOVE STORIES

*   *   *

That's where I go when I've had too much Vasil. A great place for recuperation, my uncle's restaurant, the Balkan In. No joke, that's how they think it's spelled. They have the apartment but use all the rooms as bedrooms. Well they need to. Four sons over thirty at home. My favorite is Simko, he's the one I go to see. He has this energy, this body charm. He brothers me. We get along great as long as we don't try to talk. A relief from Vasil. Vasil talks all the time. He's physically comfortable too, but in a draining kind of way. He's gotten portly but don't be fooled, he's essentially slight. When you're with him you feel you have to talk softly and somehow conceal your specific weight. To give him a chance. As a result I tend to get fey.

Anyway Simko, visiting Simko, they have a cot in the bathroom where I sleep. No problems, there's three downstairs. Two of the sons sleep on the living room sofa opened out. My aunt and uncle put their bed in the dining room where the table must have been. Simko sleeps in the kitchenette; he says it's good, he gets thirsty in the night. They all work the restaurant and get up late. That's what makes it so good for recuperation. I mean it's hell to visit people who let their alarms ring down and slam drawers and drop coffeepots and tiptoe out the door hissing "shut up" to each other, "Don't wake her, it's her vacation." Then the place suddenly gets quiet and you're left wide awake on their sofa watching sun motes drift through the blinds and staring at their furniture, waiting to be introduced.

At my Uncle Stojan's they all lumber out about noon, leave the beds in a heap, clothes dropped anywhere, pile downstairs for breakfast of coffee and french fries. Well, they want to use up the grease. If you get hungry later you can go through those little bins and get cabbage and parsnips already chopped or throw hamburger on the grill, it's handy and you never run out of plates. They each take a different booth and more or less live there until it's time to start meals. I read magazines. Since I stopped going to doctors I don't get the chance; there's the laundromat but it's risky, you never know when the light will go off on your machine, so you read short things, letters, the story complete on a page.

THE SELLER OF WATCHES

At Uncle Stojan's I catch up on "Can This Marriage Be Saved?" I discuss it with Simko. It's safe, we both agree it can't. At four when they fold up the papers and open the door to clear the smoke, I give a hand with the tablecloths and napkins. I'm fond of ironed linen, don't have any myself, it reminds me of earlier Sundays, balancing glasses on the folds, wondering who's invited. Then I retire and take in the scene: my uncle filling the cashdrawers, Simko vacuuming, shouting back to my aunt in the kitchen, but overall a calm—it's the dusky afternoon light and all those white tables. A restaurant before it opens has got to be the most satisfying place. After a week, I'm ready to leave. They always protest. They haven't taken me to the falls, if it's summer, or else the ice hockey game. This time I left early. Because of Nadine. She came into the restaurant and ordered paella. Over the Balkan In substitute (herring for prawns, pullet for crab, green plastic parsley) she told me her story of Vasil. That's it for Toronto, Rose.

Back in Detroit I decided my uncle had something and quit commuting. Split my bedroom into an office, put in a business phone. No one should occupy two addresses. Think of apartments empty all day except for a cat or a bird, the sofa grows stiff, the table's printing itself in dust; and at night, vacant office suites lit up strong enough for eye tests, for open heart surgery, oh the waste. I have to notice it in my work. I'm a freelance window washer with my own truck, a pickup I paned in glass. DAYLITE's printed in large block letters on the sides with my old office number below. I'll have to change it. Travel does that. Before I left I'd written off choice as a fake mystique. Everyone carrying on about options, it's a religion, a lifestyle, a lot they know. In my life as lived in Detroit, there's only one floor you get out on, no matter how many buttons you push.

Well all of a sudden I'm choosing: 6d or 8, sizes of nails. Grades of drywall, types of doors, I'm considering whole new things. Like, do you really want a door hollow? Think of that space in there going unused. Perfect for storing old formals. Hollow doors bother me. People think they're knocking on your door but they're not, they're knocking on *their* door; you've got a different one on the other side of the air. A small distinction, excuse me, since I stopped reading the news I find myself having to quibble about things like doors. Something else changed when I got back. My world view. I started seeing myself as living south of the border. That gives you a lot of leeway, well it's supposed to. I think that's why I said yes when Vasil's brother called.

His name is Robert, don't bother changing it, Rose, you don't know anyone like him. Retired at thirty, goes to all-day movies, hires cabs. I recognized something familiar and said I'd go to Cedar Point. At the state line a celebration. We got out of the taxi, saw it was freezing, drove back.
"What's this about state lines?" I said.
"When I found out they weren't invisible," he explained.
Is that an explanation or is it? I tried to get him to tell me how he got rich when Vasil's so broke. He won't talk business, he's retired. Won't talk about Vasil either. "We're only half brothers, you know."

That left me back with Vasil. He's been courting me through three marriages. His. It's worse on me than the wives. I give them a reason to ditch him. For me it's hard. When I was younger he was my secret from the family, too unsuitable. Well of course that's a great binder. I don't know if it's quite the same as "social cement," a phrase I've been pondering lately, but for a while it comes close. Then after ten years of acrobatics (will she let go in time to catch her mother? will he swing back too soon?) my mother raised the net. She met this man in Great Books class and tried to get us together after his marriage went bad, around about John Stuart Mill. It was the wife who had brought the books, he just came along. My mother was impressed by the way he could still discuss without them. And she thought he might be a Serb. Not that it mattered, she was too advanced for that, but she had to wonder. It was a rarity those days, meeting a Serb in culture. It's only recently we've begun to get firsts. Now she phones me up with a new one every month: Zorich, Bogdanovich, Simic, it makes you glad you didn't change your name. I tell her I'm waiting for our first astronaut, or harpist. Well of course her friend was Vasil.

* * *

144

THE SELLER OF WATCHES

I think about Nadine's story and telephone Lila.

"Nadine's a liar," said Lila. "Especially in restaurants. She hasn't seen Vasil for years."

"But she works for him, Lila."

"No, she was fired, she kept misspelling his name."

"Then why did he send her to Canada?"

"Oh that," said Lila. "Her car was in for repairs. She went to Hertz and kept driving. She's got family up there too."

"She was eating alone in the restaurant."

"Proves it," she said.

When I'm down I take on jobs, ten window minimum, lower floors preferred. Pick up Sal, a second story woman who keeps my hours. A gem: over forty and not afraid of heights. Vertigo increases as you age, a loss of inner ear fluids, not bravado as you'd expect. We do a rooming house and a gallery. I love the work. Outside, hanging off into space. The tools, squeegees, now there's an invention, you could feel proud. And ladders. You've got to sing or whistle as you climb, have you noticed? Might be air pressure, but I think it's something else. I need to talk over Vasil with Sal. She's just below me and off to the left, but the wind's wrong, I can't hear her answers, only those of a tenant sitting inside the window. "Don't sound right to me!" she yells through the glass.

I go out with Borkin. He's not a Serb but he plays in a tambouritza band. Over at a club, a real neighborhood place, where the ice is dirty so you drink the coke, it's cold. It's not licensed for dancing so everytime someone comes in the owner yells "cut it," and you stand there waiting till someone says "Oh, it's just Mike." I pick up Borkin after work and we drive to the airport, the only all-night entertainment that's safe. We do the shooting machines, the driving machines, the pinball and go for walks down the ramps. He talks about his music. He's a composer, wants to do computer but doesn't have access, so he has to use what's at hand. Illustrates with the tunnels. Gives a shout and says "Hear that? Hear that overtone? Now just keep that sound going, keep it going, got it?" A life of percussion. Plays grills, sewer covers, matchbooks, puts it all on tape. I help out. Hold the mike close to the pinballs. Up to the foot vibrator while he rides on my dime.

LOVE STORIES

*   *   *

Vasil sends me a gift. He must have heard I'm seeing Borkin. I don't like gifts. Not this one, an antique comb. I can see him in the junk shop, exercising his taste. Thumbing through greasy postcards, rejecting the oil paintings, the box of weights. He spots the comb. Did he say, "Amazing! I always find something of value in an intrinsically worthless world!" or was it only to me he made such admissions?

Will I tell him the story? My grandfather bought my grandmother combs for her hair. He worked in a lumber camp at the Soo. The boarding house, which she ran, was built directly on the railroad. Since trains often blocked the entrance, she learned to duck under the flatcars to get in. Once she came up too soon and broke one of the combs. She had a large, ugly gash on her head. Her husband said only "You broke the comb."

It's hard to think of that man as my grandfather, I knew him old. When I visited him in the rest home not far from the last woods he worked, he couldn't get over my being his. I was such a modern girl. In the movies, that thin. Was this my everyday coat? He introduced me to all his cronies: "What a beauty, she even talks Serbian." I was one item short of perfection. He suggested it shyly as I got up to go: Shouldn't I wear a ribbon in my hair?

Halfway down the block I see Vasil. This is when he appears, Rose, the rest was just talk. He's dyed his hair white. He carries a see-through briefcase filled with something liquid and brown. "You've got thirty good years!" I tell him, but he's disappeared through a door that says MOVED. I bang on the pane and yell VASIL. A man standing in the next doorwell says "They've gone to 105th."

I do a basement apartment. Not our kind of work, we're over-equipped, but this is a favor to friends. Sal's down sick, no one to talk to. It's one of those days you catch your own reflection and leave streaks. Oh well, too much job satisfaction may be an escape. An exterior cleanliness marred by the very next rain. An illusion of dangling in front of a backdrop of

146

clouds, when it's only the opposite building that's in your frame. The need for frames.

Next day I parked the truck and watched Vasil through the rear. I diagnose fugue. He's wandering towards me, abruptly turns. I back up, keep backing up, follow him into an alley. I'm terrible in reverse. I strike a larger, parked truck and lock fenders. "Hey Vasil," I say, but he's busy, he's put down the briefcase to feed some birds. I say it again, it's not Vasil. I climb back in the truck in a rage and hit the pedal, shoot out mid-block into traffic. No one's there.

I called Stan, the mutual friend, he hates one-to-one relations.

"Stanley, what's this I hear about Vasil?"

"I give up, kid, what's this you hear?"

"Nadine says."

"Don't believe her, call Vasil."

"He doesn't answer."

"I'll look into it after lunch and get back to you soon."

Mogol talk, I'm supposed to hunch by the phone while Stanley arranges and, if I'm lucky, gets back. Well I do wait. He gets back to me four days later.

"Daylite," I say.

"That you, kid?" Then, "He's made up his mind. Refuses help."

"Stanley, tell him I'll marry. No wait, let me think it over."

"You've been doing that for years."

"But he wouldn't want pity."

"You're wrong."

"But it's not about me."

"Of course not."

"You're not supposed to agree."

"I don't know, kiddo, when my father had his attack, it was my mother who aged. Forgot things, slurred her speech."

"Is that supposed to be a warning?"

"You think he's faking?"

*   *   *

LOVE STORIES

Yes, no. We said we'd remain independent. Of what? It's manipulation. Square nails, dark hairs between the knuckles. No rings. I think of Jack. In the ward for alcoholics, getting old under constant observation. He'd been in some kind of explosion that left him with webbed hands. He'd treat me to lakeside bars on his afternoon passes. Be caught and taken off privilege; I'd be given one more chance. We played yachts on his bed.

"I've signed out for church next Sunday. Asked Warnke to go with. You like her?"

"So so." I was an aide, they don't have favorite nurses.

"She said she was busy, too bad, she missed her chance. Now I'll ask Margaret. If she goes with me, we'll marry."

She did and they did. He died two years later, leaving her rich.

There's Moira. Phoned me on New Years, said "I'll be married next spring. Don't tell anyone, but it's going to be Warren or Frank." I forget which or whether it's lasted.

My great uncle Adam. Worked a mine in West Virginia. Wanted a wife. Asked the seller of watches to find a nice Serbian girl. "Know who," said the salesman, "over to Youngstown," and took him there on the train.

Now Ilenka had stayed at home, helping her mother with boarders. "Get married," the family told her, but she'd wait. "One day I'll marry a stranger, he'll knock at the door. I'll say yes and go off, I don't care if he's already married."

So the seller of watches takes Adam out to the house, knocks, and makes the introduction. Ilenka says "He's the one." Her mother says "But he's not married!"

Adam returned to West Virginia. Ilenka wrote to find out when they'd wed. He said May.

"Did you buy a watch from the salesman?" I ask them, sitting in their kitchen.

They say "No, a ring."

My sister—the one you met, Rose, remember—she talked to me on the beach. It's too cold, we're not swimming. She wears a coat and ties a kerchief back under her ears. I like her better that way. She's got red hair now and isn't the same. I am lying out flat on my stomach wrapped in a towel that keeps coming undone. She tucks it back. She's worried about my life.

"He loves you." She's an authority and one of the few who do.

She wants to say "Cut the shit," but talks of vacations instead.

I'm not young any more, I've been saying that since twenty to get in practice.

If he puts an ad in the window, opened a restaurant. If he asked me to take him to church.

Is there a way to unknow him?

If he'd come on a train and knock in Serbo-Croatian, is it the watch I'd buy, or the ring?

THE WEDDING TRIP

Lloyd Rose

The heavy feel of the satin in her arms as she lifted the wedding dress to step into her shoes, lifted it higher than necessary, exposing her slim, neatly-hosed calves, just to hold the weight, was all she clearly remembered of the wedding. She remembered other things in a vague, unstructured pattern of color and smell and sound and Arthur's curiously dry mouth scraping hers, but it was as if she had moved in a trance, slightly below the water of the world, looked up to a distorted, muted reality. She leaned against the car door with her dress bunched around her and was too tired to smile at the relatives on the church steps. Arthur smiled and waved. Yes, she thought, that was it— he would smile and wave. She floated on her cloud of satin and watched him, content to have him wave as she had been content to have him lead her down the aisle out of the church and put her gently into the car. She saw her parents at the church door, her mother wiping away tears, and, suddenly anguished, she jerked her hand up to wave. She smiled. But her stomach was hollow, and something solid seemed to be slowly filling her throat.

"Are you okay?" Arthur asked her. She looked at him. He was smiling at her. "Are you nervous?"

"Nervous?" She examined him with curiosity and realized that she had never seen him before. It was true that she had gone out with him all through school, but she had never seen him before, not as he was now, a force to make her nervous. She found herself unable to remember whether his hair had previously had such a strong red cast to it, and she did not think his eyes had been so dark, nor his mouth so small, nor his hands so capable, helping her into the car, lifting her veil over the back of the seat, packing the folds of her dress carefully around her.

"Well, you know, honey. About tonight."

His mouth, she decided, had definitely been different.

"Don't be." He removed his right hand from the wheel and placed it over hers. "I'm very proud to be marrying a virgin. I'll be very gentle."

His hand was as dry as his mouth. She looked down at it, trying to envision it a few hours from now placed on her untouched, unseen body layered now with satin. She could not imagine it penetrating the layers of the dress; within it, she felt remote and cool as stone, and the hand under his did not seem to be connected to her body under the dress but to be some false appendage placed on the end of her arm in order to give him something to touch. She looked up from his hand out through the windshield. Dark massive clouds filled the sky, tumbling against one another, racing away from the pale slit of yellow sky at the horizon. The wind turned up the silvery undersides of the leaves and bent the long grass by the road. She shivered.

"Rain," he said. "I hope it won't ruin your dress. You shouldn't have travelled in it."

"I didn't want to take it off," she said quietly.

He turned to smile at her. "Sentimental girl. Looks like a storm," he continued, squinting at the sky.

She watched the grass along the side of the road. So much of it was yellow and dead; she wondered why that was. Sudden bursts of wind bent it to the ground.

"What are you thinking about?" He put his hand on hers again. She didn't answer. "You are nervous, aren't you?" She didn't answer. "Now don't be, don't be. You know I love you. It'll be all right. I won't hurt you."

She wondered when the rain would begin. The sky was almost black. She thought about its not hurting. She could not imagine pain in that part of her, just as she could not imagine his hand on her.

"Really going to pour," he said. "I'm worried about that dress."

"Maybe it'll rain itself out," she said. The sheen of her dress was like the pearly inside of a shell. She imagined rain rolling off it. The sky was so dark. How low were the clouds? The sky was moving down to meet them.

"Is that a woman?" said Arthur.

The figure had flashed past them. A hitchkiker. Arthur slowed down. She looked back. Was it a woman? Whoever it was wore a dark, drooping, wide-brimmed hat and was gazing after the car.

"I can't tell."

"A woman shouldn't be hitchhiking alone, that's a damn fool thing to do."

Her body was being pressed slowly back against the seat: he was still slowing down. A thrill of panic ran over her skin like electricity. "Why are you stopping?"

"Well, hon, I can't leave a woman on the road like that."

She looked back again. Seeing the car continue to slow, the hitchhiker started towards them.

"You're going to pick her up?"

"If it's a girl I am, sure."

"But . . ." He was nearly stopped now; the hitchhiker was running through the long dead grass. "It's our wedding trip," she said desperately.

"Hon, I'm not taking her to the motel with us." He grinned and patted her hand.

"Don't pick her up!" she screamed. "Keep driving!" But she must not have said anything, because Arthur had stopped the car, and the hitchhiker was bending down by his window, smiling. Dark short hair curled around her ears. Her hat was black canvas and very old. Arthur rolled down the window.

"How far are you going?"

The hitchhiker smiled and shook her head and presented him with a card. He stared at it. "Well, I'll be. Look here, honey."

She took the card. It was smudged and dog-eared. I AM DEAF AND DUMB, she read, and in smaller type below: I can read lips.

Arthur took back the card. "Do you, uh, do you sell this for a living?" He started to reach into his pocket, but the hitchhiker shook her head again, took the card, turned it over and handed it to him again. Printed on it in pencil was the message: I am going to Franklin.

"We're not going to Franklin," Arthur told her, speaking more loudly than usual. "But we can take you as far as Reid. Will that do?" The hitchhiker nodded and smiled. "Well, get in." He opened the door and leaned forward, pulling the back of his seat forward. "Don't let me crumple your dress, honey."

But she had already pulled the dress around her as the woman climbed into the back seat. Now she turned and looked at her. Besides her hat, she wore an old black raincoat, buttoned to her neck, frayed leather gloves, and jeans. She carried a small case which she held on her knees. It was not like a suitcase but was metal with a double catch.

"Well," said Arthur, starting down the road again, "it's no wonder I wasn't sure she was a woman, with that get-up. I guess she dresses like that as a disguise, for protection."

But she looked back at the woman and thought that that was not why he had made the mistake, or, if it were, it should not have been. He should have made the mistake because the woman was tall and because her face, though friendly, was hard and strong-featured, and because her short hair was like a man's under her dark hat, and because of the trace of dark hair on her upper lip.

"Have you come far?" she said shyly. "And is that all your luggage?"

The woman threw back her head and made the movements of laughter. Still smiling, she opened the case. It contained tubes, jars, small brushes, a mirror. She pulled out several snapshots and handed them across the back of the seat.

"Oh." She turned to Arthur. "Look, why look, she's a clown."

Arthur glanced briefly sideways. "What do you know?"

"A real clown." She stared at the pictures: the woman in baggy black pants and coat, huge shoes, white face, red wig, a trailer in the background. A real clown. She had never been near one before. They had always moved far away, separated from her by a crowd. She had always been glad; they frightened her. She handed the photographs back. "Are you joining the circus in Franklin?"

The woman nodded. She held up a finger, then took a tube from her case, unscrewed the cap, and squeezed a soft white coil onto the palm of her hand. Balancing the case carefully on her knees and propping the mirror against its open lid, she began to put on a clown's face, spreading the make-up over her features, smoothing it evenly in spite of the poor light in the car.

When was it going to rain? The sky was black. They had picked her up because rain was coming—when was it going to start? Perfectly white now, the woman's face seemed to glow faintly in the darkness, like a moon. She picked up another tube.

"Tell her she shouldn't be hitchhiking alone," said Arthur.

"She's busy," she whispered.

"Busy?" Arthur glanced in the rearview mirror. "Well, I'll be damned. That's pretty clever."

She looked down at her dress. In the fading light it held a faint illumination of its own, like the mysterious, stored radiance of dogwoods at twilight. She slipped her hands beneath its folds and shut her eyes. She waited for the rain.

It had not come when they reached Reid and stopped at the bus terminal. It was dark by this time, and the neon letters B-U-S flashing off and on gave a lapping red sheen to the woman's clown face, white with black-rimmed eyes and a red nose and a red upturned mouth. She stood by the car window and smilingly accepted the money Arthur gave her to buy a bus ticket to Franklin and get herself some dinner. "And go in the ladies' room and wipe that stuff off your face," he said, and the woman smiled and nodded and went into the terminal.

"I think she's a half-wit," said Arthur as they drove away.

She glanced back and glimpsed through the glass doors the woman, her make-up case knocking against her thigh, her hat pulled low on her head, crossing the lobby to the ticket counter.

LOVE STORIES

They did not stop until ten o'clock when they pulled up to the Fountain Court Motel. It stood on the side of the road between an old iron fence which bounded a small graveyard with a boarded-up church in its center and the edge of a pine wood which stretched away into the darkness. It was fronted by a small, brightly-lit pebbled area containing a birdbath in which stood the plaster statue of a girl with a jug on her shoulder. Water trickled from the jug down along her left breast and thigh.

"You want to keep driving till we get to a town?" Arthur asked her.

"I'm tired," she said.

"It isn't much of a place to start a honeymoon." He ran his hand along her arm. His mouth opened a little. "When we get there tomorrow, that's when the fun starts."

She stood in the middle of the motel room, her dress as solid around her as ice, and watched him. He was pacing. His face had spotted redly, the way it did when he was upset: she remembered that.

"Is it this place?" he said. "Is that it?"

She stared at him and said nothing. The left hand double bed was turned down; their suitcases sat on the other one. Prints of hunting dogs hung over the beds. She tried to remember him.

"Of course you're nervous," he said. "I'd expect that. I'd expect you to be nervous."

She felt distantly sad for him: a small, hot, sad place deep inside her. She thought that perhaps she would remember him better tomorrow.

"I'm proud of you, honey," he said. "I'm proud to have married a virgin. This is natural. I know that. But I'm a man, after all."

"Tomorrow," she said, so low that he did not hear her and she had to repeat it. "Tomorrow. When we're there."

He stood looking at her, his hands loose and bewildered at his sides.

"I love you," he said, and she knew he would not touch her tonight.

He took the right hand bed and she took the one by the window. She sat on the bed in her dress. "Aren't you even going

156

to get undressed?" he said. "Are you scared to get undressed, for God's sake?" And when she did not answer but only looked at her lap, he thought he had hurt her, and he was sorry and kissed her and said he understood and she could sit up as long as she wanted. He said he was proud she was a virgin. He said he didn't mind waiting for a night. He said things would be fine tomorrow. Inside her dress, she felt her body growing smaller and smaller in the distance from him. The folds of her dress hid this metamorphosis and the masks of her face and hands remained deceptively in place, but she knew she was falling away, accelerating, growing tinier by the minute, ready to be folded in under the waves of sleep if he would only release her and go. She said he could turn out the light, she didn't mind sitting in the dark.

She sat in the dark and wondered why it had never rained. After a long time, when she was sure Arthur was sleeping, she lay down on her back, rustling her dress as little as possible, and closed her eyes.

She was dreaming that the woman's white mask was floating near her. She was outside the window, kneeling on the sill, her hands and face pressed to the glass. She waked to find herself staring into a moon so bright it made her blink and turn away. She struggled with sleep, unable to believe the moonlight. What had become of the black sky? The sky now was a far away darkness, hidden by the translucent, milky veil of the moon's radiance. One or two bright stars hung in that veil like ornaments. The moon burned in the sky: its brilliance had erased its features; she could not make out either the figure of the lady seated at her mirror or the face of the man-in-the-moon.

Her arm ached where she had twisted it under her as she slept. Murmuring, resisting the pain, she tried to sink again into sleep, but the moonlight was too bright in her face. She rose and stumbled to draw the curtains. Why were they open? Why hadn't she drawn them earlier? The brightness of the moon, which she had thought half a dream, did not fade as she came fully awake. She could see clearly the little white church with its short, square steeple, and the old, falling gravestones and crosses surrounding it. She looked over her shoulder into the room. The moonlight did not reach Arthur, a dark, quietly-breathing heap. It threw her shadow across the bed. Its sheen on her dress made her think of a field of unbroken snow. She looked back out the window. A figure stood in the shadow of the church. As she watched, it stepped into the moonlight. She recognized it. She was not surprised.

The woman beckoned, but she waited. Would she come closer? Was she worth coming closer for? She waited calmly, her hands still clutching the curtains. The woman did not hesitate but came blithely forward. Her make-up was gone, but her face was still white in the moonlight. Her hat and coat and gloves were gone too. She wore a white man's shirt and jeans, and her feet were bare. She did not come all the way to the fence, but stopped a few yards away. She beckoned again. And quickly, glancing at her sleeping husband, gathering up her dress, stepping out of her shoes, she slipped out the door into the night.

She hurried past the fountain, the pebbles bruising her feet, and ran down the side of the road through the long grass by the church fence, looking for the gate. It was just opposite the church, hanging open on one hinge. She raised her head, took the night into her nostrils, lifted her dress and turned restlessly, searching. She started forward into the graveyard.

The moonlight was silver on the tombstones. The shadows were blue. The woman was waiting for her by the broken cross.

"Who are you?" she whispered, but she had forgotten, the woman was a deaf mute. She stood with her dress pulled around her, waiting, uncertain. Her body felt warm suddenly, and large, straining at the seams of the dress.

The woman came forward. Carefully, she unpinned the veil and lifted it and draped it over the broken cross. She thought she should run, but she stood still. She looked across the graveyard and saw the moon gleaming on the windows of the motel, and the fountain, lit-up. She felt the woman's hands at her back and started. The woman was unfastening the dress, parting it as if it were some skin or shell she had outgrown. The night air fell cooly against her unveiled back. She bent her head. The dress fell around her feet, blue and sliver in the moonlight. She stood in her long slip, shivering a little, and the woman, still gently, took her hand and she stepped out of the dress, and the woman pulled her down to sit beside her on the ground. She could see her heavy-featured face quite clearly. A sudden panic seized her. "Oh, oh, you—" and half in fear, half in rage, she grabbed the woman's shirt and ripped it down the front. But she was wrong. The torn shirt exposed breasts.

She slid then, slid down, as the woman's hands slid up under her slip. For one fearful second her blood pounded crazily in her head and she moved to escape, but she was held and pulled down and she fell and she fell and she rose again.

Waking with the familiar body beneath her, she found that she was wet, her hair stringy and damp on her neck and cheeks. She raised her head. The woman was still sleeping. By the faint grey light of the coming dawn, she could see drops of water on her eyelids and lips, caught in the heavy brows, tracking down her cheeks. Her body had shielded her, but now the rain, gentle but steady, began to soak through her shirt—her breasts rose up against the wet cloth, clearly outlined.

She sat up. Her ruined dress lay a few feet away. Raindrops lay in her veil, still hanging from the broken cross. She smelled wet grass and trees. No birds were singing. She sat with the rain running down her face and back and breasts and arms, as the grey light grew whiter and whiter. Beside her, the woman stirred and opened her eyes, and she turned to her and bent over her and was going to kiss her, but Arthur was screaming.

"Oh my God!" He stood with her soggy dress in his hands, staring at her. Where had he come from? He was still in his pyjamas. He must have come running from the gate, from beyond the church. His chest was heaving. Had he seen them from the window? Had he waked, missed her, risen, gone to the window, seen them distantly sleeping? Had he run from the room, across the pebbles down the road, through the gate, past the church, over to them? "Oh my God," he said again, "oh my God, oh my God," and then he screamed again and threw himself at the woman.

Quickly, without panic, she rolled, seized a piece of broken stone, and, as he came at her, smashed it into his face. He made a violent, broken sound and his hands flew to his face. He fell to his knees and, on her feet, holding the stone with both hands, the woman struck him again. He did not make any sound this time, he only collapsed forward and the woman was gone. Running, she supposed, running across the graveyard, through the rain, the way Arthur had come, but she did not look to see. She sat staring at Arthur.

His left hand lay half-open by her knee. The rain was beginning to soak his pyjamas to him. There was blood in his hair and blood on the grass beneath his hidden face. She wanted to see whether he was dead, but to do that she would have to touch him, and she did not want to touch him.

NINA

Irene Tiersten

No husband, no children, no home, no money, no job.

But no pity, please. Choice was involved. Free will and determination and a willingness to live with the consequences of my choice.

"I hear you took a walk," was how an acquaintance put it at a conference I attended, looking for job possibilities.

"How on earth did you know?" I asked, stunned that she knew I had left my husband only two weeks ago.

"Word gets around," she said, patting my arm with more warmth than our tangential relationship had called forth in the past. Before Federal grant money had run out, I had conceived of and coordinated conferences similar to the one we were both at now, and had used this woman as my expert on Sex Discrimination in the Classroom. Usually, befitting the auspices of the university I worked for, the conferences were aimed at educating educators. Because my husband, an educator himself in the field of law, was involved in public policy as it related to public education, he had also had occasion to call on this woman's expertise. I did some mental spins: had Martin himself told her? Unlikely. Was the entire community talking about what I had done? Possibly. Should I press her for a definitive answer? What for? I wanted desperately to know who was saying what, but I was also afraid to find out. She smiled and asked, "How are you managing?"

"It isn't easy," I said, trying to be offhand.

"Well, I wish you the best," she said, pouring herself a cup of coffee at the hospitality table.

A good wish. A treasure, sparkling and precious and unexpected. Gratefully, I entered her into my well wishers column. She, who had worked with my pro bono lawyer husband, the public do-gooder, had wished me well in my attempt to act on my own behalf for my own good. For which most people, as I had been hearing directly and indirectly, accused me of being selfish.

I took copious notes, listing every lead that sounded even vaguely like a job possibility. I wrote my notes in a spiral notebook my sister-in-law Lainie had given me on my last birthday, a notebook with a cartoon of Snoopy on the cover. Snoopy was typing his doggy novel, thinking to himself in a cartoon balloon "Here's the world's greatest author working for his Pulitzer Prize." Lainie had written on the first page, "Dear Nina, Someday you'll win lots of prizes. Love, Lainie." I left the page intact. In the months I had had the notebook, I had used it mainly to jot down ideas for short stories. As I used it now, I felt I was sullying its pages, which stopped me for an instant until I could restructure what I was doing into a more acceptable thought, that I was integrating the different aspects of my life. So far, after twenty years, writing had brought me no money. And right now I needed money. For actual survival and for self-respect, which was part of survival.

On and on went the conference. Familiar with most of the information, I had hoped to be tapped as a resource person for one of their future conferences, but all their resource people had been hired. However, I let it be known that I was in the market and left the conference feeling hopeful that I might get a telephone call or a letter with a job offer.

More definitively, what I left with was stories of four other separations, three ending in divorce, one in reconciliation.

NINA

Driving back to the newly rented apartment, unfurnished except for a bed, some books, a counter and two stools, a place still too unfamiliar to be thought of as home even though I was sharing it with Daniel, I thought that I would tell Daniel that this should have been called a conference on divorce, that everyone was doing it, that they should refer to the current year as the "year of divorce." Or perhaps it was simply the same principle I had observed at other times in my thirty-five years; whatever trauma, delight, illness, growth, stimulation, or depression I experienced seemed to be exactly what everyone else was simultaneously experiencing.

Daniel was also doing it; he had left his wife the day after I had left Martin. Within a month, after Daniel and I had found an apartment, Janet filed her divorce complaint. Adultery of course, with me as correspondent. And an extra kicker: a ground of extreme cruelty. As Daniel and I read the two count complaint, I felt nauseated at the vindictiveness, the distortion, the rawness, the pain, the disbelief that was mine, and Daniel's and Janet's, and Martin's.

Martin had not yet filed a complaint. I imagined him sitting in our marital residence, arms folded across his chest, in custody of Karen and Bobby, either waiting for me to come to my senses and return, or figuring out how to punish me for my misbehavior, or both.

A classic situation, so predictable that it's hard to describe.

Martin and I and Daniel and Janet had been friends. We lived within four blocks of each other; we belonged to the same Temple. Our children, my two and Daniel's three, knew each other.

At the beginning, I barely knew Daniel. What began the friendship was Janet's invitation to me one morning at Temple while the two of us waited for the Hebrew School to let out. Janet, whom I had spoken to casually at various Temple functions, asked me to sit down with her. I replaced the book I had removed from the shelf and sat down with Janet at one of the library tables. The room was chilly and both of us kept on our coats.

"How are you, Janet?" I asked, sitting down. Bad question, I

163

realized as I took a good look at her. Unhappy, I answered myself before she even opened her mouth.

"I hate my life," she said.

Oh, boy, another one, was my immediate and empathetic reaction. "Is it really that bad?"

"If I had the guts I'd commit suicide," she said, looking me straight in the eye.

An over-reactor, I thought.

She set me straight. "My sister committed suicide last year."

Warning. Siren wailing for help. I may have been unhappy, but I had never contemplated suicide. This woman needed help. And her need made me see how safe, relatively speaking, I was. "No one should feel that awful," I said.

She didn't agree or disagree, but began a recitation, "My marriage is terrible. My children have behavior problems. I feel worthless. I sit at home and try to figure out what to do."

"Maybe you can't figure out what to do by yourself."

"What do you mean?" Her question was defiant. She looked sad and angry.

"I mean... why don't you get yourself some supportive therapy?"

She stuck her tongue down between her teeth and her bottom lip and worked it around, pushing out the skin in a misplaced pout. Then she said, "I tried that already; it didn't work. All I talked about was Daniel."

"Why?"

"Because it's Daniel who's making me miserable. He... he's the most selfish... He always... He never...."

"All right, never mind the details. The point is that you need professional help. Listen, I have a therapist who's helped me a lot...." Janet gave me an evaluating look. I wondered why she had chosen to talk to me. Did I also look unhappy? Or did she think I looked so well adjusted that I could give her answers? All I could do was react to her distress by directing her to a therapist. From her tone and her manner, I knew she wanted, for whatever reasons, to pull me close to her, to wind her needs around me. Such situations had occurred before, and while it was gratifying to help, it was also dangerous to fall into the well of someone else's neuroticism. I needed my energy to stay afloat on my own. "Why don't you write down her number and call her in the morning?"

The next morning Janet called to tell me that she had made an appointment with the therapist, and that she felt much better even though she was sure the therapist wouldn't be able to help her at all. I urged her not to decide on defeat before the fact. She invited me and Martin to dinner. I accepted and when I hung up, I realized I had done again what I had promised Martin I wouldn't do. I had made a commitment for both of us without consulting him. A fair request on his part. And I felt guilty as hell, despite the mitigating circumstances I immediately began to reel off for my own benefit: Martin wasn't home, Janet wasn't just a run-of-the-mill type person who had proffered a casual invitation; she was so emotionally precarious that I couldn't refuse her the instantaneous acceptance. I had reacted spontaneously to the plea in her voice. Janet had made me put myself on the spot. For a second, I was angry at her. However, when I asked Martin if he would like to go to dinner at the Wasser's on Saturday night, he said, "Oh, from the Temple?"

I said, "Yes, I've had some conversations with Janet this week and she called this morning."

"Sure, why not," he said.

I didn't know what he would have said if I had told him I had already accepted.

That Saturday night, we sat in the Wasser living room having before-dinner drinks. Janet and Martin, across the room in twin armchairs, began a discussion about paralegal training. Janet had recently completed her training and had gotten a job in the New York City Welfare Department. I sat on the couch with Daniel, who fixed me a cracker spread with a mixture of roquefort cheese, horseradish, sour cream and onion that he had made himself. He asked me what kind of music I wanted to hear. During my Saturday errands, I had heard Mozart's 39th Symphony on the car radio, and the themes still sang in my head. I wanted to hear it again.

"How about some Mozart?" Daniel suggested.

I laughed and told him why.

He smiled, "I like coincidences like that."

After dinner we went back into the living room, resuming our pre-dinner seats. This time, loosened by wine and food, a glass of brandy in my hand, I leaned against the arm of the couch and stretched my legs out across the pillow, accidentally touching Daniel's thigh with my toes. I pulled back immediately. Daniel looked at me questioningly and I flushed. A handsome man. Very handsome.

Before we left, Daniel said, "Oh, just a minute," went back into the living room and came back to the door holding a book. "I just finished reading it," he said. "Tell me what you think of it."

Once before, some years back, new acquaintances of mine and Martin's had come out from New York City to spend the day "in the country" and to stay for dinner. Upon arrival, the man had given me as a hostess gift, a book by Norman O. Brown, CLOSING TIME. Just that morning I had read a review of the book and decided I wanted it.

The gift delighted me.

That night Martin grumbled, asking me pointedly how the man had known exactly what I wanted. I gave the book to someone else within two days, as soon as I finished reading it.

While Martin was brushing his teeth, I looked through the book Daniel had chosen for me. A novel. With line drawings. Exactly what I was working on; a novel with line drawings, the first time I had done such a thing. How the hell did he know? I put the book at the bottom of the stack next to the bed, and Martin said nothing about it but turned out the light and fell asleep. I was jabbed out of dozing by the memory of my toes touching Daniel's thigh, but finally the brandy put me to sleep.

When Janet called the next morning, I felt uncomfortable since thoughts of her husband had kept me awake, but she sounded so cheerful that I began to concentrate on her and forget about Daniel.

She said she enjoyed our company enormously. I thought back and remembered that during the course of the evening she had looked angry every once in a while and also depressed. However, when she had been talking to Martin she had looked engrossed. And when she talked to me she seemed thoughtful and calm. It was Daniel who set her off. As he had carefully poured the wine, Janet told him sharply that he hadn't opened the bottle early enough. He let her comment pass. We all knew that Daniel had opened the wine well over an hour before we sat down at the table. For the next few minutes neither Janet nor Daniel spoke and I looked at Martin, remembering dinner parties during which we had publicly flayed each other. We didn't do that anymore. There were no more running sores; they had scabbed over.

It pleased me that Janet said she enjoyed herself. Gratified, I invited her and Daniel to dinner for the next weekend.

When I told Martin I had asked them, he frowned.

"Listen . . . if you don't want them to come, I'll tell her that I checked my calendar and we have a conflict," I said.

"No, no, it's O.K."

"I'm sorry I didn't check with you first. . . ."

"Well, I would appreciate it if you did."

"Did you have a good time last night?" I asked.

"It was O.K." he said, not looking up from the New York Times crossword puzzle which he always did boldly in ink.

That was all I could get out of him. I knew if I asked him whether he liked Janet or Daniel, he would be noncommittal. As for the reasons that I liked them, for Janet's taking and Daniel's giving—Martin had no need for either.

During the week Janet called me so often that when I told Martin about her calls he asked me whether I had bitten off more than I could chew. "She sounds like she could get to be a burden," he said.

"I see what you mean," I agreed, wincing inwardly as he bulls-eyed my own misgivings, "but so far it's O.K. and she's started to see Dr. Barnes."

"Hmmmmmmmm. . . ." Martin said. Both Martin and I had been seeing Dr. Barnes for over a year, individually and in joint sessions, ever since our disastrous trip to a Bar Convention in New Orleans, when I had been asked by an old mutual friend, Stan, to go for a walk. Which I did. And listened to him talk about how he and his wife, Sharon, had committed themselves to reshaping their marriage, how he was trying to be more open with his wife, and how the process of revealing himself scared the shit out of him. Anyone knowing what he was really like would surely be revolted. That handy-dandy universal neurotic truth made us both laugh. When we returned to the hotel suite party after about ten minutes, I saw Martin sitting morosely by himself, and after my attempts to talk to him met only with sulking—eyes lowered into glass of bourbon, lips barely moving in denial of "Is something wrong?" I spent the rest of the evening talking to Sharon, and dreading going back to our room with Martin.

Martin was furious. I had humiliated him, he told me as we both lay in bed, rigidly keeping our distance from each other. What did I think it looked like, he asked, when I left with Stan.

"Absolutely nothing," I said emphatically.

"How can you be so . . . so insensitive, and naive. I'll tell you exactly what it looked like. . . ."

I cut him off. "Only to you . . . I can't live like this anymore. You have to give me some leeway. I can't be chained to you. Martin, I can't stand this."

"I think you need help . . ." he said dully into the dark.

"You do . . ." I said back.

We both went. And Dr. Barnes seemed to be helping.

I hoped Janet would be helped.

The only difference I noticed as Martin and I saw the Wassers several times a week, was that Janet talked even more about her various unhappinesses. Martin listened to Janet during most of our evenings, saying very little himself. Daniel and I talked to each other. Despite the Madeira Daniel had taken to pouring for me just before the evening's end, I would lie awake for hours after Martin had fallen asleep, reliving my conversations with Daniel, tracing the pattern of his shirt with my eyes, separating the brown, russet and white colors of his beard, absorbing the resonance of his voice. A doctor by profession, Daniel's love of music had given him an encyclopedic knowledge, an extensive record collection, and a bassoon, which he had played since he was fourteen.

Janet, sitting on my back porch during the week, staring into a glass of iced tea, bridled when I mentioned how much I admired Daniel's musicality.

"He cares more for his music than he does for his family," she said, not at all admiringly.

The more Janet called and visited and talked about Daniel, the darker she became, glowering and complaining. Out of bitterness, Janet thought she had constructed in Daniel an effigy worthy of contempt. And she clearly expected me to share her feelings. Her expectation made me uncomfortable. I began to dread her visits and telephone calls. I began to wish that it would be Daniel who called me, Daniel who came to talk to me for an hour.

One night I dreamed that I woke up. My dream eyes wide open. I looked at Martin's head on the pillow, and saw that his face was grey and shrivelled, old and dull. I tried to see more clearly through the dim light. Horrified but not surprised, I looked at his face thoroughly and long, to make sure I saw it properly.

I discussed the dream with Dr. Barnes, who had become the loom on which the threads of my life, and Martin's, and Janet's, and Daniel's, were being woven.

Mutual friends began inviting us as a foursome. At a dinner party, left alone in the living room by spouses and friends who preferred the den, Daniel, obviously thinking the same thoughts as I, said, "I'll call you during the week. I think we have to talk to each other privately."

"Yes," I said, "That will be good."

At every dinner party, movie theatre, concert hall, and informal gathering, I was drawn to Daniel, sat next to him, talked to him, listened, watched him, became suffused, absorbed, enthralled, bemused, engaged, aroused.

But discreetly, I thought.

Martin didn't say anything.

Janet didn't say anything.

But my attachment, I felt, must surely be obvious. Why didn't Martin notice? Or Janet?

But, of course, I didn't want anyone to notice. I wanted to be able to see Daniel so often, so acceptably, so safely. I wanted to explore.

Symptoms of exploring:

Sudden and unaccountable desire to maintain the status quo.

Complete rejection of the status quo.

Diarrhea.

Guilt.

Insomnia.

Dreams of appetizing food, tables of canapes, entrees, salads, desserts, viewed by the hungry dreamer, but forbidden to same.

Quickened speech.

Thickened tongue.

Monday morning at 9 a.m., after the children had gone to school and Martin had left for work, the telephone rang. It was Daniel. My stomach in spasm, my mouth dry, I pressed the phone tightly to my ear.

"Something is happening," Daniel said, his voice over the telephone private for the first time. For me only.

"Yes."

"I think about you all the time. I read a description of a woman in a novel and I'm startled because the woman sounds like you. Every once in a while I stop dead on the street because someone is wearing perfume that smells like yours, and for a minute I think maybe it's you. When I play Mozart, I think of where you were sitting, how you looked, how close we were, when I played it for you. There are so many things I love, that I want to share with you. I want to give you books, and records, and wine....but how? It's not allowed. Such closeness is forbidden. But....it exists...."

"Daniel, it's the same with me. I never get to sleep after we've seen each other. I relive you completely, trying to keep you with me. What should we do?"

"I don't know."

"I don't know either."

No commitments, no arrangements; not yet. Not ready yet. Almost. But not yet.

It was impossible for me to talk to Janet now; I didn't want to pretend to be her friend. When she called, I was as short as possible. I stopped accepting her invitations, although I didn't cancel the obligations we had already confirmed.

Martin didn't mind at all that we were no longer seeing so much of Daniel and Janet.

"Daniel is a good fellow," he said, "but Janet drives me crazy."

"Janet is a good person," I said. "But you were right, she demands more than I can give."

That was the extent of our actual conversation. I knew I was being dishonest by omission, but what was there to tell Martin? I had to admit to myself that I was already past the point at which, if such a conversation had been possible with Martin, discussing my feelings toward Daniel might have defused them. At various times in the past, during various stages of friendship with or attraction to other men, I had been confused and guilty and tried to talk to Martin, but he retreated angrily, saying he never felt attracted to other women, that friendship between men and women was impossible and dangerous. So he had taught me. And my relationships with all other men became impossible and dangerous, and I never discussed them with Martin. I edited my conversations, kept my fantasies to myself, except when I wrote them.

Writing the story had made me exceedingly nervous, but I had to do it. As I wrote, I wondered what the hell I would do with it when I was finished. Send it out? Impossible. So I wrote it and put it away and a year and a half later I happened across it as I was straightening out the folders in which I kept my stories; and I read it:

BETRAYAL, TWICE

Betrayal (2)

Jimmy looked up from the story he had just begun reading and said to his wife Andrea, who had written it, "You don't intend to send this out, do you?"

"Jimmy," Andrea tried for a placating tone, but heard the high edge warning of danger in her own voice, "you haven't finished reading it yet. You've barely even started..."

Jimmy's lips tightened and he went back to the story, starting again on the first page. "Betrayal," he said out loud.

Betrayal (1)

The shower had washed away the salt and sand, and she felt
sweetly clean. In the summer her hair thickened, and when she
took off the shower cap she felt its summer weight on her lightly
tanned shoulders. Carole walked to the full length mirror on the
back of the bathroom door. She could look at herself without
fear of being discovered by Samuel or their two small children,
who would all be on the beach for at least another hour. She
wondered if Robert would have the courage, or the need, to
come to her cottage while his own wife and children were safely
on the beach. If Robert did come now he would find her naked.

She thought her breasts were fine looking. Several days ago
she had put on a polo shirt over her bare breasts. No bra. To see
how it felt. To see how it looked. For the reaction. That summer
it seemed that every woman had taken off her bra.

Samuel had said nothing when she came out of the house
and got into the car, joining him and the children for a ride out to
Gosman's dock for a fish dinner.

Then Robert came out of his cottage and waved to attract
their attention.

"I'll see what he wants," she said, already out on the road.
She ran toward Robert, feeling the looseness of her breasts.
Robert noticed. He looked away then looked back, his face pink
beneath his even tan. "What's up?" she asked.

He snorted.

She was confused. "You did wave, didn't you?"

"Oh. That. Yes. Where are you going?"

"To Gosman's for dinner. I thought you knew. You all want
to join us?"

"I wish . . . but no, it's impossible. Jean just put the kids down
for a nap. Don't have dessert there. Come back and have it with
us."

"O.K."

She ran back to the car. The wind came in under her shirt
and touched her skin. Getting in, she began an explanation of
what Robert had wanted. Samuel interrupted. His lips curled,
"Boy, you were certainly flapping in the breeze."

She looked down. Her breasts sagged humiliatingly. "Should
I put on a bra?"

"Entirely up to you," Samuel said magnanimously.

Feeling tough, she had gone to dinner braless. But she managed to keep her chest as inconspicuous as possible by slumping her shoulders, crossing her arms, and bending over the table.

That had been two nights ago. Now she looked at her naked self. She was definitely the type that looked better without clothes. Better in a bathing suit than fully dressed. Better completely undressed than in a bathing suit. She wanted Robert to see her the way she was seeing herself in the mirror. Samuel saw her that way every morning and night, but he didn't react. Samuel.

Saying his name made her feel guilty. If he saw what she was doing he would laugh at her. "Healthy people don't have to stare at themselves in the mirror," he would say. But she often caught him staring at himself. He just never admitted it. And if Samuel knew what she was thinking about Robert. . . . What if he were to know? What exactly would he do? He insisted that he never found another woman attractive. Oh, of course he did say that occasionally he was momentarily aroused at the sight of a pretty woman walking by on the street, but nothing beyond that. Nothing, from what she could gather from her oblique questions and his indirect answers, like her own wondering about what she would be like with another man.

And, after all, what did she find so unsatisfactory about Samuel? Samuel had a stable personality: he didn't swing from highs to lows the way she did. He was the fulcrum of her emotional seesaw. He balanced her, as he was fond of saying. He had started as a trainee in a small but growing computer development company and was now in line for a vice-presidency. He had said, long ago in graduate school when he was only twenty-four, that he intended to make his mark by the time he was thirty-two. And now he was only thirty. Ahead of schedule.

She stared at her breasts. They were definitely saggier than they had been when she was twenty-four. Now she was twenty-eight and trying to figure out what her own schedule was. And on what she wanted to make her mark. Before her marriage, she had studied music and taken voice lessons. Then her mother died without leaving enough insurance money for her to continue full time in school. She got a job in Barnes and Noble and met Samuel there the next September when he came into the store to buy his textbooks. The day he came in she was wearing a black turtleneck, her straight black hair was parted in the center and pulled into a barrette at the back of her neck. She was underweight. All she needed, she had decided that morning as she saw herself in a store window, was to cough blood.

Evidently, Samuel was also struck by her tragic image. When, two months later he asked her to marry him, he told her passionately that all he wanted to do was to take care of her. She warned him then that she was exhausted from her mother's death and didn't have enough energy to love anyone. He assured her that he understood. She told him, feeling relieved but uneasy, that she would marry him. The ceremony took place during the Christmas holidays that year, and when they came back from their honeymoon weekend in Bermuda, they found the letter accepting Samuel into Wharton's graduate school of business, which meant moving to Philadelphia. She continued working at Barnes and Noble, kept on with her two courses at the Manhattan School of Music, and kept planning how she would investigate the music schools in Philadelphia. When she discussed her plans with Samuel he seemed distracted and uneasy. She didn't know why.

"If I go back to school full time, I'll be finished in a year and a half. And you have two years of graduate school, so we'll be finished at about the same time. And then we can.... Samuel?" She whispered his name across the table, wondering whether he was listening to her at all, or was mentally reviewing the information he had absorbed in class that day. Samuel was a very serious student. He looked up from his plate.

"What are you whispering for?" he asked, looking at her as if she were strange.

"You didn't seem... I mean... I was trying to see... Never mind. Were you listening to what I was saying?"

"Of course. I heard you. You've been saying the same thing every night for about two weeks."

"Oh."

"Come on, don't look so insulted. But you do go on and on."

"Because you never say anything about what I'm saying, and I somehow got the feeling that you either disapprove, or there's something wrong. . . . Samuel . . . ?"

"All right. I didn't know that you'd want to go to school. We never discussed it. I thought you'd work while I finished."

"Oh."

"It will be much easier that way. When I'm finished, I'll start making money right away and then you can do what you want to do."

"But why can't we both . . ."

"Because there isn't enough money now."

But by the time Samuel was finished, their first child was due to arrive, and she made no plans to go back to school. Besides, it was far too late to consider a serious voice career. She thought she might someday take a degree in theory and then teach, but that was for the future. She was very busy now with two children, a big house, a husband, and an active social life.

And, increasingly, busy with thoughts about Robert, who had come into her life at a friend's party, who had brought his guitar, and, late in the evening after wine and cognac, had been persuaded to play. He played Bach, gently and evenly, but not through to the end, because, as he admitted with a self-amused smile, he had not yet learned the end. She had been touched by his admission, by his daring to play something he did not know perfectly. She looked over at Samuel, who was sitting on a rocking chair, looking into his cognac, frowning.

Samuel said later that he had been disturbed at being left hanging by the unfinished Bach. She was surprised at what seemed to be such a musical sensitivity; Samuel had never made such a musical statement before. But then he went on, "You'd think he would have played something he really could do!"

"What's the difference?" she asked, startled at his angry tone.

"What's the difference! He made himself look like an idiot!"

"I don't think so at all," she said softly, thinking of Robert as he had smiled at himself.

Despite Samuel's initial reaction, he agreed when she suggested inviting Robert and his wife to dinner. They all became friends, Carole and Sandy talking about children and Robert and Samuel discussing sailboats. Carole and Robert discussed singing and philosophy. Robert was an assistant professor of philosophy at a community college. The more they saw each other, the more Carole found herself thinking of Robert when they weren't together. If she heard a piece of music and enjoyed it, she thought of how much Robert would like it. Getting ready for an evening to be spent with Robert and Sandy, she saw Robert's eyes as they would look when he saw how she was dressed. She realized only gradually that she was dressing and perfuming herself for Robert. Once she realized, she avoided Samuel's eyes in the bedroom, in the bathroom, and in the mirror at the top of the stairs where they usually stopped to admire themselves and each other. Carole felt strongly that she was betraying Samuel by dressing for Robert's pleasure. But it was all so innocent. Nothing was happening. Surely a little mental pleasure never hurt anyone. Sandy didn't seem to notice the increasing attention Robert and Carole paid each other, but Carole could see that Samuel noticed and that he didn't like it.

For various reasons that he articulated as if he knew that she wouldn't understand, Samuel, in the course of their years together, had not liked a number of her friends, both male and female. Once he had said to her very earnestly that a mentally balanced person didn't need many friends. That one was enough, and that as far as he was concerned, she was the only friend he needed. She knew sadly that she could not be that devoted to him. He loved her more than she loved him and that made her feel selfish. Perhaps she lacked the ability to love as steadfastly as Samuel loved her. But at the same time, she also believed that Samuel was missing out on a lot of love from other people. Maybe if she herself stopped looking for, giving, and accepting love from other people, she'd have more for Samuel. She tried being more self-contained, even going so far as to refrain from touching other people so much, a mannerism which distressed Samuel. But she wasn't successful. And now Robert, and the urge to touch him. Robert's hair was curly and longer than Samuel's and she wanted to smooth it, to arrange it, to feel the texture of his hair, the shape of his head. But she controlled herself. Occasionally, she touched his arm with her fingertips. Surely that could offend no one.

But she knew that it did. She invented all sorts of mental subterfuges to hide her distress. She pretended that she was very young and in need of Samuel's protection and guidance. And, of course, if she were that much in need of protection and guidance, she couldn't very well be responsible for her lapses from his standards of conduct.

So when the time came to consider plans for summer vacation, and Robert suggested, with Sandy nodding pleasantly next to him, renting the house across the street from theirs in Ammagansett, Carole, with wide open empty eyes and a clear smile, convinced Samuel that it was a splendid idea.

Now it was summer. Being in a bathing suit and exposed to the sun made Carole feel younger. She felt her body tightening, firming up out of winter flab. The children shrieked in the water and kicked sand at each other, and Carole talked to Sandy as she lay next to Samuel, who was reading a mystery. While she talked, her eyes hidden by sunglasses, she stared at Robert in his snug blue bathing suit. Robert lay with his back to the rest of them, his body forming an elegant curve against the sky. He was reading Bishop Berkeley.

What Samuel didn't know didn't exist.

What, actually, did exist? She stared at her eyes in the mirror. Did she exist? She as Samuel saw her, chaste and dutiful, fulfilled by husband, children, a house? By eating out as often as she wanted, ordering without looking at the price column? And how did Robert see her? As sexually attractive, able to discuss Bishop Berkeley and Bach? And how did she see herself? As all those things. And as obsessed with how Samuel and Robert saw her and with how she saw herself.

Her voice, she had known for quite a while, had virtually disappeared. She no longer sang even in the shower.

Betrayal (2—continued)

Jimmy lowered the pages and looked at Andrea.

She sat in front of her typewriter, pretending to read some

junk mail but really following what he was reading as he finished each page. She kept her eyes down while she waited for whatever it was he was going to say.

"Why did you write this, Andrea?"

Her heart beat so strongly that her chest hurt and she realized that she needed to force herself to breathe properly, "Please, Jimmy, finish reading it before you say anything...."

"This is very painful.... this Samuel...."

She looked at the rows of letters waiting for her fingers to order them. "Please...."

He began to read again.

Betrayal (1—continued)

Samuel was not at all distressed by her loss of voice. "It doesn't matter. I love you anyway," he said.

Robert, when she had told him months ago that her voice was going, had said, "Why don't you start taking lessons again?"

The thought of starting lessons again was exciting and frightening. She didn't want to find out that what she suspected was true. Yet it was possible that she was exaggerating the damaged state of her voice; maybe all she needed to do was some scales, a little bit every day, and then ... and then what?

With two children, a husband, and a house, and money.... then what? A singing career? The drudgery of teaching? Why couldn't she just relax and enjoy what she had?

Instead she twisted through the winter months, ricocheting off the walls of a dilemma she couldn't define. After early spring, when the summer plans were made, she began to think of the vacation as a time when her problems would be resolved.

She laughed bitterly into the mirror. Her problems now seemed exacerbated. She was tan and firm and more confused than ever.

Last night she and Samuel had come back from Gosman's, put the children to bed and gone across the street for dessert. The night had gotten chilly, and Carole, still braless, had thrown a sweater over her shoulders. There was a fire going in the fireplace. Robert sat in front of it, his foot up on a stool, picking at his guitar. Sandy was reading a mystery. They both looked as if they had been in suspended animation and were released into movement by Carole and Samuel's arrival.

After coffee and fresh raspberry pie, Carole felt hot. And discomfitted from feeling she could not look anyone straight in the eye. She wanted to talk long and seriously to Robert but couldn't with Samuel and Sandy in the room. She wanted to talk about herself, in a way that Samuel would regard as private. She couldn't talk that way in front of him. Restless, she crossed and uncrossed her legs and finally announced, "I need some fresh air. My eyes are watering from the fire. Anyone else want to go for a walk?"

Robert raised his eyebrows at her, "Sure," he said slowly.

"Samuel?" Carole said, louder than she meant to.

Samuel, looking into the fire, shook his head as if hypnotized.

"What about you, Sandy?" Carole asked.

"No. You go. I just got warm. Besides, I only have about twenty pages left until I find out who dunnit."

Without looking at each other, Carole and Robert left the cottage and went out into the cool night. Still not looking at each other, they grabbed each other's hands and walked quickly toward the ocean.

"Quick, before they change their minds," Robert said.

"I can't believe this!" Carole said when they reached the sand.

"My God!" Robert laughed tensely, "All the times I've imagined something like this . . . !"

"You too? Really?"

"Oh, you knew. I could see that you knew."

"I guess you're right."

They stopped walking and faced each other. Their unfamiliar bodies came together awkwardly. Carole thought she would fall. She wanted to concentrate totally on the eroticism of the moment, but she was afraid of falling. He bent over her as if she were as short as Sandy. She pressed against him as if he were as thick as Samuel. In seconds they adjusted.

"Our bodies know each other," Robert said into her neck.

"Not yet. . . ." she surprised herself with her boldness.

"When?"

"Oh, God, not now...they're both...any minute they might...."

"Later...later. Come to the beach later, after Samuel goes to sleep...."

"But....how will you know? Are you going to sit on the beach all night?"

"If I have to. I often go out at night to walk on the beach. Even if Sandy's awake, she won't give it a thought."

"O.K. Yes. O.K. But we better go back now..."

He tried to kiss her, but she was afraid his imprint would be visible to Samuel and Sandy, "No. Later...."

Sandy was asleep at the table, her head on her arms, when Robert and Carole re-entered the cottage. Samuel looked up from the fire, his lips pursed, "Have a nice walk?"

"Sure," Robert answered in a completely natural voice, "It's nice out."

Carole tensed, waiting for Samuel to use one of his gag lines, "If it's nice out then leave it out." He didn't say it. He said nothing on the walk back to the cottage, and nothing as they got ready for bed.

She waited for him to say something. He always did if she spent more than a few minutes with a man out of his sight. He said nothing. She wondered if he would want to make love. Their cottage had only one bedroom and the children slept in it. Carole and Samuel used the small living room to sleep in, making up the two studio couches each night. If Samuel wanted to make love, he would get into her bed. He didn't. He said goodnight and almost immediately began to breathe deeply. Carole, so wide awake that she could feel the blood moving through her veins, stared at Samuel outlined by the moonlight. His couch was under the window and since there were no neighbors, they never pulled the curtains.

Was he really asleep? Could it possibly be so easy? She got out of bed, prepared, if challenged, to say she was going to the bathroom. Samuel continued to breathe easily. She left the cottage, closing the screen door carefully, avoiding the racketing squeaks and slam. At the window, she looked in at Samuel, still sleeping in the moonlight.

NINA

She was outside. Her mouth was dry. She ran toward the driveway, listening through the natural summer night music for sounds other than the ones she was making. Nothing. Samuel was not following her.

At the end of the driveway, from behind a stand of scrubby pines, she saw Robert emerge from his cottage, closing the door behind him in exactly the same way she had just closed the door behind herself.

She watched him, felt his movements, and panicked. She couldn't do it.

Robert hadn't seen her. She turned and ran silently back to her cottage.

Again she laughed bitterly at herself in the mirror, seeing herself running away, back to the unsuspecting Samuel. On the way to the beach just two hours ago, Carole found herself walking alone with Robert for an instant.

"What happened?" he asked softly, keeping his face conversational.

"I couldn't. . . . Samuel read until so late . . . I fell asleep before he did."

"What about tonight?" Robert looked at her.

"Yes. Yes. I'll try again."

On the beach they had all gone into their characteristic beach positions. But Carole couldn't keep her eyes away from Robert's back. She became intensely nervous. She could smell her bodily secretions . . . sweat, vaginal discharge. Surely her physical distress would be obvious to Samuel and Sandy.

"I'm getting a headache," she said, after rehearsing the excuse for long minutes, "I've got to get out of the sun."

Samuel looked up from his mystery, "You O.K.?"

She gestured vaguely toward the sky.

"Do you mind if I stay for about an hour?" he asked.

"Not at all. Maybe I'll lie down for awhile . . ."

"Go ahead. . . ." he was back to his book.

Sandy raised her head long enough to wave.

Carole tried not to look at Robert but couldn't help herself. He raised his eyebrows at her. She raised her eyebrows at herself in the mirror and tried to interpret what they might mean. Her mouth was dry again. Would Robert come? She willed him to leave the beach and come to her. "Please, Robert. I'm ready now." She filled her mind with pleading and left no room for consideration of what would happen if he actually appeared.

She heard the slurred noise of footsteps in the long grass. She saw her startled eyes in the mirror and was frightened for an instant at her power to make things happen.

The footsteps came closer to the house. And the sound of voices. If it were Robert, there would be no voices. Then a high whine, and Samuel's voice saying sternly, "I told you if you couldn't behave yourself I would take you off the beach. It's your own fault."

She quickly locked the bathroom door and with trembling fingers put on her clothes.

Betrayal (2—continued)

Andrea could see Jimmy's body tensing as he read. She thought that perhaps she had made a mistake by giving it to him. But she had changed all the details. It was the best story she had ever written, the most honest. She should just have sent it out, and if it got accepted, shown it to him then. Then he would be able to see it as a story, from a distance, the way she was trying to see it. Maybe she could still take it back; he wasn't finished yet. She could take it back and say it was only a rough draft of a story she was thinking about doing in the future. Her armpits smelled sour.

Jimmy looked at her before he went on to the next page. His face was pained and accusing. "Why didn't you end the story there," he whispered.

"You can stop now. You don't have to finish reading it. It's only. . . ."

"No. I can't stop now," he said, lowering his eyes to the next page.

Betrayal (1—continued)

When she came out of the bathroom, she avoided Samuel's eyes. She didn't want him to suspect anything, yet she was surprised that he didn't. To her ears, her voice sounded excited. Her movements were nervous. She blinked a lot and laughed at nothing in particular. But Samuel noticed nothing. He went on doggedly disciplining the children, catching them up on months of his not having enough energy to do more than kiss them goodnight when he came home from work.

The afternoon passed, punctuated by a phone call from Sandy suggesting that they all, including the children, have dinner together, potluck, in the grape arbor.

During dinner, as she sat at the wooden table lifting forkfuls of cold barbequed chicken to her mouth, she felt as if a screwdriver were rapidly tightening all her joints. Her jaw ached. Robert stared at her blatantly. She wanted to warn him that he was being obvious, but then again, she also wanted him to continue staring at her. His attention reassured and excited her.

As they left, Robert said as he always did, "Bye, see you later."

She jumped and looked quickly at Samuel.

Samuel answered, "Sure. See you later."

Carole shuddered.

"Cold?" Samuel asked, putting his arm around her protectively.

"It's getting chilly," she said, walking rapidly so that he had to remove his arm.

Several hours later, Samuel was again asleep, breathing evenly in the moonlight. Carole, doing her best to read, looked over at him every few minutes until she was sure he was really asleep. This time she did not stop at the window to look in at him. She ran to the end of the driveway, where Robert was already waiting for her.

Without speaking they joined hands and walked toward the beach. The absence of words, the pressure of their joined palms, made her feel adolescent. Nothing had to be explained. Mostly because what was happening could not be explained. No analyses, rationalizations, judgments. None of that business. They just walked.

At the edge of a path through the salt grass, Robert stopped, "In here. This house is vacant."

On the deck of the dark house, Carole took off the long polo shirt she used as a nightgown and spread it out to protect them from splinters. She pulled off the dungarees she had put on silently, not disturbing the sleeping Samuel. Robert took off his shirt and dungarees. They lay down on Carole's shirt and kissed. There was no breath. Her mouth was dry, he tasted bitter. She hadn't expected his mouth to be bitter. He rolled her on her back and stroked between her legs, missing the particular spots that she knew excited her. Open-eyed, she stared at the brilliant summer stars, closer, it seemed, than Robert's hand, his strange fingers.

He climbed on top of her before she was ready and entered her. Despite not being prepared, the delight was excruciating, the culmination of hours of staring—Robert's eyes, Robert's fingers on his guitar, Robert's voice illuminating Bishop Berkeley, Robert's snug blue bathing suit. This was Robert. Inside her.

"Robert," she said.

He pulled back, "What?" he asked, as if she had called his name in order to tell him something.

"Nothing. I just wanted to say your name."

"Oh," he said. He put his head on her shoulder.

He moved inside her hard and rapidly and in a few minutes groaned and arched his neck back. Finished. His breathing returned to normal and he lay on her quietly. She was hot and hanging, but didn't know what to say to this man who excited her but didn't know her body. Next time would be better, she decided, trying to regularize her breathing. Robert rolled off and settled beside her. She was prepared to lie if he asked her if she was O.K., but he didn't.

"Thank God," he said quietly.

"We'd better get dressed," she said, sitting up, pulling on her pants.

Robert moved to let her get her shirt, and put on his clothes.

They sat on the steps, breathing together, leaning against each other.

"I don't want this to end," Robert said, "I want us to be together as much as possible."

"But how?"

"I don't know. We'll figure it out. I need you so much. Sandy, Sandy puts me to sleep...."

"Yes. Samuel. . . . Samuel. . . . he doesn't put me to sleep, it's as if I am asleep and he doesn't want me to wake up. Or. . . . he's asleep and he doesn't want to wake up. . . ."

"Well, we're awake. . . ."

"Yes." There was a question she had to ask, "Robert. . . . what is it you want from this. . . . Is it. . . . what. . . ."

She stopped. This question was for herself too, and she wasn't sure what she was asking. Thinking, she was aware of a sound she hadn't heard before. A sandy sound. Footfalls on the beach. She grasped Robert's arm when she saw the fuzzy, searching beam of a flashlight. "Robert! It's Samuel! I know it!"

Robert jumped up, then stood still, paralyzed. She saw his rigid outline against the swaying salt grass.

"Go back to your cottage. I'm going out to the road. I'll say I couldn't sleep and went for a walk," she spoke quietly, almost hissing.

She made it several yards down the road before the beam focused on her. She turned, prepared to act startled, and was actually startled by the shock of the light.

"Where were you?" Samuel asked grimly.

She gave her prepared answer.

"With whom?"

"What . . . ? What are you talking about? By myself, at this hour of the night. What time is it anyway?" She was being long-winded and her tone of voice was twisted. She shut up.

"Do you really expect me to believe that you were out here alone?"

"Why on earth should you think anything else?"

"Because your diaphragm is not in the cottage."

Stunned, she sputtered, "My diaphragm . . . you . . . you. . . ." She saw herself sitting on the toilet, inserting her diaphragm while Samuel slept. She saw Samuel, awakening—or had he really been asleep at all?—and rummaging through her drawers next to her empty bed.

"Take it out."

They had reached their cottage. "What?"

"I said," he said, shining the flashlight on her face, "that you should take it out."

Beyond guilt and fear and pain, she shook her head dumbly.

She put up her hands to shield herself from the light, "Please...."

He kept the beam on her, "If you were alone, you would have no objection to removing your diaphragm. We haven't done anything in days."

He had caught her. Dismayed and relieved, she said, "Let's go inside."

They talked all night, he lying open-eyed in his bed, she in hers. Her chest ached, she had cried until she was dry. Yes, yes, she had admitted, I betrayed you with Robert.

"But why?" he asked, agonized.

"I don't know. Maybe I just wanted you to pay more attention."

"I pay attention...."

"I don't know how to say what I mean."

"And why Robert? What does Robert have?"

"I don't know. I don't really know him.... I think maybe I just made him up, because.... because...."

"Because what...?"

"I don't know."

"Let's go home in the morning. Pack and go home."

"Yes," she said exhausted.

"And when we get home...."

"Do you want a divorce?" The word sounded ridiculous.

He waited a few seconds. "No."

She tried to figure out her reaction. Release? Disappointment? Both.

"It has to be better than this, Samuel..."

"I agree. You are very confused. You need counselling."

"Yes. Maybe. And you...you too."

"I don't see it that way. I don't feel confused."

That night, at home in their own bed, they made love and Samuel relieved the awful tension Robert had left unresolved. They agreed never to see Robert and Sandy again. They agreed that they would work on their marriage. And they agreed that Carole would go into therapy.

Betrayal (2—continued)

Jimmy put the manuscript down next to the typewriter. His voice strained, he asked Andrea, "That's it? That's the end of the story?"

"Well... I thought so. Doesn't it work that way? Isn't it a story?"

"Do you really think I can possibly give you an objective answer?"

"Oh. It's just a story. It isn't real...." she stopped. "What are you staring at?"

"I'm waiting for you to say that it never really happened. That you made it all up and that no one will know what you're writing about."

"Jimmy...."

"What do you intend to do with this?"

"I thought.... I thought, depending on your reaction, that I'd send it out..."

"Why?"

"Because I think it's the best story I ever wrote."

"It's too bad you really aren't a singer; you could go out on the streets and sing it. Complete with costumes and scenery. You could call it 'Public Betrayal'."

"Jimmy.... I won't send it out if you feel this way." He stared at her. She remembered the glare of the flashlight. She reached for the manuscript.

He got it first and held it in both hands. "I didn't say that...."

"You didn't say what?"

"That you shouldn't send it out."

"Maybe not in so many words. But that's what you feel. And if that's what you feel, I won't. It probably isn't a finished story, anyway. I'll put it aside for a while." She waited for him to look relieved. She had seen his feelings; she wanted him to acknowledge them so she would know that he knew what they were. Since that summer, the summer past, the summer that was the time of the story, Jimmy had not talked about what had happened. When she told him about the therapist's suggestion that he, too, come in for some sessions, he had replied strongly, "I don't think that's necessary."

"It would be helpful..." she had said, keeping her voice calm.

"I was not the one who created the situation. I am not confused."

"I didn't say you did . . . but, Jimmy, this has to do with the two of us. . . ."

Now he said nothing. He didn't look particularly relieved. He looked pained. His eyes, wide under the ridges on his forehead, proclaiming distress. This was the way he communicated. Wondering how long she wanted to live with such obliqueness, she jumped from her chair and snatched the manuscript.

Stunned at her quickness, Jimmy said alarmed, "What? What are you doing?"

Standing directly in front of him, filled with a thrill which made her bones shaky, she said slowly, "I will not cause you such pain. . . ."

"No . . . no, it's not. . . ." Jimmy muttered vaguely.

She knew what to do. Looking into Jimmy's eyes, she tore up the story, seeing herself distantly as she committed her act of passion—ripping, shredding, and very aware that she could still read her words as they lay on the floor.

"Stop! What are you doing?" he lunged toward her, but the manuscript was gone. "I didn't mean. . . ."

"It's all right, Jimmy. Really. Someday I'll write a better one."

I wept as I read it, and then put it back in the folder and thought I would show it to Daniel someday, perhaps after Martin and I came back from the vacation we were about to take.

Several days prior to our leaving, Janet telephoned to ask why I had suddenly discontinued our friendship. I had been dreading that conversation, predicting it, suffering through what to say and what not to say. I discussed my predicament with Dr. Barnes, who was seeing Janet twice a week, me once a week, Martin once a week, but had not yet met Daniel. Dr. Barnes advised me to tell Janet the truth; that Janet talked so much to me that she was siphoning off her emotional energy, deflecting and diffusing it, instead of using it in therapy where it would benefit her most. A truth. The other truth was distressing: that I didn't want to speak to Janet because I was probably in love with Janet's husband.

Nevertheless, Janet wrote to me twice while we were away. Daniel didn't write at all. Yet I felt very close to Daniel, thought about him calmly, even wrote his name in the sand as if I were an adolescent. Of course I only did this when Martin was off on one of his long walks down the beach. At night when I was in bed reading Colette, and Martin was in the living room reading a John MacDonald, I thought about Daniel. And during the mornings while Martin played tennis and I worked on my novel, I thought of Daniel as I sipped my coffee. In the ocean, with the children, tangled in water and seaweed, I laughed and thought of Daniel.

The night after Martin and I got back, we went to a chamber music concert at Carnegie Hall with Janet and Daniel. The tickets had been sent for months before, and I couldn't think of an excuse not to go, nor could I think of a more immediate way to see Daniel.

During the intermission, Janet asked exuberantly, "How was your vacation?"

"Very relaxing" I said. "After years of practice, Martin and I have learned to ignore each other creatively." I really meant that; I thought it was an achievement.

"I wish Daniel and I could do that. When we ignore each other it's hostile. Even when we pay attention to each other it's hostile. I can't imagine going away with my husband for a whole month. I'd be bored out of my mind."

Daniel winced.

Martin looked at the ground.

I realized that I had been bored out of my mind for a whole month and for far longer than that.

The next morning Daniel called me and we agreed that the time had come for us to meet. Alone.

Calmly, amazed at my calm, I bought a new diaphragm, and on the morning I was to meet Daniel, I showered, washed my hair, and before putting on what I had carefully chosen to wear, I inserted the diaphragm. Traffic into N.Y.C. was horrendous and when I reached the right corner, I couldn't find a legal parking spot. I sat in the car, sweating, forty-five minutes early, looking into the rear-view mirror from time to time at my very flushed face. I looked at my watch every two minutes, trying unsuccessfully to make the time pass quickly. Only fifteen minutes had passed when Daniel opened the car door and got in. We stared at each other.

"How was the traffic?" he asked.

"Awful," I said.

We put our arms around each other and sat for long minutes without moving, barely breathing. I had no idea what would happen next. Would he suggest going to a hotel? Should I? I had no idea how one registered for adultery. Did Daniel know? There was a lady-killer air about Daniel, and in the preceding months, one mutual friend had said straightforwardly, "I noticed how Daniel was noticing you the other night. . . ."

Caught by surprise, I nodded. "He. . . . I don't know what's happening."

"Well, if you're looking for an affair, Daniel seems like a good choice. I'm sure he's quite experienced."

I wasn't sure whether he was or he wasn't. He suggested putting the car in a parking lot garage and going for a walk. We walked toward the Hudson and sat down on the Fortieth Street Pier. Our conversation was about how we were entitled to do what we were doing, which I wanted to believe but didn't. By the vehemence of his arguments, I knew he didn't quite believe himself either. Nevertheless, we were doing what we were doing. What we would be doing in an hour, I had no idea. I knew what I wanted to do.

With an innocence I hadn't felt since I was fifteen years old, we sat on the pier and held hands. We were warm and the sun made us warmer. We talked earnestly until we kissed, and when we stopped kissing, we looked around simultaneously and discovered that a trucker, motionless in his parked rig, was watching us. We waved to him and laughed at our shared impulse. Unintimidated, the trucker kept staring.

"Where should we go now?" Daniel asked.

Up until then I had been fairly convinced that Daniel knew exactly where we would go, how we would get there, and what we would do when we did get there. But he didn't know any more than I did. We wandered around Greenwich Village looking for a hotel until he mentioned that it was entirely possible that we might run into his in-laws who lived on Eighth Street. We drove uptown, parked again, and after one try at a hotel that only had suites available, found a modest hotel where Daniel registered under a name he thought up during the subway ride to meet me, the only thing he did, in fact, know ahead of time.

It was strange and not strange at all to take off my clothes in a hotel room with a man who was strange to me and yet familiar beyond our limited experience of each other. Would he find me pleasing? Would I find him pleasing?

Before vacation, after a dinner with Daniel and Janet, Daniel had said to me as we sat on the floor in his living room, listening to Sibelius, "I finished reading *Jumps*. I see why you liked it so much. There was one thing Alberto Cardona said that really jumped out at me.... it is impossible for a relationship to be consummated without anything physical."

I had held on to that during vacation. Now we had gotten to the physical.

It was an explosion. It was unexpected.

Peaceful after months of agitation, I knew I was ready to move.

I was ready to move away from Martin. Martin and I were going to separate. It was due, overdue. Late one night after the children had gone to bed, we sat in the breakfast nook drinking brandy and talking about our marriage.

"I can admit for the first time," Martin said, his lips turned down from the strength of the brandy and from the bitterness of his words, "that our marriage is not satisfactory to me either. If it continues on the present basis, it's not worth it."

"We've tried to change it for a long time." I said, seeing an unfamiliar configuration of lines on his face—sadness.

"I'm willing to try some more...." he looked into his brandy.

"I don't know...." I wanted to say 'yes, we'll try again' but I was seeing Martin more and more distantly. Most of what we said to each other was rooted so far in our past that it made no impact on our present, a present that I was coming to see as two diverging courses. Just that afternoon, Martin and I had gone for a long walk. During the past several weeks we had done a great deal of walking and talking. It was easier to talk if we did not have to look at each other directly, if the movements of our bodies could relieve the tensions that our emotional state imposed on our muscles.

"You know," Martin said as we walked close together but not touching, "I've come to admire you for your...your physicality before you knew me."

I wasn't sure what he meant. For years....ever since the beginning when I told him I had had intercourse with the man—a boy, really, since both he and I were eighteen at the time—I had been seeing regularly before meeting Martin, Martin had been dismayed and disappointed. Although we were engaged for many months, he remained a technical virgin until our wedding night. I carried the weight of his disappointment at my impurity during all the years of our marriage, and as Martin gradually loosened up and wanted to try new things with me in bed, the weight of my early sexual experimentation made me loathe to further soil the image I knew Martin had of me. And now, after fifteen years, what was he saying?

"What..."

"You were right...you had a lot of feeling for him, and you went to bed with him. You were free enough to do it....I wish I....And when you wanted me and I couldn't...." He kept leaving his sentences unfinished.

"How long have you felt like this?" We had stopped walking. I looked at him.

"Oh, I'm not sure...A couple of years."

"A couple of *years*? Why didn't you tell me?"

"I thought you knew."

"But how could I know if you didn't tell me? All these years I thought you thought I was dirty."

"Well, I used to. But I don't any more. I respect what you did." He looked at me appealingly.

"Oh, God, Martin. I don't know what to say....I think it's too late. I needed to know that so long ago...."

"But you know it now."

And now we sat drinking brandy and he said, "If you want the marriage to end, you must know that you are the one who will have to leave the house and leave the children. I will not leave this house. And you will not have custody of the children."

I was going to leave. "If there were no Daniel," Dr. Barnes asked me, "would you be leaving now?"

"If there were no Daniel, I would be leaving now. And if there hadn't been any children, I would have been long gone."

"If you leave, you will lose custody of your children," she said.

I had been walking up and down the narrow consulting room. I sat down as her words ripped into me, "Oh, God." I held my hands over my face and rocked back and forth.

"Martin is not going to leave the house. He's adamant on that," Dr. Barnes said. "Can you stay there with him?"

For months, Martin and I had been drinking and taking tranquilizers, although neither of us had been drinkers or pillpoppers. In the last weeks, in an attempt at courtship, Martin had been buying me gifts—a leather bag costing more than all the bags I had ever bought in fifteen years combined—writing me notes, and following me through the various rooms of the house, searching my face for a sign that his courtship was effective. He had an anxiety attack in the middle of the night and took to keeping a yellow pad beside the bed on which to write his dreams. He stopped eating. When I looked at him and saw Martin suddenly behaving in ways that were more typical of my own past neurotic behavior, I was saddened, disoriented, and resentful. He was going to extremes. It was too late.

"No, I can't stand his pain. Or my own. It has to stop."

But I stayed for days and days, wandering like a visitor in the house I had lived in for years, staring at my own children like a relative from another country. My children. The years of mothering. The distortions of love—"Practice, the piano—you will love it for the rest of your life." "Don't pick your nose, it's not nice." "Stop rocking back and forth; you're nauseating me." "Can't you give me a minute of peace and quiet." "Leave me alone, I'm working." "Of course I love you." Round and round the rooms. At night, getting out of bed to walk off insomnia, leaving the room silently to avoid waking the finally sleeping Martin, walking barefoot into my son's room, smelling the woody odor of his sleep, watching his face that resembled my own. How could I disturb his peace? If he woke during the night and called me and I wasn't there....And my daughter, a teenager, smelling in her sleep like a woman....even though she was not yet woman enough to comprehend, to understand what she would have to understand in order not to feel deserted. How could I leave my children?

But how could I stay? My body consuming itself, smelling of acetone as I breathed and spoke. Eating was impossible. Sleeping was impossible. Only as I considered actually leaving was I present to any degree.

In the morning, I sat in my sister-in-law's kitchen as I had done several times a week for as many years as she had been living around the corner, and looked into my coffee cup and wondered how she couldn't know that my life was coming apart. Yet how could I expect her to know? All of her energy at the moment was going into consolidating her own life. Pregnant with their second child, she and my brother were in the final stages of buying a new, more spacious house. I stirred my coffee and mentally chose the room in their new house where I would live until I found a job and could afford my own apartment. Martin had told me that he would give me half of our saving's account, which, if I lived a frugal, bohemian life would enable me to support myself for over a year. That he would do for me, he said. And from then on it would be up to me. And he would keep and support the children. With his money. My contribution to the children's support had never had a dollar value. What was I worth? To whom? Was I about to leave Martin, or was Martin getting rid of me?

"You're going to stir the bottom out of that coffee cup in another minute," my sister-in-law said as she sat down across the table.

I tried to smile.

She pushed a plate of bread toward me. "Eat," she said, "you look like a stick. Why are you losing weight?"

"No, thanks, I'm not hungry." But every night I had dreams of starvation; cafeterias, banquets, supermarkets—full of unpalatable food. Or visions, in full color, of delectable food that I couldn't have.

"What's the matter with you?"

I tried to smile again. "I think...." As was happening very often, my eyes filled with tears. If I said another word I would cry.

"I'm going crazy," she said suddenly, her own eyes reddening.

"What's the matter?" I asked, reaching for her hand.

"Everything. I can't stand being in this house every single day. Jeffrey is driving me crazy...."

"All two year olds...."

"...and why I ever wanted another one is beyond me. I must have been out of my mind. And on top of that, Steven has been working even longer hours than usual, and when he comes home he has two drinks and sits down in front of the television. He never talks to me. I feel like I'm living alone. I feel like Jeffrey has only one parent...." She wiped her eyes.

"Ah, yes. Martin works like that, too. At least my children are older now. They're not as physically demanding. Look, have you talked to Steven about how you feel?"

"It's like talking to the wall."

"You have to try. You must try. You can't let it go on and on and on. You still have a chance.

"A chance...? But...."

"You have a good relationship, I can see it."

"Oh, sure. I wasn't questioning.... But sometimes...."

"I know, I know...." I was tempted to say more than I wanted to say, to compare my situation with hers. But I stopped. Lainie didn't have enough energy to deal with my problems, too. "I have to go now."

She looked startled at my abruptness, "Where are you going?"

In imitation of a vaudeville exit, I spread my arms, bent one knee, and sang, "To live my life."

She narrowed her eyes and said, "Be careful."

I was going to meet Daniel, who, picking up on my tone of voice over the telephone, said he was leaving his office and would meet me in an hour in the park. The hour was up.

We sat at a picnic table in a secluded grove, "It's coming to a head, Daniel.... I'm going to see Dr. Barnes at 4:30. I'm exhausted and full of nervous energy at the same time."

"Yes," he said. His hand on mine was slightly damp and tense, but warm.

"I'm going to leave Martin. I'm telling you because you're involved. I mean, because I love you. But I'm not leaving for you or because of you. I'm leaving because it's long overdue. Of course, what happens with you and Janet. . . . I'm involved in that, too. But I don't know if you'll work out your problems and walk off into the sunset together, or. . . ."

"Stop! That isn't what's going to happen. You and I are going to be together. I just don't know when. I'd like to know that Janet is on an even keel. . . . All her talk about suicide . . ."

"Oh, God. With all this horror, how is it that I feel so strongly that what I'm going to do is the best thing?"

"Because it is."

Half an hour later, Dr. Barnes put me through the question routine again, forcing me to consider the bottom lines on every issue—the children, the house, supporting myself, living alone. Then she asked me to come back at 7:30 with Martin. When I left her office, I wandered distractedly around town waiting for Daniel, who was taking his turn talking to Dr. Barnes, as we had decided he would do when we spoke on the phone in the morning. Daniel had already seen Dr. Barnes twice, in joint sessions with Janet. I looked in the record shop window, in the shoe store window, at the drug store display and the handicrafts. Back to the record shop window, the shoe store. . . . What was going on in Dr. Barnes' office? Was she encouraging? Discouraging? Committal?

Finally Daniel was striding toward me, smiling. Dr. Barnes had asked him all the questions he had been asking himself, and he felt good and strong about his answers. He dropped me off two blocks away from my house and we said goodbye, knowing that I would tell Martin that our marriage was over.

Martin was not surprised that I suggested we both see Dr. Barnes after dinner. When we told the children where we were going, their interest flickered for an instant, then went back to the television.

During the ten minute drive, Martin and I said nothing. Absolutely nothing. I looked at his profile from time to time. His face was set, ready. I kept my mind as blank as possible, trying not to rehearse. What was Martin thinking? Did he know it was to be essentially a replay of a session we had already had six months ago with Dr. Barnes, when I said I wanted to leave? Then I was convinced by Martin to give it another try.

This time I couldn't. Martin was exhausted. I was exhausted.

"Go to your brother's house for the night," Dr. Barnes said to me while Martin waited in the anteroom—several times during the session she spoke to each of us alone. "Don't take any of your things or do anything definitive without talking to a lawyer. I think it best that you and Martin not be in the same house tonight. You'll tear each other apart. Why don't you go home first and tell the children. I'll drive Martin home in about forty-five minutes."

Home. Tell the children.

Children.

Home.

They were in the bedroom watching T.V.

"Please turn it off," I said as normally as I could, "I want to talk to you."

The T.V. off, I said, "Daddy and I are going to separate. We tried very hard, but it didn't work. I know you won't be able to see it now, but we will all be happier...."

"What!" My daughter's face reddened. She said tearfully, "I don't believe it.... you and Daddy? But you were always holding hands...."

"Yes...but.... you were always asking me whether we were going to get a divorce.... we all knew this was coming..."

"Oh, no!" My son was weeping. "Don't leave, Mommy! Can't you just live in the attic? You don't have to sleep with Daddy."

Even through my numbness I was astonished at the pain. "No, it doesn't work that way. I'm going to Steven and Lainie's for tonight. I'll see you tomorrow...."

"But where's Daddy?"

"Daddy is here now. I just heard the car door slam. Dr. Barnes brought him home."

"Dr. Barnes!" Karen said bitterly. "It's all her fault! If you didn't see Dr. Barnes none of this would be happening!"

"Oh, Karen.... how can I explain.... you'll have to understand a little at a time...."

Martin came into the bedroom, red faced and tight lipped. "Daddy!"

As I left the room, I could hear the dryness of his voice as he answered.

Downstairs, I called my brother and asked if I could spend the night there. "Wait, what's happening?" He picked up immediately on my voice.

"I'll tell you when I get there. I'm coming right now."

"Don't do anything until you talk to me!"

"I did it already."

"What did you do?"

"I'll tell you when I get there."

Steven met me at the door with a drink in his hand. "You left Martin."

I nodded. "Are you surprised?"

"How could I be?"

Two years ago I had driven to Steven and Lainie's house at ten-thirty p.m., in my pajamas, bathrobe and slippers. Steven and Lainie had been in bed. "Who died?" Steven had asked when he saw my face.

"No one, yet," I said, beginning to pace in the living room, "but I will be dead very shortly. Martin is destroying me."

This was like a replay. I heard the echo as I said again what I had said two years ago, "Martin is destroying me."

"All right, calm down," Steven said, also pacing. "Do you want a drink?"

"No. Yes...." I followed him into the kitchen where he made us all bourbon and water. Lainie took hers looking distracted; she was waiting for Jeffrey's wail.

"Now....what happened?" Steven sat himself on the counter.

"Nothing in particular...no, everything....he....I...."

Lainie stared at me.

"I have to get away from him. I want to leave him. This isn't the first time....I felt this way soon after we were married. Scared the shit out of myself. I was only a kid. Karen was already born. I went and had a long talk with Aunt Sally. You can ask Aunt Sally. She knows...."

"I'm sure she does. Stop defending yourself and just tell me what happened."

"I told him that I want to stop working at the University and devote my time, full time, you know, from nine until when the kids come home at three, to writing. I've never done that. When the kids were little I had virtually no free time. And then when they both got to school, I had gotten involved in doing conference work.... I've enjoyed that, a pay check, having a finished project and the gratification of being told that I've done a good job.... it's been very good for me. But it takes more than half my time, and the kids and the house and Martin take more than the rest of the half that's left, and I don't have enough time to write. And it's time. I can't fool myself anymore. Writing is what I should be doing. I have enough courage to say that now. I can do it...."

"So what's stopping you?"

"Oh, God ... that's what I wanted Martin to say...."

"But he didn't...." Steven poured himself some more bourbon.

"No. He doesn't want me to write. It scares him."

"Well, sometimes you do write things about him that aren't very nice.... you must give him credit for dealing with that."

"Nice! I have to censor and edit myself all the time. I am a writer! Yes, I understand that, given his personality, he's put up with a lot. What I'm saying is that we have conflicting personalities."

"You're both the same," Lainie said from her side of the table.

"We are completely different," I said, "except for the fact that we're both stubborn."

"All right. Did he tell you that you shouldn't write?" Steven was maintaining his lawyerlike neutrality.

"Not in so many words.... I told him that I wanted to stop working at the University, that I wanted to give myself at least two full years of doing nothing but writing ... to train myself, the kind of training he had in law school when I wasn't going to school because we couldn't afford to have both of us go. He told me then that someday it would be my turn, and now it's my turn!"

"O.K...." Steven came across the room with the bourbon and refilled my glass. I didn't remember drinking the first drink.

"*You* say O.K. But *he* didn't. He got insulted."

"Insulted?" Steven said.

"What do you mean, insulted?" Lainie echoed.

"Defensive. Said I was demanding a quid pro quo and he didn't see it that way. He said he didn't think I ought to give up my job because why should all the financial responsibility be on his shoulders. An appeal to my feminism...A perverted appeal—all I made at my job was only as much as his cost of living increase!"

"Go on...."

"I can't. I'm tired. I'm going crazy...." I started to cry.

Lainie reached across the table and held my hand. "You're not going crazy," she and Steven said simultaneously. They smiled at each other, and I saw again the look of private satisfaction I had often, with envy, seen them exchange. Seeing them made me feel what I was missing with Martin, and also that what was missing was possible to have. I closed my eyes.

"No, I know I'm not crazy. But Martin....I really think he thinks I am. He's always waiting for me to have a nervous breakdown. He said that to me once."

Lainie's eyebrows went up, "A nervous breakdown? You?"

"Well, you know, you do sometimes get overwrought." Steven said in a fair-is-fair tone.

Lainie and I glared at him.

"All right, all right...you're not nervous breakdown material."

"You know, Steven, sometimes...." Lainie began, then looked tired.

"What?" Steven said.

"Nothing. Never mind," Lainie sighed.

"Now don't you two start," I said. "I've always envied what you have together."

Ignoring that, Steven asked, "Well, my dear sister, what do you intend to do now?"

It was eleven o'clock. I had told Daniel, after his appointment with Dr. Barnes, that I was going to tell Martin I was leaving that night and then go to Lainie and Steven's. Daniel said he would call me there at eleven. Lainie and Steven knew nothing at all about Daniel. "I'm expecting a phone call. Don't be surprised."

Lainie and Steven looked at each other.

"You don't know him. Although I have mentioned his name to you, Lainie, in a very neutral way. . . ."

"Daniel . . . it's Daniel! All that talk about Daniel and Janet!"

"Yes."

The phone rang. Steven picked it up, listened and said, "Yes, she's right here," and handed it to me.

Daniel said he had had a fight with Janet and left the house. All he could think about was what I was going through. He wanted to see me. I covered the phone. "Daniel would like to. . . ."

"Sure. . . ." Steven said, anticipating, "we might as well meet him sooner than later. I have a few things I'd like to say to both of you."

And he did. Daniel sat at the kitchen table; I sat on his knees. Both of us were aware that the sight of us together to relatives who had been seeing me with Martin for sixteen years and who had never seen Daniel before, might be provocative, but the importance of feeling each other's solidity went against prudence. Lainie alternated between staring at us and staring at the table. Steven, into his third bourbon, sat on the kitchen counter, removed from the rest of us, and higher, playing father/brother/judge/advocate.

"May I ask what the hell is happening?" Steven waved his glass at us.

We told him. That we loved each other. That, as Steven well knew, I had left Martin because the situation was impossible; I had not left because of Daniel. That Daniel was going to leave Janet, but he didn't know when.

When his questions were answered, Steven looked at us thoughtfully, nodded, and said, "Please be careful. Don't jeopardize yourselves. Come on, Lainie, let's go to bed."

I called up after them, "Daniel will be leaving shortly." Neither of them answered.

Daniel and I made love on the couch. When he ran his fingers over my body, I could feel the bones of his fingers against my ribs, my pelvis. There was very little flesh left after five months of not eating and very little sleeping.

"You have a good brother," Daniel said as he got dressed. "I love him for the way he loves you."

"I saw how he was looking at you. He will reserve judgment for a while, but I think he thought well of you. . . ."

"I don't want to leave. . . ."

"Daniel. . . ."

"I'll call you first thing in the morning. Try to sleep. You did a very courageous thing tonight. You awe me with your courage."

I shrugged. I didn't feel courageous. I felt intensely alive in the present moment, because my past, and as far as I could see, my future, had been amputated. I had no life beyond the moment.

Alone in the spare bedroom, I tried to sleep. It was a relief not to worry about whether Martin would read my thoughts or whether Martin would want to make love. . . . I could still smell Daniel. I couldn't allow myself to think of the children's red faces as I had seen them hours before. They were sleeping in their own beds. Their mother was sleeping four blocks away. Finally I dozed off.

Pain woke me. I had been sleeping lightly enough to know exactly where I was and why. The pain was familiar; how ironic to get a bladder infection now. I went into the bathroom and urinated excruciatingly. I went back into the bedroom and lay down. I sat up. Pain. There were only two things to do: take aspirin and a hot bath.

The bathroom door didn't close completely. I didn't want to wake Steven and Lainie, but there was no way to avoid the noise of running water. Lying in the tub at five a.m., I wondered why Lainie, who had surely heard the noise, or Steven, hadn't come to the door to find out what was wrong. Did they think I always bathed at five a.m.? I did my best to convince myself that the aspirin had begun to work and the tub had soothed the pain. I got out, dried and got back into the nightgown Lainie had lent me. Back in bed, I had to sit up again after ten minutes. The need to urinate was uncontrollable although I knew my bladder was empty. Before I flushed the toilet, I looked down and saw blood in the bowl. I wiped myself again, and the paper came away red. This had never happened before. I needed Daniel as a doctor and comforter and couldn't call him; he was home in his bed with Janet.

Downstairs, I called Harry, a neighbor and long time friend, whom I often described as the family's court physician.

"Harry, it's Nina."

"Nina. What can I do for you?" His voice cleared immediately of sleep. "What time is it?"

"It's five thirty and I have a bladder infection and there's blood in my urine. What should I do?"

"It's probably a virus. Don't worry. Either have Martin drive you to the hospital or call the emergency squad."

"Harry. I'm not at home. I'm at Steven and Lainie's. I've left Martin."

Only a small silence ensued. "Oh. Then have Steven take you. And call me as soon as you can after they treat you. Don't worry, you'll be fine."

I felt anything but fine as I walked painfully back upstairs and stood in the doorway of Steven and Lainie's bedroom. They seemed to be asleep, but I couldn't believe that after the noise of my self-ministrations. "Steven," I whispered.

He raised his head. "What?" he whispered.

"Can you take me to the hospital? It's nothing, but I'm bleeding."

"Oh, Jesus," he said. Lainie sat up. Steven dressed in two minutes as I explained what had happened.

"We heard you running the bath," Lainie said, "and we were furious. I said to Steven that if you were going to be living with us, we would have to lay out the ground rules—no baths at 5:30 in the morning. . . ."

I laughed. Lainie laughed. Steven said, "All right, let's go."

They put me in an examining room in the emergency room after I had given them the insurance information that identified me as Martin's wife and Martin's responsibility. I felt like a liar, but how could I start explaining to the nurse that I was nobody's wife and nobody's responsibility, and had no current home address. The nurse asked me to urinate into a sterile jar, but I couldn't.

"Lie down here," she said brusquely. I did. She left the room and closed the door.

I lay on an examining table in what seemed to be an equipment storage room. The air conditioning was on full blast, chilling me under the sheet I had pulled up. Between my legs the discomfort throbbed. There was no color in the room, only white, black and grey. I tried to do yoga breathing. Over the paging system I listened for familiar names. There weren't any. What was Steven doing? How long had I been lying there? If I didn't feel so lousy, I would get off the table, get dressed, and go home. Home? Who would call my children to tell them I was in the hospital? What would Martin say? Would he feel concern? And Daniel? How would Daniel find out? I needed to get in touch with Daniel. Blood in my urine. How long would it be until someone acknowledged my presence? Maybe they had forgotten that they put me in there. Blood and pain. Leave home and die. My insides were putrefying. Cells were eating each other. I would lie still, control my breathing, and accept my punishment. But for how long? Empty. Cold. Colorless. Blood. Pain.

The door opened. Steven stuck his head into the room. "Hey!"

"Oh, it's you!"

"Who were you expecting, King Kong?"

"No, but maybe a nurse ... or a doctor?"

"Listen, I have to be in New York at eight o'clock and it's already seven. I have to go. . . . I'm sorry. . . ." He ran his fingers over his unshaven face.

I did not whimper "don't leave me here alone," but nodded cooly.

"Lainie will be here as soon as Jeffrey gets picked up for nursery school. I called her. O.K.? Hang in there, kid."

When the door closed, the sense of isolation increased. I folded my hands across my chest. Emptied. Belonging to no one. No belongings. Another few seconds of immobility and I would cease to exist. I got off the table, left the room and found that they had in fact forgotten me. The nursing shifts changed at seven o'clock, and the new nurses hadn't yet gotten to my chart. The new nurse was human. For her I urinated, and when she looked into the thick dark liquid in the cup, she clucked her tongue.

"Can I ask you a question?" I barely whispered.

"Of course."

"Do I. . . . I mean, does that ... all that blood. That's never happened to me before. I know blood in the urine isn't a good sign. I mean, you . . . do you think I have cancer?"

Her laugh was gorgeous. "Good heavens! You have a bad bladder infection. This isn't unusual. Now sit down here and wait for the doctor."

The doctor, an Asian, arrived twenty minutes later, looked at the lab report, told me I had an acute infection, high white cell count, and that he was going to admit me to the hospital.

"Oh, no. Not today. Impossible." To lie in a bed, completely separated from whatever parts of my life that I still had?

The doctor blinked in disbelief, "What do you mean, not today? It is today that you are sick. Do you want to get better? This lab report tells me that this is the kind of infection you have had for a very long time. Is that not so?"

"Well. . . . I do get bladder infections from time to time. . . ."

"No. It is the same one. You never get rid of it properly. And you are run down."

"Look. . . . I'm not staying in the hospital. At nine o'clock I'm calling my own doctor. I can't reach him right now."

"Who is your doctor? He is a urologist?"

"Dr. Wasser. No. . . . he's not a urologist."

The doctor shrugged. "Then why must you call him?"

"It's personal."

We were having our discussion in the main section of the ward, adjacent to the nurses' station. The telephone rang. "Yes, yes, she's here," I heard the nurse say. She called me, "It's a Dr. Wasser to speak to you."

His voice sounded far away, strained, "Darling, how are you?"

"Daniel! How did you find me here? How did you know? I was going to call you. . . ."

"I'm at the train station. I couldn't wait to get to my office. I wanted to know how you were, so I called you at Lainie and Steven's and Lainie told me what happened. Are you in pain? How are you?"

"I'm frightened . . . They want to admit me. I can't be admitted today."

"No, of course not. Don't worry. Just sit down and wait for me. I'll be there as soon as I can. Tell them your own doctor is on his way!"

As I put the phone down, I heard the shaky echo of Daniel's voice. Daniel was frightened, too. Maybe I would have to be hospitalized. Would they let the children in to see me, if in fact, the children would even want to see me? Maybe they would be glad I was sick, served me right for leaving. And Martin. Did Martin know yet that I was in the hospital? Would Lainie or Steven call to tell him? Impossible to stay in the hospital. I wouldn't be able to lie still.

The doctor said, "Well? Have you come to a decision?"

"What? Oh. No, no, no. My own doctor is coming. He told me to wait for him here."

The doctor shrugged and said, "I do not understand. He is not a urologist. But . . ." He went into the nurse's station and I sat down in the hall.

All the questions attacked again. I got up. It was still painful to walk. In the telephone booth, I could both sit and be doing something. I had to do something. I called Lainie. No one answered. I called Harry, remembering that he had asked me to.

"Hello, Harry, it's me."

"Nina, my dear. Are you feeling better now? What did they say?"

"It's a bad infection. They want to hospitalize me."

"Oh, my. That seems excessive. There's no reason you can't be treated on an outpatient basis."

"I hope so. I can't stay here. Not . . ."

"I understand. Listen, Nina, do you want me to come up there now?"

"Thank you Harry. I know your office hours start soon. You don't have to. Daniel Wasser is on his way."

"Daniel . . . Good, good. Daniel is a good man. Very sound."

"Yes, Harry . . ." Harry knew Daniel not because they were both doctors but because they were both musicians. They played in two local orchestras together. One night when Harry had gathered a chamber quartet, as he regularly did on Friday nights in his cavernous living room, Martin and I, who had a standing invitation, had asked if we could bring Daniel and Janet. We did, and it was then I discovered that Harry and Daniel knew each other so well that Harry was a standing joke in

Daniel's house. Harry always called at the dinner hour to discuss orchestra business, and when the telephone rang just as everybody sat down, the kids would shout, "It's Dr. Harry! No dinner without Dr. Harry!" The children had never met him, but he was part of their lives. I wanted to tell Harry that Daniel was now part of my life. But I didn't want to do it over the telephone. "Thank you, Harry. I'm sorry I woke you up so early. You're always so good to me."

"Listen, Nina. Call me later in the day and tell me how you are. Don't forget. Thank you, dear." Harry always thanked me after doing or saying something for which he deserved the thanks. I hung up feeling loved.

Calmer, I went to the waiting room and sat in a soft chair, just as Lainie, carrying a brown paper bag, bustled in, looking harried, frantic, and excited. "Oh, there you are, Nina! I didn't know what to expect. But there you are, all regular...."

"Well, sort of. Sit down. Calm yourself...." It was so soothing to tell someone else to be calm. "Daniel is on his way."

Lainie sat next to me and rattled the bag, opened it, and handed me a thermos. "Coffee. Drink it. I'll bet they didn't give you anything to eat. Here's bread and butter, too. Yes. Daniel called about eight. I told him...."

"Yes, I know ... He told me. Did the kids ... my kids.... did anyone else call?"

"No."

"Oh."

"Well, don't be so upset. They had to go to school. And it's only five minutes to nine. No one else has been up all night.... Give them a chance."

"I know.... Daniel!"

Daniel hurried through the waiting room, doctorly in a vested suit, a watch chain, his neat beard, gold rimmed glasses: an image of intimacy in the sterile room. He took my hand and kept his fingers on my pulse as he questioned me. His body touching mine. Doctor—patient. The same bodies touching in a different way than the way they were touching ten hours ago. Lainie said, "How is she, doctor?"

We all laughed.

"Nina," Daniel said, now holding my hand in the usual way,

"I'm sorry if I frightened you over the phone. I should have known better and reassured you. This is only a bad infection that you must have been carrying around for months. . . . I panicked and I shouldn't have."

"Ah ha, you thought God was punishing me too, then."

"Us."

"Well, I feel better already. Let's get out of here."

"Slow down. You're going to be looked at by the best urologist in the hospital, who happens to be a friend of mine. I've already had him paged."

Two hours later, with medicine, I was back at Lainie's and Daniel was on the train into New York, where he would be just in time for a lunch interview with the Chief of Pathology of a Manhattan hospital. Daniel was looking for a new job, and this was the one that interested him the most.

At Lainie's urging, I tried to sleep. Impossible. Pain alternated with relief at the abatement of the pain. Anxiety about the children alternated with relief at having finally made the definitive break with Martin. Where would I live? I couldn't go back to my house with Martin still there. The children, when I told them about the separation, had said immediately that they wanted to stay in the house. What could I do about that? I had disrupted their lives so much already. If I said, "Come with me," where would we go? There wasn't enough room at Lainie and Steven's. I had not thought any of it through. I had acted on the most immediate need, to get away from the mutual torture of myself and Martin. Now what? I smelled coffee and went downstairs, hearing the telephone ring.

"For you," Lainie said, "Dr. Barnes."

I looked questioningly at Lainie. Dr. Barnes had never called me before. Lainie shrugged. "Hello?" I said.

"Hello, Nina. How are things going?"

From her tone I knew she didn't really want an explanation.

"Well, they are going, that's about all I can say with assurance."

"Good. The reason I called is that Janet was just in my office and I've been trying to get in touch with Daniel. Do you know where I can reach him?"

"You can't reach him now. He's having a lunch interview—that job he's after.... They're at some restaurant in Manhattan, that's all I know."

There was a silence. "All right. Look, Nina, I wouldn't ordinarily do this, but Daniel should be prepared and he will surely be in touch with you...."

"Yes."

"Janet knows about the two of you and she wants Daniel to leave. She said she was going home to pack his things."

"Oh! How....all this time she didn't....you said just the other day that she had defended herself against seeing what was going on and you didn't think....How...?"

I sat down on a kitchen chair. Lainie stared at me, open-mouthed, as if she were watching a horror movie.

"In the course of our session today, she talked about how you were no longer speaking to her and how Daniel was more withdrawn than usual. I had to ask her what the sum of one and one was."

"You told her!"

"No. She added one and one."

"But, you...."

"Nina, she had been threatening suicide. I wanted to see her through the worse part, to help her with her anger."

"Now what happens?"

"Tell Daniel what I just told you and ask him to call me, please."

When I hung up, my tongue and limbs felt so heavy that in answer to Lainie's questioning look I could only say faintly, "She..."

Lainie nodded.

"I...."

Lainie reached for my hand. "Nina..." she said, "this is all very hard to believe. Now what are you going to do?"

When Daniel called I gave him Dr. Barnes' message and asked him the same question. "I guess I better go straight home," he said. "Maybe this is the best thing all around. What good would it have been to prolong everyone's agony.... I'll call you as soon as I can."

Steven came home for dinner before I heard from Daniel. I filled him in about my hospital adventure and then tried to explain Dr. Barnes' call.

"She said *what* to Janet!?" Steven, drink in midair, actually screamed.

I cringed and told him again.

"I never in my life heard of such unprofessional conduct on the part of a psychologist."

"But, Steven, she didn't actually *tell* Janet anything...."

"Bullshit! All these psychologists think they're God! Christ, I don't believe it. Well ... what can I tell you? First you move out of your house *before* getting legal advice.... I told you not to do that...."

"But, Steven, it was impossible to...."

"And now Daniel is going to leave and she'll charge him with adultery...."

"Steven...."

"You are going to find this very amusing, but what I was going to tell you when I first came home was the name of the best matrimonial lawyer in the state...."

"But you...."

"You didn't think there was a chance in hell that *I* would be your lawyer, did you? For God's sake, I'm your brother! Daniel wouldn't treat his own family, would he?"

"No, but I thought maybe Howard Stern would...."

"Well, he won't. You can't have him. Sure, he's really the best, he and I, but in this case using my partner is just as bad. No, it's better to use someone else. Call him first thing in the morning. Although I have the feeling that there won't be much anyone will be able to do for you.... A woman leaves at her own peril...."

"The peril would have been worse if I stayed."

"That's why you can't mix legal principles and emotional relationships. As your brother, I have to say that what you said is more right than what I said ... but as a lawyer...."

The telephone rang. Lainie, with the wide-eyed look that had come to mean that she perceived a new development, handed me the phone, "Daniel," she said.

Shakily, he asked me if he could come over.

When I asked them, Lainie said, "Sure," simultaneously with Steven's muttered, "I knew it ... here we go...."

I looked at him.

"Oh, God. Don't look at me that way. Of course he can come over. Absolutely. I have to talk to both of you."

For the second time in twenty-four hours, the four of us sat in the kitchen, in basically the same seating arrangement. From his counter perch, Steven waved his glass at us, "Now what," he demanded.

"Steven...." Lainie said in a voice meant to gentle him.

"Don't interrupt me when I'm hollering. I'm hollering. I have to. I'm not going to apologize. There are things I have to say, and when I'm finished, I will never say them again."

"Go ahead," Daniel said. "We're listening." He tightened his arm around my waist.

"What happened? Have you left your wife?"

"I think you can safely say that." Daniel said, looking over his shoulder at the suitcase he had left in the hall. "My car is full of stuff. She had it all sitting near the door. You might say that she threw me out."

"Why?"

"Steven," I said, "you know perfectly...."

"Nina, do not interrupt," he said in such an authoritarian manner, that I laughed.

"You are younger than I am," I said.

"That happens to be totally irrelevant," he said, "and if you can't shut up, I'm going to tell you to leave the room."

I laughed again at the absurdity of being reprimanded by my brother.

Daniel continued, "She told me that she knew that Nina and I were having an affair and that she didn't want me in the house anymore."

"And did you deny it?"

"I didn't say anything. She told me to leave and I left."

"What are you going to do now? That question is for both of you."

Daniel and I looked at each other. For months, during our telephone calls, we had talked about living together someday, as if it were a possibility only on a mythical level; first the dragon had to be killed, the sword extracted from the stone, the foot fitted into the glass slipper. There had been no fairy godmother, but the wand of motion had been waved. We nodded. "We're going to live together as soon as we find an apartment...."

"I was afraid of that," Steven shook his head. "Don't do it. You will both jeopardize your legal situations if you do that. You will each have an aggrieved spouse to hang charges on you, and you'll be socked for the maximum the court will allow. The law is punitive you know...."

"So what should we do at this point? We should live separately and not see each other? Or we should live separately and see each other chastely, with a curfew and four feet on the floor? Or just make believe we're living separately and waste money on two apartments, and wait for the private detectives to take pictures? Why can't we just be honest and do what everyone with half a brain will know and expect us to do anyway?"

"Look, Nina, I'm not telling you what to do. You do what you have to do. I'm just telling you that you're making problems for yourselves. And also showing you why I couldn't possibly be your lawyer."

"I guess I need one now, too...." Daniel said.

"Yep," Steven said exhaling, "most people consult one first, but all I can say is 'better late than never.'"

"Steven...."

"Yes, Nina...."

"Do you think we've ruined ourselves.... people will think we're evil.... we don't have any money.... What were we supposed to do? We didn't plan this. I had no idea last night, after I left Martin, that we would be sitting here again like this. I did what I had to do because I was waking up every morning with what felt like a block of concrete in my stomach.... after not sleeping. I've lost twelve pounds... Steven, even the children had been asking whom they would live with if Martin and I got divorced...."

"Nina, please, I'm not asking you to justify yourself. Please. Look.... all of this doesn't exactly make me feel too good about myself. You're not in a good legal position now because of Daniel—and vice versa." He looked down into his glass, then back up at me with the appeal of a younger brother. "Nina.... when you came to me two years ago, saying that Martin was destroying you... if you had been a client in my office, telling me what you told me, I would have started a divorce action for you. But you're my sister, and don't forget that I love Martin, too, and I had a vested interested in the status quo. I apologize."

"Steven. . . ."

"And furthermore—it's important for me to say this—I think you're doing the right thing now."

"Oh, God, I hope so. Just call me every ten minutes during the next six months to remind me."

Lainie asked, "Well, here you are, the two of you.... what are you going to do about tonight?"

"We could go to a motel. . . ." Daniel said.

Steven sighed loudly. "You might as well stay here tonight. Tomorrow we'll talk about what comes next."

We used the sofa bed in the living room instead of the spare room. Lainie was afraid we would disturb Jeffrey if we used the bedroom. I was slightly insulted when she said that. "Did she think we're going to carry on wildly?" I whispered to Daniel.

"Maybe..." he grinned. "But actually, she probably didn't want to hear us herself. After all, this is all very strange to everyone."

"Including me. . . ." I said. "A honeymoon night suddenly in the middle of my life. A switch from. . . . from. . . . I can't even talk."

"Don't. . . ." he said.

The entire night passed in total awareness of each other's body, the shape of each other's voice and presence.

In the morning, saying that he felt amazingly refreshed. Daniel went to his hospital. He promised to be back as early as possible so we could decide what to do next. I was sure Lainie and Steven would let us stay until we found an apartment.

Over coffee, Lainie said, "Nina, Steven and I.... Well, you know.... You and Daniel will have to find someplace else to stay."

Lainie too, I thought. Evicted and rejected.

"Nina," she said quickly, "don't look like that. It's not that we don't want you to stay. . . . I wish. . . . It's that, in the long run it may be harmful. I mean, we have to consider Martin, too. And the kids. . . . If you stay here, it will look like we're taking sides."

I couldn't say that what I wanted was for her to take sides. She of all people. All those morning cups of coffee we had together, after my children went to school and I drove Martin to the train. When, against the pressure of the work I knew I had to do—the laundry, the food shopping, the cleaning, the typewriter waiting—I pulled the car into Lainie's driveway and went in without knocking, usually to be greeted by Lainie in her bathrobe, saying, "Oh, there you are. I just called you to come for coffee, but you weren't home."

My line was, "Of course, I wasn't home. I was on my way here."

And then the conversation, each of us recapitulating domestic, parental, marital anecdotes, sometimes because they were funny, sometimes in a funny manner because what we were saying was not funny at all. Now I sat in Lainie's kitchen, coming not from my own house because I didn't have one anymore, but from her own living room.

"But. . . ." I stopped. I couldn't pressure Lainie. She was doing what she thought was best.

"Of course we're not going to kick you out when you have no place to go. What I mean is, you have to find a place."

That morning, she and I looked at ads for apartments. Nothing. Undaunted, we dressed like ladies—no dungarees and stained polo shirts for superintendents with an eye for respectability—and visited all the apartment houses in the area. Brief visits, because in our suburbia there aren't many apartment houses and, in the few that exist, the superintendents don't answer their buzzers.

Back at Lainie's, depressed, I called Daniel and told him we were still homeless.

"Don't you worry. Today we'll find an apartment."

"But. . . ."

"You don't know the Wasser determination. I'm taking the rest of the day off and by tonight we'll have an apartment."

I met him at the train station, we bought a local paper, called the telephone number given in an ad and ten minutes later we were following a superintendent through a high-ceilinged ground floor apartment, convenient to the train, my children, and Daniel's children. The three rooms, laid out eccentrically, were spacious, especially compared to the non-space we now had in Steven and Lainie's house, and to Daniel's tiny Fiat, crammed with his suitcases, paper bags of shoes, piles of sheet music, and his bassoon—our home away from home.

"What do you think, do you like it?" Daniel asked, as the super, unaware that we had stopped for consultation, walked into the bedroom a second time, spieling to himself.

"I can't believe it. It's perfect."

Daniel nodded. "Want to take it?"

I nodded. Such luck. Then a panic reaction set in, left over from living with Martin: we hadn't looked long enough, maybe we could get a lower rent, more rooms, a quieter location, a bigger kitchen, a nicer superintendent. How could we actually take the very first apartment we saw? I looked at Daniel for help.

"Great," he said. "The Wasser determination works again."

Daniel. Not Martin. Trust. Relax. It's O.K. It is not necessary to check and double check. The apartment is perfect.

The superintendent said we could move in in two days. All that had to be done was a quick paint job.

Because it was only a two day wait, Lainie and Steven consented to our staying with them during the interim, provided that Daniel pulled his car to the rear of the house so that should Martin happen to drive by, he would not see the yellow car flashing Daniel's presence, symbol of Steven and Lainie's acceptance. Steven and Lainie preferred neutrality.

And the children. Karen, that afternoon, asked to take a walk with me and brought me a single red rose. Blood red. Her blood. My blood. We walked through the familiar streets, the four or five blocks between Steven and Lainie's house and the house where I used to live, where Karen and Bobby and Martin still lived, and I did my best to reassure Karen that I was still her mother, that I loved her dearly, that I had to do what I did, that someday, maybe not until she was an adult, she would understand that having a more peaceful and satisfying relationship with a separated parent was better than having a hostile and angry relationship with an unhappily married parent.

Pain and anger walked with us, obscuring our vision, clotting the air between us like fog hovering between beach and ocean. I tried to evaporate it with my assurances. Mostly, I felt frustration, mine and Karen's. But some hope. Before we got back to Lainie's, I put my arms around Karen and hugged her. She hugged me only slightly, rejecting what she couldn't help perceiving as my rejection of her. As we approached the driveway, Lainie burst through the door, her face pinched, "Go away! Don't come in! Your father's on his way over! I'm getting out with Jeffrey. I don't want to be here when that madman gets here—you should have heard him raving on the phone, Nina! Take Karen home and then you go somewhere...." Lainie bounced up and down in her agitation, wringing her hands on a dishtowel.

Karen shrivelled away from me, away from Lainie. Her mouth got smaller and tighter, like the lips of an old woman sucked in in toothless grief.

"Karen...." I put my hand on her arm. She moved away.

"Lainie," upset, I tried to be calm for Karen, "why should I run away? He's my father. I know he's maniacal. I didn't expect him to be overjoyed at this, but I have to face him sometime! Please, calm yourself."

"Look, Nina, do what you want to do, but I'm leaving. Take Karen back home ... to.... her house. She doesn't have to hear his craziness."

For years my father had been on an even keel, passing as a normal father, making me almost forget the three year period after the birth of my son, when he didn't talk to me because I didn't name my child after his tyrannical and finally dead mother. But I never quite forgot. And neither did Lainie, or Steven, or Martin. Dealing with my father was like walking on eggs. I had tried to shield my children, especially Karen who was very perceptive and even aged in her youth, from my father's unpredictable rages, his judgmental pronouncements. Up until now I had succeeded pretty well.

Karen shrank away from me, telling me with her body that it was all my fault, this mass causing of pain. "Come on Karen. I'll drive you home," I said, as normally as I could, trying not to catch on the word "home." We got into Lainie's car—Daniel had taken his to run some errands. Wordlessly, I drove the four or five blocks we had just walked. As Karen opened the car door, I decided to say a quick word about her grandfather, to give her some perspective, to defend myself. "Karen," I began, when Martin ran down the driveway, looking concerned.

"Go away, Nina," he said. "Your father's on the rampage and he's headed over here. Take Karen with you, I don't want her here if he's going to carry on."

On the way back to Lainie's, Karen slumped down on the seat and wailed, "Oh, Mommy, I have no place to go, I have no *home*."

"Oh, my darling," I said and couldn't continue. Neither of us had any place to go. Out of habit, I assumed that Martin's judgment of the situation had more validity than mine or Lainie's; so to protect Karen, I decided that the two of us should seek refuge back at Lainie's. I pulled into her driveway, parked, and as Karen and I got out, Ceil, Lainie's mother, pulled up behind us, all smiles, and Lainie, obviously waiting for us by the door, came out on the porch looking more frantic than before.

"Oh, Nina, I told you to go *away*. He's coming! Oh, this is awful!"

"For God's sake, is he coming here or is he going to Martin's? Has everyone gone crazy?" I looked toward Ceil, who saw our distress.

"Hey!" she said, "What happened? Is...."

"Nothing happened yet," Lainie began, and then turned to stone.

We all looked where she was looking. My father had pulled up across the street.

"Mother!" Lainie hopped up and down, wringing her hands, looking anguished and absurd. "Take Karen for a ride. I'll explain later."

Ceil and Karen left so quickly my father, grey and shaking in his rage, wasn't even aware of them. Lainie faded into the kitchen as Sol crossed the lawn toward the house. Behind my father, her face red and miserable, trotted my step-mother, Freya, who had spoken to me earlier in the morning, sadly, and said, "I can't say this makes me happy, Nina, but I know you well enough to say that if you did it, you must have had very good reasons. I'm not even really totally surprised. I guess I noticed that you and Martin were.... unsuited. I'll try to explain it to your father. But you know how he is."

And there he was, being how he was, imagining that everyone else's life was lived wholly and solely to cause him to suffer. I tried to convince myself that he was nothing more than the personification of arrogance as he came closer to me, into the house, shaking his finger as soon as he saw me. I could see spittle at the corner of his lips. His eyes protruded like the marble eyes of a statue. The figure of outrage.

"Nina!", he shouted, "Are you happy?"

"Well, Dad, I'm trying to be...."

He waggled his finger so close to my face that I stepped back, "Ah ha! That's just what I thought! *You're* happy! That's all you care about! *Your* happiness. You don't give one good god damn about the misery you're causing. You don't care about your children, you...."

My stepmother put her hand on his shoulder, "Please, Sol, don't." He shook her hand off and shot her a quick silencing look.

"You...." he continued, his spittle sour on my face, "are a wicked, selfish...."

"Dad, Dad," I kept my voice even, "if you'll just calm down and give me a chance to talk. Please, sit down and let's talk."

"Talk? You want me to talk to *you*? You left that wonderful man up the street, who...."

"Dad, do you care about *me*? I'm your daughter, I want...." My voice rose.

"Oh, no! You're no daughter of mine!" His eyes narrowed. I could see the popped veins in his temples and across his lids. He was ugly. Stony.

I was not stony. I answered with my own rage. For the first time I shouted at the man who was my father, "Well, you're not my father, either. You've never been a father to me, I don't know why I expected you to be any different now. Get out!"

He did, dragging my stepmother along like a ragdoll.

Furious and triumphant, I slammed the front door and watched the two of them stagger to their car and drive away. Seconds later, Ceil and Karen pulled into the driveway, and Daniel pulled up behind them. Relieved, impatient to recount the story, to define what had happened, I pulled the doorknob to get out to them. But the door was jammed. In my fury, I had broken the door.

Neither Daniel nor I slept that night. How to explain one's nonparent. When, despite the attainment of age thirty-five, despite some years of therapy, despite an intellectual and practical grasp of the fact that one's father had never loved, supported, or appeared when needed, one still had trouble accepting the fact emotionally. One must distance oneself. Daniel told me to stop referring to myself as "one." He congratulated me on my door-slam.

At about 2 a.m., we gave up on sleep. We were both thirsty but didn't want to clatter around at that hour in Lainie's and Steven's kitchen.

"How about going to the apartment? There's orange juice in the refrigerator." Daniel sounded excited. An adventure.

"Let's go."

Two a.m. We quickly pulled on our pants and shirts and let ourselves out the back door. In the car, we began to laugh. The thrill of being the only ones on the suburban streets, of stealthily entering our own furnitureless apartment that smelled of paint, and drinking orange juice from the carton, in the light of the open refrigerator. . . . we drank and laughed, saw each other laughing and stopped, silenced by our need to kiss, to love, to touch.

The living room rug—a selling point for the apartment—received us hospitably, cushioning our bodies, welcoming us to our new lives.

Which began in earnest the next morning when we officially moved in. Moving in consisted of emptying Daniel's car of the suitcases, paper bags full of shoes, piles of sheet music, a bassoon, a bottle of scotch, two bottles of wine, four glasses, piles of books, ties that slipped off their hangers—all stuff that had been in the car for four days since Daniel had been out of his house.

On one of those four nights, Daniel had taken his sons out to dinner.

"But did you fit them all into the car?" I asked. "With all your things. . . ."

"They sat on top of them," he said, trying to smile, exhausted from trying to convince his children that he was still their father, that he hadn't left them.

Once the car was emptied of its initial load, we made several trips to Lainie and Steven's to pick up my clothes, some miscellaneous linen and towels I had had the presence of mind to take from the house that had been mine for years, and the set of silverplate I had inherited from my mother before my marriage to Martin—my lawyer told me I was entitled to take that, as long as there was another set of eating utensils in the house. And my books and typewriter and manuscripts.

We carried our belongings in as if each one were a treasure. What we had was all we had. After all of our belongings were put away, the apartment remained empty, spacious, full of possibility. Daniel and I walked through each of the rooms: in the living room, the rug and a coffee table that Daniel had taken from his garage where it had lain for years developing a patina of rust, insect leavings and the powder of dried leaves; in the galley kitchen, an old drainboard and dishrack donated by Lainie and Steven; in the bedroom, a new mattress and box spring on a metal frame that Daniel and I had bought, after deciding that it was a necessity whether we had any money or not, and which had been delivered as we were moving in. There it sat, regal, made up with the sheets I had brought, Daniel's pillow, and my pillow. Our bed. In the bathroom, two toothbrushes and two towels.

The apartment was set into the side of a sloping lawn. Forsythia bushes and rhododendron hugged two windows in the living room, and in front of the third, heavy auto and pedestrian traffic flickered the streaming autumn light into a strobe pattern.

"Our cave," Daniel said, "carved out of the side of the hill just for us. . . ."

"How is it possible," I said as he hugged me, "that I felt so crowded in my big house, and here in this two room apartment I feel I can expand. . . ."

At four o'clock, Daniel left for the junior high school to watch his oldest son compete in a gymnastic meet. I decided to take a shower, my first in the apartment, to be fresh when Daniel came home and we both prepared our first meal in our first apartment.

NINA

The rush and splatter of the water masked the silence. Four-thirty and silent. Silence at four-thirty in the afternoon, a time which, for years, had been the children's witching hour, the nagging, either bored-to-death time before dinner when they insisted they would die of starvation unless they ate immediaely despite the fact that I was making the supper they had requested, or the frantic oh - my - god - I - have - too - much - homework - and - my - practice - and - now - you - want - me - to - take - out - the - garbage - why - me? Pressure. Cooking. A glass of wine for the five o' clock nerves. Six o'clock. Dinner ready except for the finishing touches. House clean. Children under control. Ready. Ready for adult companionship. Telephone ringing at 6:10, one minute before the time to pick up Martin at the station. Answer it or not. Martin frowns when I'm late. Answer it, though. It is Martin. Not coming home for dinner. Unavoidable. Sorry.

Oh, sorry, very sorry. Sorry children. Your father is unavoidably detained. Too busy. No temper tantrums. Eat it anyway. I am not drinking too much. I don't know the answer. What is this eat and run business? I expect a little help around here. I am not a nag. I am not shouting. I am not mean.

Not not not.

Descending to a childish level.

So much noise.

Silence.

Water, only water.

I turned off the shower.

Very quiet. I dried myself, the towel made no noise against my skin. I stepped out of the brightly lit bathroom into the bedroom, where my clean clothes were piled on the closet shelves. Dark. Five o'clock in late October in a cave-like apartment is dark. I flicked on the light switch. Nothing. In the light overflowing from the bathroom, I saw that there were no light fixtures in the bedroom, only switches connected to outlets. We had no lamps. I located my bathrobe and put it on. Found my watch on the bed and brought it into the bathroom. Five-fifteen and quiet. No telephone until the end of the week. No piano practice. No drum practice. No whining. No thudding. No laughing. No voices.

Silence.

Calm. Be calm.

Daniel will be back soon. How long can a gym meet last?

I picked a book out of the carton in the hallway and went into the living room to sit on the rug and read. I flicked on the light switch. Nothing. No fixture. No lamps.

Kitchen: fixture but no furniture. Bedroom: bed but no light. Bathroom: light and a toilet. I sat on the toilet and tried to read.

Five-thirty. No dinner cooking. No noise, very little light. Virtually no furniture.

Limbo.

No nagging. No whining. No music. No telephone. No cooking. Nothing.

Had I chosen limbo? I felt a painful nostalgia for the old pressures of the old witching hour.

But no.

At the end of the witching hour had been Martin.

No.

The constriction. Tightness.

No Martin.

Just Nina now.

Nina alone.

Nina expanding.

Nina who would mother her children because she wanted to mother them.

This was just the first afternoon. There would be lamps. Music. Chairs. A table. Telephone. Children's voices.

I pressed my hands against my knees and sat up straight. Very straight.

The sound of the key in the lock was startling. Loud.

Daniel. Daniel was home. I reached the door to open it for him.

BIOGRAPHIES

HELEN BAROLINI's poems, stories and essays have appeared in American and Italian publications. She has written two novels and lives in Ossining, New York, where she writes for a county magazine.

MARGARET GIBSON has published short stories in the *Red Clay Reader, Shenandoah, The Georgia Review, The Southern Review,* and *Contempora,* and she is the author of two published books of poetry, *Lunes* and *On The Cutting Edge,* and has a third volume that will be published by LSU Press. She lives in New London, Connecticut.

KATHRYN KRAMER lives and works in Boston, Massachusetts. Her stories have appeared in *Cromo-Uri* and *Generation.* She is working on a novel called *A Handbook for Visitors from Outer Space.*

As well as writing poetry and fiction, TIRZA LATIMER builds, remodels and restores houses. She lives in Berkeley, California.

BARBARA LOVELL lives in Charlotte, North Carolina, where she teaches at the University of North Carolina. She has had poems published in *Women, Southern Voices, Crucible, White Trash, Contempora,* and *Southern Poetry Review.*

Among DEENA METZGER's extensive publications are a novel, *Skin: Shadows/Silence,* a radio play, *The Book of Hags,* and a book of poetry, *Dark Milk.* In 1974, she was co-filmmaker of *Chile: With Poems and Guns,* a full length documentary on the revolutionary government and the fascist coup in Chile. She lives in Los Angeles where she teaches workshops in the Re-Creative Writing Process.

PAMOLU OLDHAM was born and grew up in North Carolina. She has published poetry and fiction in various college literary magazines and presently teaches English at Fayetteville Technical Institute in Fayetteville, North Carolina.

LLOYD ROSE has done extensive work in theatre production, acting, and directing. Living in Charlotte, North Carolina, she is currently at work on an autobiography, *Sherlock Holmes Meets Dracula.*

SARA ROSE is a pseudonym for a woman writer who lives in New York.

LOVE STORIES

CAROLE ROSENTHAL's short stories and essays have appeared in a number of magazines and anthologies, including *Transatlantic Review, New Dawn, Gallimaufry, Masterpieces of Mystery,* and *Woman in the Year 2000.* Currently, she is completing a novel about love and arson. Her home is in New York City.

JUDITH SERIN lives in Berkeley, California, where she teaches creative writing classes in adult education programs. Her poetry has been published in various literary magazines, including *New Poets Women,* and is forthcoming in two anthologies, *Mothers, Daughters* and Merlin Press's anthology of contemporary Californian women poets. A group of her short stories will appear in *Gray Sky* magazine.

LEE SMITH's most recent novel, *Fancy Strut,* was published by Harper & Row. She has just completed a fourth novel, *Black Mountain Breakdown,* and lives in Chapel Hill, North Carolina.

Lullaby is LEE SOKOL's first publication. She has been Film Maker in Residence in both South Carolina and Georgia. Currently, she is living in Atlanta, Georgia and working with the Atlanta Women's Art Collective, making a series of video tapes on Atlanta women artists.

A volume of LAUREL SPEER's one act plays is due to be published by Holmanger's Press. She writes full time and lives in Tucson, Arizona.

ANN TAYLOR has worked in film production, sculpture, furniture making, and wardrobe design. She lives in Savannah, Georgia in a Victorian house which she restored.

JEAN THOMPSON has had fiction published in *Carolina Quarterly, Ploughshares, Descant, fiction international, Mississippi Review,* and *Ascent.* She currently teaches fiction writing at the University of Illinois, Urbana, Illinois.

IRENE TIERSTEN lives in Maplewood, New Jersey, and currently works as a paralegal in a divorce law office. She has completed five novels, won the Fels Award for Short Fiction in 1976; and has had her work published in numerous little magazines. In 1977, her play, *Connections,* was read in the Off Center Theatre in Manhattan, New York.

DIANE VREULS worked for ten years as a painter. Her publications are many: a book of poems, *Instructions,* a novel, *Are We There Yet?,* short stories in *Paris Review* and *Iowa Review,* a children's picture book called *Sums.* She teaches in the Creative Writing Program at Oberlin College in Ohio.